As I crossed the living room, a pop-pop-pop followed by the peeling of tires shattered the morning calm. I dropped to the floor. I knew that sound. Still, Fourth of July was only days away. Maybe I was wrong. Maybe some of the neighborhood kids had gotten hold of some firecrackers.

I crawled toward the windows and inched my way up until my eyes were slightly above the sill. The Escalade was gone, the red Mercedes convertible was still parked in front of my house, and Jared Oberman's body lay sprawled in the street.

Acclaim for the Anastasia Pollack Crafting Mysteries

Assault with a Deadly Glue Gun

"Crafty cozies don't get any better than this hilarious confection...Anastasia is as deadpan droll as Tina Fey's Liz Lemon, and readers can't help cheering as she copes with caring for a host of colorful characters." – *Publishers Weekly* (starred review)

"Winston has hit a homerun with this hilarious, laugh-until-your-sides-hurt tale." – *Booklist* (starred review)

"A comic tour de force..." – *ForeWord Magazine* (Book-of-the-Year nominee)

"North Jersey's more mature answer to Stephanie Plum." – *Kirkus Reviews*

"...a delightful romp through the halls of who-done-it." – *The Star-Ledger*

"Make way for Lois Winston's promising new series...I'll be eagerly awaiting the next installment in this thoroughly delightful series." – *Mystery Scene Magazine*

"...once you read the first few pages of Lois Winston's first-in-series whodunit, you're hooked for the duration..." – *Bookpage*

"Anastasia is as crafty as Martha Stewart, as feisty as Stephanie Plum, and as resourceful as Kinsey Millhone." – Mary Kennedy, author of the Talk Radio Mysteries

"Fans of Stephanie Plum will love Lois Winston's cast of quirky, laughable, and loveable characters...clever and thoroughly entertaining—a must read!" – Brenda Novak, *New York Times* bestselling author

"What a treat—I can't stop laughing! Witty, wise, and delightfully clever, Anastasia is going to be your new best friend. Her mysterious adventures are irresistible—you'll be glued to the page!" – Hank Phillippi Ryan, Agatha, Anthony, and Macavity award-winning author

"You think you've got trouble? Say hello to Anastasia Pollack, who also happens to be queen of the one-liners. Funny, funny, funny—this is a series you don't want to miss!" – Kasey Michaels, *USA Today* best-selling author

Death by Killer Mop Doll

"Anastasia is a crafting Stephanie Plum, surrounded by characters sure to bring chuckles as she careens through the narrative, crossing paths with the detectives assigned to the case and snooping around to solve it." – *Booklist*

"Several crafts projects, oodles of laughs and an older, more centered version of Stephanie Plum." – *Kirkus Reviews*

"In Winston's droll second cozy featuring crafts magazine editor Anastasia Pollack...readers who relish the offbeat will be rewarded." – *Publishers Weekly*

"...a *30 Rock* vibe...Winston turns out another lighthearted amateur sleuth investigation. Laden with one-liners, Anastasia's second outing points to another successful series in the works." – *Library Journal*

"Winston...plays for plenty of laughs...while letting Anastasia shine as a risk-taking investigator who doesn't always know when to quit." – *Alfred Hitchcock Mystery Magazine*

Revenge of the Crafty Corpse

"Winston peppers the twisty and slightly edgy plot with humor and plenty of craft patterns. Fans of craft mysteries will like this, of course, but so will those who enjoy the smart and snarky humor of Janet Evanovich...." – *Booklist*

"Winston's entertaining third cozy plunges Anastasia into a surprisingly fraught stew of jealousy, greed, and sex...and a Sopranos-worthy lineup of eccentric character..." – *Publishers Weekly*

"A fun addition to a series that keeps getting stronger." – *Romantic Times Magazine*

"Chuckles begin on page one and the steady humor sustains a comedic crafts cozy." – *Library Journal*

"You'll be both surprised and entertained by this terrific mystery." – *Suspense Magazine*

"The book has what a mystery should. Like all good sleuths, Anastasia pieces together what others don't." – *The Star-Ledger*

Decoupage Can Be Deadly
"*Decoupage Can Be Deadly* is the fourth in the Anastasia Pollock Crafting Mysteries. And the best one yet." – *Suspense Magazine*

"What a great cozy mystery series...Every single character in these books is awesomely quirky and downright hilarious. This series is a true laugh out loud read!" – Books Are Life–Vita Libri

"This adventure grabs you immediately delivering a fast-paced and action-filled drama that doesn't let up from the first page to the surprising conclusion." – Dru's Book Musings

A Stitch to Die For
"If you're a reader who enjoys a well-plotted mystery and loves to laugh, don't miss this one!" – *Suspense Magazine*

Scrapbook of Murder

"This is one of the best books in this delightfully entertaining whodunit." – Dru's Book Musings

"...a perfect example of what mysteries are all about—deft plotting, believable characters, well-written dialogue, and a satisfying, logical ending. I loved it!" – *Suspense Magazine*

"I read an amazing book recently, y'all — *Scrapbook of Murder* by Lois Winston. – 5 Stars, Jane Reads

"...a quick read, with humour, a good mystery and very interesting characters!" – Verietats

Drop Dead Ornaments

"I always forget how much I love this series until I read the next one and I fall in love all over again..." – Dru's Book Musings

"...a delightful addition to the Anastasia Pollack Crafting Mystery series. More, please!" – *Suspense Magazine*

"I love protagonist Anastasia Pollack. She's witty and funny, and she can be sarcastic at times...A great whodunit, with riotous twists and turns." – Lisa K's Book Reviews

"*Drop Dead Ornaments* is such a fantastic book...I adore Anastasia! She's clever, likable, fun to read about, and easy to root for." – Jane Reads

"...readers will be laughing continually at the antics of Anastasia and clan in *Drop Dead Ornaments*." – The Avid Reader

"I love this series! Not only is Anastasia a 'crime magnet,' she is hilarious and snarky, a delight to read about and a dedicated friend." – Mallory Heart's Cozies

"It is always a nice surprise when something I am reading has a tie in to actual news or events that are happening in the present moment. I don't want to spoil a major plot secret, but the timing could not have been better...Be prepared for a dysfunctional cast of quirky characters." – Laura's Interests

"*Drop Dead Ornaments* is an enjoyable...roller-coaster ride, with secrets and clues tugging the reader this way and that." – Here's How It Happened

"...a light-hearted cozy mystery with lots of energy and definitely lots of action and interaction between characters." – Curling Up By the Fire

Handmade Ho-Ho Homicide
"Handmade Ho-Ho Homicide" is a laugh-out-loud, well plotted mystery, from a real pro! A ho-ho hoot!" – *Suspense Magazine*

"Lois Winston has brought back Anastasia's delightful first-person narrative of family, friends, dysfunction, and murder, and made it again very entertaining!" – *Kings River Life Magazine*

"Once again, the author knows how to tell a story that immediately grabbed my attention and I couldn't put this book down until the last page was read.... This was one of the best books in this delightfully lovable series." – Dru's Book Musings

"The story had me on the edge of my seat the entire time." – 5 Stars, Baroness Book Trove

"Humor, twists and turns, adorable characters make this story truly engaging from the first to the last page." – LibriAmoriMiei

"Take a murder mystery, add some light-hearted humor and weird characters, sprinkle some snow and what you get is *Handmade Ho-Ho Homicide*—a perfect Christmas Cozy read." –5 Stars, The Book Decoder

A Sew Deadly Cruise

"*A Sew Deadly Cruise* is absolutely delightful, and I was sorry when it was over. I devoured every word!" – *Suspense* Magazine

"Winston's witty first-person narrative and banter keeps me a fan. Loved it!" –*Kings River Life Magazine*

"The author knows how to tell a story with great aplomb and when all was said and done, this was one fantastic whodunit that left me craving for more." – Dru's Book Musings

"Overall a fun read that cozy fans are sure to enjoy." – Books a Plenty Book Reviews

"Winston has a gift for writing complicated cozy mysteries while entertaining and educating." – Here's How it Happened

Stitch, Bake, Die!

"Lois Winston has crafted another clever tale...with a backdrop of cross stitching, buttercream, bribery, sabotage, rumors, and murder...vivid descriptions, witty banter, and clever details leading to an exciting and shocking conclusion...a page-turner experience to delight cozy fans." – *Kings River Life Magazine*

"...a crème de la crème of a cozy read." – Brianne's Book Reviews

"...a well-plotted mystery that takes the term 'crafty old lady' to new heights." – Mysteries with Character

"...fast-paced with wacky characters, a fun resort setting, and a puzzling mystery to solve." – Nancy J. Cohen, author of the Bad Hair Day Mysteries

"Lots of action, a bevy of quirky characters, and a treasure trove of secrets add up to another fine read from Lois Winston." – mystery author Maggie Toussaint/Valona Jones

"...another great addition to this engagingly entertaining series." – Dru's Book Musings

Guilty as Framed
"Engaging and clever!" – *Kings River Life Magazine*

"This is another great entry in the Anastasia Pollack series." – Dru's Book Musings

"Winston not only combines (New) Jersey, well-crafted characters, and tight plotting, but she adds her own interpretation and possible solution to a factual museum art crime." – Debra H. Goldstein, author of the Sarah Blair Mysteries

"Reading a book in this series is like visiting an old friend." – Nancy J. Cohen, author of the Bad Hair Day Mysteries

A Crafty Collage of Crime
"Rich in descriptions of the countryside, and alive with characters you'd recognize if you saw or overheard them, it's a delightful read." – *Kings River Life Magazine*

"Winston imbues her story with current references, an appealing setting, layered plotting, and an unsinkable sleuth. Well done!" – Muddy Rose Reviews

"*A Crafty Collage of Crime* is yet another terrific cozy mystery featuring reluctant amateur sleuth Anastasia Pollack." – Lynn Slaughter, author of *Miss Cue*

"*A Crafty Collage of Crime* was a cute, fun, and entertaining read with independent, engaging, and delightful characters, and the mystery was outstanding, too!" – 5-stars, Novels Alive

"The author's style of writing was fresh, crisp, and entertaining. She kept the story moving without filler, and provided the solution to the murder at just the right time." – Tam Sesto, Cozy Review Crew

Sorry, Knot Sorry

"If you like your mysteries with a healthy dose of humor, Winston delivers... A delightful read whether you're at the beach or in your favorite recliner with a glass of wine." – Kings River Life Magazine

"A twisty-turny plot spiked with red herrings and a double shot of moxie." – award-winning author Maggie Toussaint

Lois Winston serves up another fast-paced cozy mystery that will have you chuckling through to the end. Add to your beach reads basket for a fun escape!" – Nancy J. Cohen, author of the Bad Hair Day Mysteries

"A humorous quick reading release from the real world." – Debra H. Goldstein, author of the Sarah Blair Mysteries

Seams Like the Perfect Crime

"I found myself unable to put the book down until I'd read the very last sentence." 5-Stars, Kim Davis, author of the Cupcake Catering Mysteries and the Aromatherapy Apothecary Mysteries

"Wit and humor abound in this crazy cozy caper as Anastasia and her husband aid their detective friend in hunting down a killer. The tips for memory quilts at the end are a bonus. Highly entertaining!" 5-stars, Nancy J. Cohen, author of the Bad Hair Day Mysteries

"Cozy mystery lovers will devour Seams Like the Perfect Crime! It's an entertaining and amusing mystery that shines through with authentic characters." – 5 Stars, Novels Alive

Books by Lois Winston

Anastasia Pollack Crafting Mystery series
Assault with a Deadly Glue Gun
Death by Killer Mop Doll
Revenge of the Crafty Corpse
Decoupage Can Be Deadly
A Stitch to Die For
Scrapbook of Murder
Drop Dead Ornaments
Handmade Ho-Ho Homicide
A Sew Deadly Cruise
Stitch, Bake, Die!
Guilty as Framed
A Crafty Collage of Crime
Sorry, Knot Sorry
Seams Like the Perfect Crime
Embroidered Lies and Alibis

Anastasia Pollack Crafting Mini-Mysteries
Crewel Intentions
Mosaic Mayhem
Patchwork Peril
Crafty Crimes (all 3 novellas in one volume)

Empty Nest Mystery Series
Definitely Dead
Literally Dead

Romantic Suspense
Love, Lies and a Double Shot of Deception
Lost in Manhattan
Someone to Watch Over Me

Romance and Chick Lit

Talk Gertie to Me
Four Uncles and a Wedding
Hooking Mr. Right
Finding Hope

Novellas and Novelettes

Elementary, My Dear Gertie
Moms in Black, A Mom Squad Caper
Once Upon a Romance
Finding Mr. Right

Children's Chapter Book

The Magic Paintbrush

Nonfiction

Top Ten Reasons Your Novel is Rejected
House Unauthorized
Bake, Love, Write
We'd Rather Be Writing

Sorry,
Knot Sorry

LOIS WINSTON

Cover design by L. Winston

ISBN: 978-1-940795-75-1

DEDICATION

To my incredibly awesome blogging partners at Booklover's Bench and The Stiletto Gang who are always there for each other during both the highs and lows of this life we've chosen. I'm so honored to call you my friends.

ACKNOWLEDGMENTS

To Ibba Surface, the winning bidder at the First Unitarian Universalist Church of Nashville's FUUNtastic Fall Auction, for the right to have her name as a character in *Sorry, Knot Sorry*. I hope you enjoy your new career as a creative arts agent and intellectual property attorney.

Special thanks to CrimeSceneWriter members Wesley Harris, Wallace Lind, John J. Robinson, and Alanna Weaver for their technical expertise in police procedures, cybersecurity, and ballistics. You've kept me from making what might have been really dumb mistakes!

To Shelley Noble, best of friend and Broadway companion, for providing me with an escape back to New Jersey whenever I need it and a sympathetic ear at all times.

And as always, my undying appreciation to Donnell Ann Bell and Irene Peterson for their superb editorial skills as well as their continuing friendship.

ONE

"Have you signed the contract?" asked food editor Cloris McWerther.

We stood in the break room, taking part in our morning ritual of coffee and whatever sugar and calorie-laden goodie Cloris had whipped up overnight. Breakfast of champions. Or sustenance for a magazine crafts editor who rarely had time to eat before rushing out the door each morning.

I shook my head as I swallowed a mouthful of blueberry lemon muffin. "Not yet."

"Why not? It would wipe out your remaining debt, wouldn't it?"

"But at what cost?"

My name is Anastasia Pollack. I'm the crafts editor at *American Woman*, a third-rate women's magazine sold at supermarket checkout counters. A year and a half ago, thanks to the death of my duplicitous first husband, I was yanked out of my comfortable middle-class existence and deposited into the Land of

One-Step-Away-from-Living-in-a-Cardboard-Box-Over-a-Subway-Vent.

As a single parent, I barely cover essentials, leaving nothing to whittle down the unexpected and unwelcome debt I'd inherited. If I had any extra cash, I'd have *Clueless Wife* tattooed in reverse across my forehead. Every time I stared into the mirror, I'd have a stark reminder of my obliviousness and naiveté.

Good thing too many creditors are queued up with their hands out. I already have too many regrets. I don't need to add a graffitied forehead to the list.

However, through a combination of luck and moonlighting, I'd managed to whittle down a sizable chunk of that debt. Unfortunately, the whittling tool came with strings attached. Deadly strings that had forced me into the role of reluctant amateur sleuth.

Prior to the death of Karl Marx Pollack, every dead body I'd ever encountered had reposed peacefully in a silk-lined coffin at a funeral home. And thankfully, each of the deceased had succumbed from natural causes.

Post Karl? All had died at the hands of others. Worse yet, those corpses continue to arrive in my life on a far too regular basis. In the past eighteen months, my encounters with murder victims (and by extension, murderers) has exceeded the career totals of the average suburban homicide detective.

The one bright spot in my life has been my new husband, photojournalist Zachary Barnes. But even he arrived with strings. I'm convinced photography is a cover for his real gig, spying for one of the government alphabet agencies. Zack laughs away my suspicions, claiming I have an overactive imagination, but isn't Deny and Deflect the first chapter in the *Official Book of Spying*?

Anyway, this all brought me back to Cloris and her question about the contract.

Two weeks ago, while on our honeymoon in Tennessee wine country, Zack and I stumbled across—wait for it—*another* dead body. Bad enough that I can't even get away from murder on my honeymoon. But while in the bucolic hamlet, I also became aware of an unauthorized true crime podcast that featured *me* and my reluctant crime-solving exploits.

Naturally, I blew a Vesuvian level gasket.

I'd worked my tush off to keep Karl's financial malfeasance limited to as few people as possible. Although the results of my sleuthing occasionally wound up on local news, none of the stories had gone national. Until the Sleuth Sayer podcast.

Five days ago, I'd learned the identities behind the Sleuth Sayer—my own two sons, Alex and Nick, and Alex's girlfriend Sophie Lambert. They exposed my life to every true crime junkie in the world because they'd wanted to help dig me out of debt. Talk about vying emotions!

But the shock didn't end there. Their honorable intentions had paid off beyond their wildest expectations. Flix Entertainment wanted to option the podcast and my life as a reluctant amateur sleuth for a TV series.

Hence, the still unsigned contract, which Alex had snatched from the mail and hidden from me. The teens had decided to wait until the right moment to spring the news on me. They'd fessed up a few days later at a dinner celebrating Alex and Sophie's high school graduation.

"Seems to me," continued Cloris, "you have two choices. Either sign the contract—"

"Which strips me and my family of whatever privacy we have

left—"

"Or take Zack up on his offer to pay off the remainder of the debt. It's not like he can't afford it."

I scowled at her. "I don't suppose there's a Plan C?"

Cloris shrugged. "Lottery tickets?"

"Really?" Karl's gambling had created my problem. No way would I ever gamble so much as a dollar. Besides, before his death broadsided me, I'd occasionally bought a lottery ticket. I'd never won more than seven dollars. Most of the time, I didn't even hit one number. Lottery tickets were hardly a sound fiscal plan for erasing massive debt.

Cloris topped off our coffees. As we headed to our cubicles, she said, "I guess we can scrap Plan C. If I think of a Plan D, I'll let you know."

"Much obliged. Anyway, nothing is happening until Zack's agent speaks with the production company, and that's not happening until she returns from vacationing in the Greek Isles."

Zack had connections and not just in areas that added credence to my spy theory. He'd taken one look at the contract and called his representative, who wore a dual hat as an intellectual property attorney.

"I thought you said Sophie's dad had his lawyer look over the contracts."

"Shane's lawyer handles his charitable trust. Zack convinced me we needed advice from someone whose law expertise is in entertainment and publishing."

We had arrived at our cubicles and were about to part ways when both our phones simultaneously pinged incoming texts. "This can't be good," I said, staring at the message on my screen.

Cloris pulled her gaze from her phone and shot me a worried

look. "We already have our monthly meeting scheduled for later this morning. Why would Naomi call a surprise last-minute meeting hours ahead of time?"

I'd already suffered enough physical and emotional whiplash in June to last an entire year. And we still had a week remaining in the month. The last thing I needed was another lollapalooza whammy. I could think of only one reason for an unexpected meeting, and it sent panic coursing from my split ends down to my toenails. "Do you suppose those layoff rumors are more than rumors?"

Cloris groaned. "With the state of the publishing industry in general and magazines in particular? What else could it be? We're dead editors walking toward our execution."

With that somber thought ringing in my ears, we headed for the conference room.

Silence reigned as the various *American Woman* editors, their assistants, and ancillary staff crammed into the small conference room. With nearly every seat already filled, the overflow leaned against the walls. Cloris and I squeezed in next to decorating editor Jeanie Sims. Expressions glum, no one made eye contact. We all braced for the expected bad news.

Finally, Naomi Dreyfus, our editorial director, and her ever-present assistant Kim O'Hara entered the room. Naomi settled into the seat at the head of the table, Kim took a position standing slightly behind her. All eyes turned to Naomi.

Naomi took a moment to settle her gaze on each one of us, then cleared her throat before speaking. "As I'm sure you all know, Trimedia, our parent company, has gone through some difficult times of late."

Understatement of the century. Murder is never good for the

bottom line, and Trimedia had had its share of both murders and murderers among its ranks since moving us from Manhattan to the middle of a cornfield in Morristown, New Jersey.

"Here comes the axe," mumbled Cloris, low enough that only I heard her. Or so I thought until Naomi paused and raised an eyebrow in our direction.

She turned back to the full room and continued. "For the past several months, Hugo has been in negotiations with a group of investors."

Hugo Reynolds-Alsopp had been the head of the family-owned Reynolds-Alsopp Publishing Company prior to Trimedia's hostile takeover. He had remained at Trimedia as publisher in name only, relegated to a closet-sized office with no windows and no responsibilities. He was also Naomi's longtime partner outside the office.

Ever since, Hugo had plotted to regain control of what was left of his company. Trimedia had already folded nearly half our publications. But why would Hugo be talking to investors if we were all about to lose our jobs?

"Now that things have been finalized," said Naomi, "I'm at liberty to tell you that *American Woman* will be moving in a new direction."

"What sort of direction?" asked Tessa Lisbon. "I haven't heard anything."

Tessa's uncle held a seat on the Trimedia Board of Directors, which explained why the position of fashion editor had gone to someone with neither editorial nor fashion industry experience. She was also the only staff member with a sizable trust fund, making her the sole person in the room not worried about receiving a pink slip.

In an extremely calm but imperious voice, Naomi stared down Tessa and said, "I wasn't aware all corporate decisions passed through you."

Tessa's jaw dropped, then immediately slammed shut. She crossed her arms over her chest and silently speared Naomi with an evil eye.

Naomi picked up where she'd left off. "Hugo has partnered with Creativity Books."

"I've heard of them," I said. "They specialize in craft and hobby publications."

"And culinary," added Naomi.

A boulder thudded into my stomach. Creativity Books was located somewhere in the Midwest. Did Naomi expect us all to relocate?

She continued. "*American Woman*, along with several of the other magazines that fall into the craft, hobby, decorating, and culinary categories will be merging with them. As of next week, Trimedia is officially out of the magazine business."

"Are we staying in the cornfield?" asked beauty editor Nicole Emmerling.

Naomi nodded. "Part of the negotiations included assuming the remainder of Trimedia's lease on this building. Until the lease expires, which isn't for several years, we're stuck in the cornfield."

But she didn't mention where we'd relocate after the lease ended. Would we trade a New Jersey cornfield for a Nebraska cornfield?

"Does this mean we all still have jobs?" asked Cloris.

"The only change for now will be the new company name on your paychecks."

Naomi really hadn't answered Cloris's question, and I didn't care for the ominous sound of *for now*. I bit my tongue, though.

Naomi stood, indicating an end to the meeting, However, before she exited the conference room, she turned to Jeanie, Cloris, and me. "I'd like to see the three of you in my office."

TWO

Shades of junior high school. "I feel like we're about to receive detention," I whispered as we followed behind Naomi and Kim.

"At least it beats a pink slip," said Jeanie.

What if it didn't? What if the new direction for *American Woman* involved replacing us with Creativity staff? Naomi's *for now* comment had invaded my amygdala, releasing a torrent of stress hormones. I glanced down the hall toward our editorial director's office. Only a few yards separated us from possible impending doom.

Once inside her office, instead of heading toward her desk, Naomi motioned to the small seating area to the left. "Have a seat, ladies."

Cloris, Jeanie, and I shared the sofa. Naomi and Kim settled into the two matching chairs on the opposite side of a live edged walnut coffee table with hairpin legs.

Naomi smiled at us before speaking. Her eyes gave no indication that our next stop would be the unemployment line. I grabbed onto that tiny sliver of hope as she began speaking.

"As I mentioned earlier, we're taking *American Woman* in a new direction. Our recent market research has indicated a shift in the focus of our core demographic. They want even more crafts, recipes, and decorating ideas, less fashion and beauty unless the fashion and beauty articles are aimed specifically at middle-aged women and seniors. Our readers aren't interested in makeup and fashion tips geared toward Millennials and younger women."

Not breaking news. None of us ever understood why Trimedia had hired Millennial fashion and beauty editors for a magazine that catered mostly to women who fell between perimenopause and Social Security. However, since everyone in the room held the same opinion, I held my tongue.

Such an editorial pivot wouldn't phase Nicole. Our beauty editor lacked any diva genes. However, Tessa would have a cow.

A quick glance to my left told me Cloris was on the same wavelength. To my right, Jeanie released a lungful of relief. It didn't appear a trip to the unemployment office loomed in our immediate futures.

I did see one problem, though. "Does less fashion and beauty mean more editorial pages for us each month?" More pages meant more work, which meant cramming more than forty hours into a work week. I hoped that translated into a heftier paycheck, but I sensed this, too, was not a subject to broach now.

"Not necessarily," said Naomi. "Fashion and beauty will remain but concentrate entirely on the needs of more mature women. However, in addition to the magazine, the three of you will work on a new project. We're partnering with Creativity Books to release a series of *American Woman* DIY books focused on crafts, recipes, and decorating."

Once again, Cloris and I exchanged a quick look. We could both juggle a few more editorial pages a month, but where in the world would we find the time to write and edit books along with our magazine duties?

"I hope you've discovered a way to clone us," I said, punctuating my words with a laugh to mask my apprehension.

"And if not," added Jeanie, "have you found a way to add more hours to a day or more days to a month?"

Kim chuckled as she glanced at Naomi. "Unfortunately, neither option is in our skill sets."

"However, we've come up with what we think is a fabulous marketing idea," said Naomi. "*American Woman* has been around for decades. We have a huge archive dating back to the early nineteen-sixties. With the current interest in all things retro, we've planned a series of books featuring projects and recipes from each decade, beginning with the sixties. We'll showcase the originals as they appeared back in the day along with updated versions."

Cloris wrinkled her nose. "Like Jell-O in a can?"

"And macramé?" I added. *Did anyone still do macramé?*

"Exactly," said Naomi.

"I don't exactly see hordes of housewives willing to give up their hardwoods for shag carpeting," said Jeanie. "Or switching out their stainless-steel appliances for avocado green."

"This project will involve a lot of time," I said. "Maybe you should rethink the cloning option."

"You won't work on your own," said Naomi. "The Creativity Books staff will assist you. They'll be moving into the space Trimedia is vacating. Plus," she added, "the three of you will receive an advance and split the standard ten percent royalty on the sale of each book."

For that, I could get on board. However, Naomi hadn't mentioned the amount of the advances, and ten percent royalties split three ways wouldn't come anywhere near the amount of money awaiting me if I sold my soul to Flix Entertainment.

Unless written by A-list celebrities, craft books rarely made bestseller lists. Even then, hitting one of the major lists wasn't guaranteed, no matter how high-power the celebrity. Celebrity cookbooks did better because more people cook than craft, but I doubted that Cloris, Jeanie, and I would land on any national bestseller list.

Before Cloris, Jeanie, and I departed Naomi's office, Kim handed us folders containing specifics regarding our new projects, including a timeline and all contact information for the Creativity Books staff who would be working with us.

"What do you think?" asked Cloris as we headed down the hall to our cubicles.

"In theory, it sounds exciting," I said.

"I hear an unspoken *but* hanging in the air," said Jeanie.

I waved the file in front of Cloris and her. "In reality? It still means extra work. Lots of extra work. And Naomi made no mention of a salary increase."

"There is the advance and royalties on each book," said Cloris.

"We all know royalties are tied to sales. If the first books don't sell well, we won't earn out our advances, and they'll pull the plug on future editions."

"There is one bright side to all this," said Cloris.

"What's that?" asked Jeanie.

"Tessa won't be around for long. She'll balk at the new fashion direction, and with Trimedia out of the picture, she can't run to her uncle to intercede on her behalf."

Not that he ever had. Tessa's uncle may have secured the job for her, but that's where the nepotism had ended.

Our fashion editor was the thorn in the side of every other *American Woman* staffer. Although, as evil fashion editors go, her dead predecessor topped the list. "I often wonder if self-centered egotist is a fashion editor prerequisite."

"Maybe we'll have better luck with her replacement," said Jeanie. When Cloris and I offered her identical looks of skepticism, she shrugged and added, "A girl can hope, can't she?"

"Spoken like a true cockeyed optimist," I said.

~*~

To sign or not to sign? That was the question which continued to plague me as I sat in rush hour traffic on my way home that evening.

On the one hand, my financial situation was nowhere near as dire as when I was first booted out of the middle class. Unlike Blanche DuBois, I hadn't depended on the kindness of strangers, but I had benefitted from a few lucky breaks and the generosity of others. I tried not to think about how each resulted in nearly getting myself killed. In *A Streetcar Named Desire* Blanche had never had to confront any killers.

Although the debt remained, I'd reduced it from the GNP of Uzbekistan to the GNP of Djibouti. With any luck, I could be debt free before my grandchildren had grandchildren.

On the other hand, if I signed the contract with Flix Entertainment, I'd wipe out the balance of the debt and have money in the bank. You'd think it was a no-brainer. And it would be if I didn't mind relinquishing my privacy.

I don't know which would be worse, being shunned as the

Typhoid Mary of Murder or constantly swarmed by true crime groupies. What would they call themselves? Pollack Peeps? Anastasians? Some people dream of becoming celebrities. I was never one of them. The idea horrified me.

~*~

In contrast to my possibly-a-spy husband, I had never mastered the ability to mask my emotions. The moment I entered the house, Zack's expression told me he knew something was up.

After a kiss hello, he stepped back and scrutinized me. "Do those worry lines creasing your forehead have anything to do with the TV offer, or is it something else?"

"Both, actually." I glanced toward the stove. The ziti casserole I'd prepared last night and left in the refrigerator was baking in the oven. "How long before dinner?"

"Half an hour. Need a drink?"

"You read my mind."

He reached for my hand. As we headed for the back door, an angry "*Brrrack!*" stopped us. Ralph, the Shakespeare-quoting African Grey parrot I'd inherited from my Great-aunt Penelope Periwinkle, squawked at us. Zack held out his arm for the bird to join us.

The apartment above my detached garage had once served as my home office and studio. My first post-Karl cost-cutting measure was renting it out. That's how Zack entered my life. Now the apartment served as both a dual workspace and getaway for the two of us.

"What's your pleasure?" asked Zack once we had stepped inside.

A loaded question, one I'd spent the past few days silently debating. Unlike the conundrum of the lady or the tiger, my two options consisted of a tiger behind both doors.

When I didn't immediately answer, Zack said, "Red, white, or something stronger?"

At least that choice was easy. "White."

He placed Ralph on the bird perch in the corner of the room, reached into his shirt pocket and offered him a sunflower seed before heading across the room to the small kitchen area.

Once he'd poured two glasses, he joined me on the sofa and handed me my wine. "I have news that might help. I heard back from my attorney. She wants to set up a meeting with Flix for a week from Thursday, late afternoon."

"Just me and her or all of us?"

"The two of you to start. Me if you want me to accompany you."

"Of course, I want you to join us. But why isn't she including the kids and Shane?"

"Because you're the lynchpin. Without you on board, Flix pulls the option offer."

"They told her that?"

"She had a brief email exchange with the employee who sent you the contract."

I huffed. "They've listened to the podcasts. If they want to create a series about a suburban reluctant amateur sleuth, they can change my name, make up their own murders, set it anywhere in the country, and leave me out of it. It would still be inspired by the podcasts. The kids should get paid for that."

"But it then becomes nothing unique, just another mystery series in a long line of *Murder She Wrote* clones. They'd argue that it has nothing to do with the Sleuth Sayer podcast. They want to produce something beyond a standard mystery show. Besides, I thought you wanted the money they're offering."

I sighed. "It's the only reason I'm considering their offer."

He removed my glass before I'd taken a sip and placed both glasses on the coffee table. Then he turned and cupped my face in his hands. "You have options, Sweetheart. You can rip up that contract right now. As a matter of fact, I wish you would. No one would blame you, not even the kids. They created the podcast to help you, not cause you more stress."

"I know. Their hearts were in the right place, but that podcast is a perfect example of how the teenage brain is not yet fully developed."

His eyebrows knit together. "How do you mean?"

"All actions have consequences."

Ralph squawked. "*Strong reasons make strong actions. King John.* Act Three, Scene Four."

I shot a glare at Ralph before continuing. "Alex, Nick, and Sophie had tunnel vision. They only focused on the upside of creating a podcast about my exploits. They never considered the downside."

Zack reached for the glasses and handed me my wine. "For now, let's table the contract until after we meet with my agent and the people at Flix. What else is bothering you?"

I drained half my glass before answering. "Nothing much other than my already complicated life just got a lot more complicated."

"How so?"

"Before I explain, I don't suppose that among your diverse contacts you know someone with cloning skills."

"Afraid not."

I downed the remainder of my wine and shrugged. "It was worth a shot." I then told him about the changes at the office.

I ended by saying, "In a perfect world, it's a fabulous opportunity, but it's a costly undertaking. Mid-century modern might be all the rage in home décor right now, but I'm not sure how many crafters will shell out twenty or twenty-five dollars for a book of macraméd plant hangers or tie-dyed tote bags, especially when the Internet is filled with freebie directions."

"Creativity Books must have done some market research to support the decision."

I snorted. "Market research is like statistics. You can skew the numbers to any outcome you desire. That doesn't mean the consumer will buy into it. There are warehouse shelves all over the country brimming with dusty pet rocks and fidget spinners. Remainder tables at every bookstore overflow with books publishers need to dump at deep discounts because they never sold. If the DIY books don't sell, Cloris, Jeanie, and I will get blamed for the company's losses."

Then again, the same could be said about the Flix offer. If the series flopped, would the blame for that also land at my feet? Worse yet, would Flix demand their money back? Other than the amount, the contract I'd received lacked specifics, especially regarding payment details. Was I handed the full amount upon signing, or were payments stretched out over a longer period?

THREE

To justify leaving work early the following Thursday, I had set up an appointment in the garment district to view a new line of ribbons and trims from one of the magazine's advertisers. Afterwards, armed with samples, I walked the short distance to meet up with Zack and his agent/attorney at a coffee shop near the office building that housed Flix Entertainment.

Talk about jumping to an erroneous conclusion! Ibba Surface was the antithesis of the image my brain had conjured up for an intellectual property attorney. Instead of someone in a power suit and stilettos, Zack's agent gave off an ex-Flower Child of the Sixties vibe but with a modern sophisticated twist. She had paired a white silk blouse over wide-legged navy raw silk pants and topped the outfit with a lightweight Shibori print jacket. Soft umber waves framed her face. A quick glance at her feet revealed she hadn't forsaken the stilettos, though. From the ever so slight wrinkles at the edges of her eyes and corners of her lips, I pegged her as somewhere in her mid-fifties.

After Zack introduced me, we grabbed cups of coffee and found a table in a quiet area toward the back of the café. Once seated, Ibba Surface transformed into all-business mode. "To be honest with you, Anastasia, I find the agreement you received a bit odd."

"Odd? In what way?"

"I've negotiated film and TV rights for many authors. Unless you're extremely famous, most option offers are a modest amount of money given to tie up the rights of the work for a short period, usually six months or a year. During that time, if the project is green-lit, you receive a larger amount for the rights to your work, or in this case, the rights to your adventures as laid out in the Sleuth Sayer podcasts."

"Explain green-lit."

"That means the production company has been given permission to go ahead with the project."

"Are you saying Flix is working on spec?"

"Most likely. Until they have a commitment from a studio, they won't invest a huge amount of money. The option is a way of tying up the property to keep anyone else from making a better offer."

"What happens if the project isn't green-lit within that period?"

"They either pay you to extend the option for another set period of time or drop the project."

"Are you suggesting there's something fishy about the offer they extended?"

"Let's say it's highly unusual."

"In what way?"

"For starters, the contract mentions no option period. And the amount is more in keeping with a finalized deal, not an option. You haven't received offers from any other production companies, have you?"

"No, why?"

"That might indicate a bidding war going on behind the scenes, but even that would be highly unusual."

"Why?"

"Bidding wars are generally initiated by agents. Unless Flix has some insider information about another production company's interest in you, I'm baffled. In all my years in the business, I've never seen a contract as ambiguous as this one. The way the offer is worded sends mixed messages. Normally, after an option is signed, the production company produces a treatment."

"What's that?"

"It's a summary of the proposed movie or series that includes all the essential elements of the work—the main characters, scenes, tone, and theme. Think of it like a book report. The treatment is then sent to studios to generate interest."

"And that isn't done prior to signing the option?"

She shook her head. "Before we head over to the meeting, I want you to understand that no matter how good this offer sounds, it may be too good to be true."

"I guess we'll soon find out. Have you ever done business with Flix?"

"No, but I researched the company."

"So did I. I wanted to watch some of their other movies and TV shows. I couldn't find anything."

"That's because they're a relatively new startup. They have several projects in the works but nothing airing yet. The first isn't scheduled for release until the fall."

I frowned. "How does a startup with no track record have such deep pockets?"

"Possibly private investor backing."

"The kind of backing that allows them to offer a six-figure deal to a nobody like me? Does that make any sense to you?"

She shrugged. "It happens. Some of these companies are owned by trust fund babies who dream of scoring it big in Hollywood. Others made it big in tech and want to branch out into entertainment and other industries. They have plenty of money to throw around. However, that's not the norm."

"And not in this case?"

"My research found no indication of either. The company is owned by two brothers, Jared and Devin Oberman. Both worked in the entertainment industry for about twenty years, Jared on the production side, Devin in finance."

"I still haven't decided if I want to get involved, no matter the money."

"I understand. I'm here to make you aware of all aspects of the agreement, negotiate on your behalf if you decide to move forward, and prevent anyone from pressuring you or taking advantage of you."

She reached into her briefcase, withdrew a printed sheet of paper and a pen, handing both to me. "For all of that, I receive a fifteen percent commission on whatever you earn from the deal. If you're in agreement, we can move forward and head over to the meeting."

"And if I decide to reject their offer?"

"You owe me nothing."

I lowered my head and began reading. The one-page contract was straightforward, written in English, not legalese. Zack had told me Ibba had negotiated all his photography books, merchandising deals, and gallery shows from the beginning of his career. He called her his legal barracuda.

He'd remained silent throughout my conversation with her. When I finished reading and glanced over at him, he nodded. Ibba was taking more of a risk on me than I was on her. I'm sure she only offered me representation because of Zack. After all, she may invest considerable time on my behalf and never see a penny for her efforts if I decided to walk away from the deal. No matter how you looked at it, fifteen percent of zilch equaled nada. I picked up the pen and signed my name.

As she placed the signed contract in her briefcase, she said, "Once we sit down with Ellis Cummings, I'll do the talking. Are you okay with that?"

"Absolutely." After all, wasn't that how she'd earn her fifteen percent?

~*~

The offices of Flix Entertainment took up the third floor of one of the many narrow older brick structures sandwiched between more modern high-rises along the westside of midtown Manhattan. Some had started life as sweatshops, others as tenements, in the late nineteenth and early twentieth centuries. After modernization, they had transformed into pricey real estate for companies that wanted a prestigious Manhattan zip code but didn't require huge amounts of square footage.

Stepping from the elevator, we found ourselves directly in front of a reception desk. Not only was the area devoid of any signage to indicate we'd arrived at our destination, but the desk looked like Ikea, circa nineteen-nineties. Certainly not what I'd expected from a Manhattan production company, especially one that had offered me enough money to pay off Djibouti.

A twenty-something with chartreuse-streaked blonde hair, gold nose ring, and an abundance of tattooed flowers peeking out from above the neckline of her scooped-neck, tie-dyed T-shirt sat behind the desk. I focused on the kaleidoscopic multi-colored neon swirls of her shirt. Perhaps Creativity Books knew something I didn't about the fashion trends of Gen Z. If so, the nineteen-sixties inspired DIY book might not lay a giant goose egg.

The receptionist didn't glance up from scrolling through her phone until Zack cleared his throat. With a look of irritation, she forced her attention from her social media of choice and asked, "May I help you?"

"We're here to see Ellis Cummings," I said.

Scowling, she studied us for a moment. "Are you family or something?"

"No," said Ibba. "We have an appointment."

This seemed to puzzle the receptionist. "With Ellis?"

I nodded. "Yes."

"You're sure?"

"Definitely."

She shrugged. "If you say so. Wait here."

She pushed away from her desk and headed down a narrow corridor, ducking her head into each open office she passed along the way and knocking on the doors of those that were closed.

"Odd that she didn't pick up the phone to call her," I said.

Ibba scanned the claustrophobic area where we stood taking up most of the floor space between the elevator and the desk. "Odder still that their reception area, if you can call it that, doesn't even have a couple of chairs."

Eventually, the receptionist returned. As she settled back into her chair, she once again picked up her phone. Almost as an afterthought and without looking at us, she said, "She'll be with you shortly." Then she resumed her social media scrolling.

She? In my mind I had assigned Ellis Cummings one X and one Y chromosome. Obviously, I'd jumped to the wrong conclusion.

We continued to cool our heels in the miniscule area between the elevator and the receptionist's desk. *Shortly* is a subjective word, meaning different lengths of time to different people. At Flix Entertainment, *shortly* meant nearly fifteen minutes. Standing in heels on a polished concrete floor with barely any room to move made those fifteen minutes feel more like fifteen hours.

Finally, we saw another young woman, a clone of the first but with lilac-streaked blonde hair and minus the decolletage tats, approach from the far end of the corridor. She, too, checked each open office door as she neared us, but rather than appearing in search of someone, her furtive glances led me to believe she feared running into someone. After passing the last office, her posture straightened. She pasted on a smile and strode the remaining distance.

Stepping in front of the reception desk, she extended her right hand toward me. "I'm Ellis Cummings. It's a pleasure to meet you in person Mrs. Pollack."

Not that we'd ever met any other way, neither virtually nor via phone. Our only communication had been in a one-way direction, the offer letter she'd mailed me. Ibba had emailed her on my behalf to set up the appointment. However, Ellis Cummings had done her homework, most likely checking out the *American Woman* website or one of the magazine's other social media sites, because she hadn't confused me with Ibba. Or maybe with a fifty percent chance of being right, she'd taken a gamble and gotten lucky. Obviously, she could rule out Zack.

Without introducing herself to either Zack or Ibba, she turned to the receptionist and said, "We'll be in the conference room. Hold all my calls, Miss Smith, and make sure we're not disturbed."

The receptionist pulled herself from her phone and raised an eyebrow. "Seriously?"

Ellis affected an imperious tone. "You heard me, Miss Smith."

Miss Smith sniggered. "I certainly did, *Miss Cummings*."

Ellis ignored her. Instead, she flashed me another Crest smile and said, "Follow me, please." Then she pivoted to head back in the direction she'd come.

When I passed by the desk, I heard Miss Smith mutter something indiscernible under her breath.

As we followed behind her, Ellis apologized for her coworker, adding, "It's so hard to find good help these days."

I stifled a snort of my own. She sounded like she'd worked at Flix for decades, but from the looks of her, she wasn't so much as a pea in the womb decades ago. Like the tech industry, I knew the entertainment industry was populated with plenty of wunderkinds. However, I didn't expect that someone close to Alex's age would have enough authority to offer a six-figure deal. Ellis Cummings didn't look old enough to order a glass of wine. Either she'd discovered the Fountain of Youth or had graduated college in her early teens.

Her wardrobe, which screamed Old Navy, did little to disabuse me of those thoughts. I had expected someone with so much authority to dress in corporate attire, not torn jeans and an off-the-shoulder Taylor Swift T-shirt, but what did I know of the entertainment industry? Judging from the only two staffers I'd seen so far, maybe Flix subscribed to a Casual Friday Everyday policy. Or perhaps it was Wear What You Want Week.

As we strode along the corridor, I noted the walls were dotted with posters of recent Emmy and Oscar-winning productions. Given Flix's startup status, was this an attempt at misrepresentation, leading prospective clients and investors to assume the company had worked on these productions?

At the far end of the building, Ellis led us into a small conference room that looked out onto an air shaft. Once we took seats around a battered table, also Ikea circa nineteen-nineties, I introduced my entourage. "This is my husband Zachary Barnes, and this is my attorney Ibba Surface."

Ellis's eyes widened. "Your attorney?"

Ibba took over. "Why are you surprised, Miss Cummings? When I emailed you, I mentioned I was contacting you on behalf of Ms. Pollack. The sig line on my email states my credentials."

Ellis attempted a recovery by sweeping a hand in the air as if shooing away a dust mote. "Of course. I juggle so many projects all day long it slipped my mind."

"You didn't expect Ms. Pollack to agree to your terms without benefit of counsel, did you?"

Before Ellis had a chance to answer, someone rattled the doorknob. She froze in her seat. With panic written across her features, she stared wide-eyed at the door while Zack, Ibba, and I stared at her. This wasn't the White House Situation Room. We weren't discussing a top-secret operation. Why on earth had she locked the conference room door?

The person on the other side of the door refused to give up. He banged hard enough to rattle the pens in a cup on the table as he yelled, "Cummings, my office. Now!"

FOUR

Ellis forced a smile as she pushed away from the table. "Excuse me for a moment. It sounds like we have an emergency that needs my attention."

Shortly after she slipped from the room and closed the door behind her, we heard a nearby door slam. More shouting ensued, all from the same male voice, but the walls muffled his words. For ten minutes we listened to the rumble of a nonstop, one-sided rant.

When the tirade ended, the minutes ticked away, but Ellis Cummings failed to return. Various scenarios churned around in my brain, but one stood out the most. "I think we've seen the last of her."

"You may be right," said Ibba. "Everything about this place feels off."

Zack turned to me. "Any theories, Nancy Drew?"

"I think—"

The door swung open and a man somewhere in his late forties

or early fifties entered the conference room. His wardrobe of black long-sleeve T-shirt and black jeans mimicked the late Steve Jobs. The resemblance continued with his wire-rimmed glasses and closely cropped, graying hair that rimmed a receding hairline.

With his mouth pulled into a tight line and his brows knit together, he strode to the head of the table. Instead of taking the seat Ellis had vacated, he pushed the chair aside, placed his phone on the table, and leaned over, his arms straight, his palms flat on the surface. Without introducing himself, he eyed me, then Ibba.

His phone buzzed. He scowled at the screen, rejected the call, then returned his attention to us. "Which one of you is Anastasia Pollack?"

"I am," I said. "And you are?"

"Jared Oberman, owner of Flix Entertainment. I'm sorry to inform you that the offer you received was not made in good faith."

"Explain," said Ibba.

"Who are you?" he demanded.

"Ibba Surface. I represent Ms. Pollack." She reached into her briefcase and passed a business card across the table.

"I see." He straightened and crossed his arms. Then he zeroed in on Zack. "And I suppose you're the muscle?"

The muscle? This guy might look like Steve Jobs, but he sounded like a bit player from *Goodfellows*. Or every Mafia guy who'd crossed my path since Karl had died. "In a manner of speaking," I said. "He's my husband."

Oberman opened his mouth to respond, but before he said anything, I continued. "I take it Miss Cummings wasn't authorized to offer the contract I received?"

"Definitely not. She acted on her own, behind my back, and

without consulting our legal department."

"Which explains the odd wording in the contract," said Ibba.

"Not to mention the obscene sum Flix offered me."

Oberman's eyebrows formed an even more pronounced V as he glowered at me. "And yet you readily accepted."

"I haven't accepted anything yet, Mr. Oberman."

His attitude shifted, sounding less accusatory with more than a slight hint of relief. "Then why are you here?"

Before I could answer, the door swung open. Another twenty-something blonde, this one with shocking pink streaks and a trellis of tiny pink rosebuds tattooed around her neck, stuck her head in the room.

Oberman glared at her. "What?"

"Sorry to interrupt, Mr. Oberman, but your brother is on the phone. He said he's been trying to reach you all day, that it's urgent."

"Global warming is urgent. My brother's calls are never urgent. Tell him I'll get back to him when I have a free moment."

"Got it."

"And to stop calling me every ten minutes."

After she nodded and closed the door, he turned back to us, "Well?"

"We came to learn more," said Ibba. "I'm sure you know what they say about offers that are too good to be true."

He tightened his mouth and nodded.

"Why did she do it?" asked Zack.

Oberman straightened and began to pace alongside the length of the table from the door to the windows. "We have three summer interns working for us. Each is jockeying for one full-time work-study position we plan to fill at the end of the summer.

Along with typical gopher duties, they were each tasked with searching out material for a possible new movie or series. None were given permission to do anything beyond presenting me with the best options they found."

"Did you phrase it that way?" I asked.

He stopped pacing and turned toward me. "What do you mean?"

"If you said you wanted them to bring you the best options, Miss Cummings may have interpreted that to mean she had the authority to offer options for anything she thought promising."

"That's ridiculous. It's not how this business works."

"Did she know that?"

"She should have."

"Why?"

He exhaled forcibly as he scrubbed the stubble on his head. "Because anyone who wants a job in this industry should know how it works."

"Did you offer any orientation or training beforehand?"

"They were receiving on-the-job training."

"To answer phones and make lunch runs? Forgive me for saying so, Mr. Oberman, but you're partly to blame for what happened. Your intern is just a kid. You can't blame her for being a go-getter, especially since you set up a competition between your interns."

He slumped against the wall, shoved his hands in his pockets, and stared up at the exposed pipes suspended from the ceiling. The last thing I expected was what he said next. "You could be right, Ms. Pollack. I suppose I overreacted."

He turned toward Ibba. "Where do we go from here?"

"That's entirely up to you and Ms. Pollack."

He turned back to me. "This is the first I've heard of you. Leave me a copy of your book. Maybe I'll be pleasantly surprised, but don't expect the kind of option offer you received from my former intern. We're a small startup with limited funds. Most of our options are only for a few hundred dollars. We negotiate beyond that after we receive financial backing and a studio commitment."

"There is no book," I said.

He raised an eyebrow. "You're a journalist?"

"I'm a magazine crafts editor."

"We don't produce craft shows."

"No problem. I wouldn't want to star in one."

He threw up his hands. "Then why on earth are you here, Ms. Pollack?"

"I'm a dead body magnet." I went on to explain my status as a reluctant amateur sleuth and the series of podcasts the kids had created. "Your intern wanted to option the podcasts for a TV series."

"And my client's life," added Ibba. "According to my email exchange with Miss Cummings, Flix Entertainment wanted to create a quasi-reality TV series using actors to portray Ms. Pollack and her family, not a show loosely based on or inspired by her crime solving exploits."

"Hmm." His expression grew thoughtful. He pulled out his phone and tapped an app. "What did you say this podcast was called?"

"I didn't, but it's The Sleuth Sayer."

He picked up Ibba's business card from the table. "I'll give a listen and get back to you."

~*~

"Definitely one of the strangest meetings I've ever attended," said

Ibba after we exited the building.

"I doubt you mean that in a good way," I said. "What would you advise?"

"Walk away. From what Zack has told me, that six-figure deal was the only reason you considered accepting the offer. Even if Flix wants to go ahead with the project, my guess is they'll offer no more than five grand per episode. I doubt you want to risk exposing yourself and your family to a fishbowl existence for that amount of money."

No matter how much I'd like to pay off my remaining debt, five grand an episode would hardly make a dent in Djibouti and wasn't worth risking my privacy and my family's privacy. I extended my hand. "I'm sorry I wasted your time, Ibba. If Jared Oberman calls, please inform him I'm not interested."

She grasped my hand in both of hers. "At least I've had the chance to meet the woman who stole my favorite client's heart. From everything I've heard about you, Anastasia, I know we would have had a great working relationship. If I can be of service in the future, please don't hesitate to call."

She turned to Zack. "We'll talk soon."

After he hailed her a cab, we made our way south toward Penn Station.

~*~

I exhaled a deep sigh as I plopped into a window seat on the train back to Westfield. Zack settled in next to me and reached for my hand. "For what it's worth, I'm glad it went down this way. You made the right decision."

"I know. I just hope the kids aren't disappointed."

"They won't be. They've seen how stressed this has made you."

"Good, because for the first time since learning of that podcast,

I'm inching closer to a possible Zen moment."

He half-snorted. "You? Zen?"

"Don't look so skeptical. It could happen."

He leaned over and kissed me. "Before or after the arrival of the flying pigs?"

"I'll get back to you on that."

~*~

Trimedia had arranged to depart the cornfield on Friday morning. Creativity Books planned to move part of their staff in that afternoon and the remainder in the weeks ahead. Given the expected chaos, those of us remaining in the cornfield were told to work from home for the day.

Zack had left the house early to catch the train to D.C. for a meeting at the Smithsonian. Or so he said. For all I knew, he was really heading to the FBI, CIA, or NSA. Maybe some other government alphabet organization so covert that its very existence was on a need-to-know basis. I certainly didn't have need-to-know clearance. Since he said he'd be home in time for dinner, at least I didn't have to worry he was off to Madagascar or Malawi or Mongolia—neither Inner nor Outer.

Alex and Nick were getting ready for their shifts at Starbucks and Trader Joe's. My mother-in-law was in the bathroom, taking one of her five-minute showers that lasted half an hour and drained the forty-gallon hot water tank. I had just poured myself a second cup of coffee when the doorbell rang.

"I'll get it," yelled Alex. A moment later he yelled again. "Hey, Mom, there's a guy here to see you."

Coffee mug in hand, I walked from the kitchen through the dining room and living room to the foyer. I found Alex and Nick standing side-by-side at the open front door. Leonard, the French bulldog previously known as Manifesto before he transferred his allegiance from my mother-in-law to Nick, stood sentry between the boys.

On the opposite side of the threshold stood Jared Oberman. In his arms he held an enormous floral arrangement and an equally enormous box of chocolates.

"Mr. Oberman? What are you doing here?" *And what's with the flowers and candy?* He looked like a nervous suitor.

"May I come in, Ms. Pollack?"

When I nodded, the boys stepped aside and allowed him to enter, but worry clouded both their faces. Leonard emitted a low growl. Nick asked, "You want us to stay, Mom?"

"No need." I reached out and hugged both boys goodbye. "Have a good day." Then I whispered in Alex's ear. "I'm fine. Don't worry."

He stared at me for a beat before nodding. Then he turned to his brother, deposited a playful punch on his bicep, and said, "Let's go, dude."

Nick hesitated, his eyes narrowing as he telegraphed a look toward Oberman that meant only one thing: *Mess with my mom and live to regret it.*

Oberman offered him a weak smile before Alex grabbed Nick's arm and dragged him out of the house.

I closed the door behind them. Oberman held out the floral arrangement and candy. "I wanted to apologize for my behavior yesterday. You must think I'm a real jerk."

I had but didn't nod in agreement. I stared at the overture, hesitant to accept. Flowers and candy seemed too personal. The man was a virtual stranger. But then I glanced at his face. Either he possessed excellent acting chops or genuine remorse stared back at me. I gave in and reached for the offering. "Thank you, but a phone call would have sufficed. You didn't need to drive all the way from Manhattan to Westfield first thing this morning."

"I didn't. I commute into the city from Summit. We're practically neighbors."

Not that a six-mile distance qualified as living in the same neighborhood. However, I suppose if he drove into work each morning, I was only a slight detour. I placed my hand on the doorknob. "I appreciate the gesture."

He didn't take the cue. "Is there something else, Mr. Oberman?"

"Actually, there is. I listened to the Sleuth Sayer podcast after you left yesterday and immediately called your attorney. She said you're no longer interested."

"That's right."

"Because I acted like a total jackass?"

I didn't want to have this conversation with him. However, I decided his remorsefulness required a more detailed explanation. "How about a cup of coffee?"

With Leonard close on my heels, I led Jared Oberman into the kitchen, placed the flowers and candy on the table, and started a fresh pot. In the podcast, the kids had spared me the embarrassment of diving deep into the weeds of Karl's financial deceit. All they had said was that he'd died, leaving us with a huge amount of debt.

There's debt and then there's debt with a capital D. Many people have a mortgage, car loans, and credit card balances that carry over month after month. Most don't find themselves saddled with the equivalent of Uzbekistan's GNP, even if I'd now trimmed Uzbekistan down to a semi-manageable Djibouti.

I had nearly finished giving him a more detailed version of life post-Karl and why I'd considered accepting the option, when Lucille hobbled into the kitchen. She took in the flowers, candy, and the guy sipping coffee at my kitchen table and issued one of her classic harrumphs. "Already cheating on your new husband, I see, Anastasia."

Oberman took one look at my mother-in-law, turned to me, and asked, "The commie?" When I nodded, he added, "My condolences, Ms. Pollack."

"Don't call her that!" Lucille pounded her cane on the floor. "That hussy is no longer a Pollack. She's forfeited the right to use my son's good name."

Lucille then reached out and grabbed the box of chocolates from the table. "Come, Manifesto," she said as she hobbled back in the direction she'd come.

Leonard shifted his jowly head from Lucille to me, then back to Lucille, finally deciding the commie with the chocolate cremes won out over the woman who supplied his kibble. After one last sorrowful look at me, he followed his mistress.

"Don't feed Leonard any of those chocolates," I yelled after her. The last thing I needed was another vet bill.

"His name is Manifesto!" she yelled back, punctuating the last word with a pounding of her cane on the hardwood floor. "And I'm not stupid, Anastasia."

"Could've fooled me," I muttered under my breath.

Oberman chuckled before growing serious again. "I wish you'd reconsider your decision. Ellis was right about the potential of the podcast. She's got good instincts."

"And yet you fired her."

He huffed out a huge sigh. "I'm trying to rectify that, but she's ignoring my texts and calls."

"Keep trying."

"I will. Anyway, I think we could create something unique from the podcast. I can already picture several character actors perfect for the role of your mother-in-law."

I took a sip of coffee, then eyed him over the rim of the mug. "I'm a very private person, Mr. Oberman. I don't crave attention. I've already had enough to fill several lifetimes. Although the option offer tempted me, learning I never should have received it made my decision easy. No matter how much debt I still have, I'm not willing to risk Kardashian-type exposure for a few thousand dollars an episode."

He grew thoughtful, scrubbing his jaw, then said, "Let me talk to my business partner and put a few feelers out to backers we've worked with in the past. I can't promise anything, but we may be able to sweeten the deal."

"Talk all you want. I seriously doubt you're going to come back with anything close to six-figures."

"I can be extremely persuasive when I want a project, Ms. Pollack." He paused. "Or should I be calling you Mrs....what was your husband's name?"

"Zachary Barnes. Either Ms. Pollack or Mrs. Barnes works." What did it matter? Jared Oberman wasn't going to come back with anything close to a six-figure deal. We both knew that. And I wouldn't agree to anything less. If I agreed at all.

It was past time to end this conversation. I stood. "I'm sure you need to get to work, Mr. Oberman. Thank you again for the flowers...and the chocolate."

Not as dense as some men, he took the hint and rose. I walked him to the foyer and swung open the door. He thanked me once more for accepting his apology, turned to leave, and froze. "What the—?"

I searched for what had caught his attention. Two unfamiliar cars were parked on the street. A red two-seater Mercedes convertible with the top down sat in front of my house. An enormous black SUV with black tinted windows was parked across the street in front of the McMansion that had sprung up in place of Betty Bentworth's bulldozed house. "Is something wrong?"

He hesitated before asking, "Does that Cadillac Escalade belong to your neighbor?"

"I have no idea."

"You don't know what cars your neighbors drive?"

"Why would I? Especially those neighbors. They haven't moved in yet."

"Have you seen the Escalade parked across the street before?"

I glanced at the massive vehicle. "Sorry. As a card-carrying member of the Estrogen Brigade, I don't pay much attention to automobiles. Why?"

He shook his head. "I suppose it's nothing."

Nothing? Then why the obsession? Between the worry on Jared Oberman's face and the furtive glances he shot up and down the street, it didn't take Westfield's own Jessica Fletcher to realize something had spooked the guy. "Are you sure nothing's wrong?"

"Yes, I'm fine. For a split second I thought I recognized that car, but I'm mistaken. I'd better run." And he did, literally, jogging down the front path to his car. After closing the door behind him, I headed toward the kitchen.

As I crossed the living room, a pop-pop-pop followed by the peeling of tires shattered the morning calm. I dropped to the floor.

I knew that sound. Still, Fourth of July was only days away. Maybe I was wrong. Maybe some of the neighborhood kids had gotten hold of some firecrackers.

I crawled toward the windows and inched my way up until my eyes were slightly above the sill. The Escalade was gone, the red Mercedes convertible was still parked in front of my house, and Jared Oberman's body lay sprawled in the street.

FIVE

I pulled my phone from my jeans pocket and called 9-1-1. When the operator answered and I gave my name, I heard a groan on the other end of the line. "Don't tell me. Another dead body?"

"In the middle of the street in front of my house."

"Are you sure he's dead?"

"No, but he's not moving. I haven't gone out to check yet."

"Hit and run?"

"Shooting."

"Stay inside. I'm sending the EMTs and law enforcement."

"And Detective Spader?"

"Of course."

I've suspected for some time that the Union County dispatchers have a standing order to notify Detective Samuel Spader whenever a call came in from me.

At that moment, Lucille shuffled down the foyer toward the front door. "Lucille, stay in the house," I yelled, pulling myself to my feet.

She spun to confront me. "How dare you tell me what to do!"

"Please, do not go outside right now."

"I'll do what I want." She swung the door open. From my vantage point at the window, I watched her hobble to the curb.

A moment later, Harriet Kleinhample, my mother-in-law's number one minion, pulled up in her VW minibus and idled behind the convertible. After Lucille hauled herself into the passenger seat, they drove off, oblivious to the dead body sprawled in the street. Or maybe they just assumed it was business as usual these days. After all, what's one more dead body around Casa Pollack? At least Harriet hadn't run over the corpse as she pulled away from the curb.

Within minutes, an ambulance, the SWAT team, two squad cars, and Detective Spader's unmarked sedan converged from opposite ends of the block. A few of my braver neighbors opened their doors a crack, but no one ventured outside.

The SWAT team fanned out. The EMTs rushed to the body, but when they made no attempt to render aid, I knew for certain Jared Oberman was dead. Spader strode over and studied the body for a moment before conversing with the other law enforcement officers.

Less than two minutes later, he concluded his conversation and strode up the path to my house. I met him at the door. Before I had a chance to invite him inside, he took one look at me, shook his head, and asked, "Who'd you piss off this time, Mrs. Pollack...uhm...Mrs. Barnes?"

I swung the door open wider. "Come in, Detective."

He shook his head and flashed a grin as he stepped into the foyer. "Sorry, not yet used to your new name."

"No problem, but really, at this point in our relationship, don't you think first names are in order?"

He offered a sheepish grin as he pulled a notepad and pen from the inside pocket of his suit jacket. "I'd have to get used to that as well. So, who is he, and what happened this time?"

"What makes you think I know him?"

His mouth quirked. "Because it's you."

He had me there. "His name is Jared Oberman. He owns a TV production company in Manhattan. I first met him yesterday."

"What was he doing here so early this morning?"

I gave him the Reader's Digest condensed version. His eyebrows rose at the mention of the television series. "Tell me you weren't considering doing a reality TV show."

"Not me. They planned on hiring actors."

"To portray your adventures sticking your nose in police business?"

I gaped at him. "Really? How many crimes have I helped you solve, Detective?"

"Touché. You do have a knack for seeing what others miss."

"Including you."

He offered a reluctant nod. "Agreed."

"Anyway, I turned him down."

"Probably for the best." When I raised an eyebrow he added, "I wouldn't want my life splashed across TV screens."

"Exactly."

"Any idea who had it in for the guy?"

"Not really, but there was a black Escalade parked across the street when he left. He grew agitated and asked me if I knew who owned it."

"Did you?"

"I don't think I know anyone who owns an Escalade. I told him it might belong to the people who bought the house across the street. When I asked him if anything was wrong, he waved my question away and headed for his car, but his body language told a different story."

"You didn't see any interaction between him and the occupant of the Escalade?"

"No, I closed the door behind him. I heard the gunshots a few seconds later."

"Have you checked your security footage?"

"Not yet." I pulled out my phone and opened the app. Sure enough, the cameras from the high-tech system Zack had installed had not only captured the Escalade's New York license plate, but also the shooting when the Escalade's driver lowered his window and pointed a gun at Oberman. Unfortunately, the shooter wore a black ski mask and gloves, making it impossible to determine the killer's sex, let alone anything else.

I tapped my phone to send Spader the footage. "I wouldn't be surprised to learn the Escalade was stolen."

Spader shot me a *no duh* look. "What else can you tell me?"

"Not much, except yesterday he fired the intern who offered me megabucks to sign a contract."

Spader paused in his note taking. "Do you know why?"

"She wasn't authorized to make the offer. As I learned afterwards, their option deals are never more than a few hundred dollars."

"I see. Do you know why she did it?"

"Killed him? I don't think she had anything to do with that. She's just a college kid."

Spader rolled his eyes. "I meant why she offered you so much money."

"Oh." I told him about the competition between the interns. "I did notice hostility during a brief encounter between two of them."

"In what way?"

"The one who had offered me the option contract lorded over the intern sitting at the reception desk."

"Do you know their names?"

"Ellis Cummings is the intern who contacted me. She referred to the receptionist as Miss Smith."

He scribbled a few more notes. "Anyone else?"

I shook my head. "Like I said, I hardly knew him. I spent less than twenty minutes with him yesterday and even less time this morning."

"If you turned him down, why was he here?"

"He listened to the podcast last night and realized the intern was right. Not about the money but about the potential for a TV series. He came to apologize and try to get me to change my mind."

"But you didn't."

"No."

"Anything else you can tell me that might help?"

I thought for a moment. "Apparently, his brother had been trying to get in touch with him yesterday, and he wasn't taking his calls." I explained the brief exchange when the third intern with the shocking pink streaks interrupted our meeting yesterday. "I don't know her name."

After Spader finished jotting his notes, he thanked me. As he turned to leave, I stopped him before he reached the door. "What about his car?"

"CSI will call in a tow truck. They'll impound it for a few days to do a more thorough search for evidence before releasing it to his next of kin. Why? You in the market for a used convertible?"

"Hardly. I just didn't want it sitting at the curb when my sons come home. They were here when Oberman arrived."

"It's going to be hard keeping the murder from them."

"I don't plan to, but I'd rather tell them on my own terms."

"Assuming they don't hear about it before they get home."

I frowned. "I'm hoping they don't. This is not a conversation for a phone call or text in the middle of their workday."

Spader reached for the doorknob. "Good luck with that."

Given my good luck to bad luck ratio so far today, the odds of Nick and Alex arriving home blissfully ignorant of the Oberman murder ran about a million to one. I crossed my fingers anyway because hope springs eternal.

If it weren't so early in the morning, I'd head up to the apartment for a glass of liquid nerve-calming reinforcement, but I was too responsible a person to drink so early in the day.

I thought about calling Zack or at least sending him a text but decided against it. I'd tell him about Jared Oberman's unexpected visit and his subsequent departure once he got home. As much as I hated to, I'd also have to tell Alex and Nick.

Instead, I decided to call Cloris and suggest we meet for lunch, but at that moment, my phone rang.

"Anything you'd like to tell me?" asked Zack, dispensing with any pleasantries and getting right to the point.

He could only be referring to one thing. "How did you—?"

"How did I know Jared Oberman was shot and killed a few minutes ago in front of our house?"

"I'm guessing clairvoyance is another one of your superpowers."

"That and the local news app on my phone. It lit up with a

breaking news alert about a murder in Westfield. I figured you couldn't possibly be involved. You were supposed to work from home today."

"That was the plan. And just so you know, I haven't left the house."

"I know. I checked the cameras. It didn't seem to matter, at least not for Jared Oberman. What are the odds?"

I let loose a huge sigh. "Given my luck? At this point, I'd think you'd know the odds are pretty good."

"What was he doing there?"

I explained what had happened. When I'd finished, silence greeted me on the other end of the line. "Are you still there?"

"I am."

"You're not saying anything."

"I'm trying to come up with a suitable response that won't make me sound like a Neanderthal. I'm not having much luck. I suppose you wouldn't agree to me locking you up in an impenetrable ivory tower to keep you safe."

"I see logistical problems, but if you allowed visitation rights, especially conjugal ones, I might consider it. At least until Spader catches the killer."

"Except with your track record, there will always be another killer waiting to strike."

I heaved another sigh, this one deeper and louder. "It's beginning to look that way."

"Are you going to be all right until I get home?"

"I'm fine. I was going to call Cloris and suggest we meet for lunch."

"Stay out of trouble."

"Now you're beginning to echo Spader's refrain."

"Sound advice no matter who delivers it."

After promising to steer clear of any murders or murderers, I hung up and called Cloris.

~*~

I found Cloris waiting for me inside the Westfield Diner. She took one look at me as I scooted into the booth and said, "Spill. And don't tell me nothing's up. It's written all over your face."

"You're not going to believe what happened."

Her eyebrows rose under her gingerbread pixie bangs. "If you're involved, nothing surprises me anymore. I'm guessing this has something to do with your meeting in the city yesterday. What happened?"

So much had occurred between the short time I stepped foot into the offices of Flix Entertainment yesterday and Jared Oberman's murder this morning that I was having a hard time processing all of it. Rather than pause mid-explanation, I waited until the waitress poured us coffee and had taken our orders. Then I launched into a chronological recitation of the events, ending with, "Zack is threatening to lock me up for my own protection."

"Not a bad idea."

"Et tu, Brute?"

"If the shoe fits."

Both Zack and Cloris had a point, but I decided not to make any further comments regarding my propensity for finding myself in the vicinity of murder victims. Thankfully, the waitress chose that moment to arrive with our sandwiches.

Cloris took a bite from her BLT, then returned the sandwich to her plate. She leaned back in the booth and crossed her arms. As she chewed, she cast a discerning eye across the table at me. Once she'd washed the mouthful down with a swig of coffee, she said, "I'm beginning to think you're a human manifestation of Joe B-t-f-s-p-l-k."

I squinted at her. "Joe who?"

"A character who appeared in the Li'l Abner comic strip by Al Capp back in the last century."

"I've heard of Li'l Abner. I remember watching the movie version of the musical on television years ago. But who's this Joe guy? I don't remember him. And what's with the crazy surname? How do you even pronounce B-t-whatever?"

She shrugged. "I have no idea why his name has no vowels, but according to Capp, the name is pronounced like a raspberry or a Bronx cheer." She grinned. "I didn't think you'd appreciate me spraying spittle over your lunch."

"Much appreciated. Now, why are you comparing me to this obscure comic strip character?"

"Because although well-meaning, he was the world's worst jinx. Capp always depicted him with a black cloud over his head. You, my friend, have an invisible black cloud over your head."

"Gee, thanks. Although I'd trade the dead bodies for a black cloud any day. Where did you come by such esoteric knowledge?"

"Jeanie found a collection of popular mid-century syndicated comic strips at a yard sale. She brought it into the office while you were on your honeymoon."

"Sorry I missed it." Not. "Did everyone immediately decide I had something in common with this Joe what's-his-name?"

Cloris shrugged. "Only me. Then again, I know more about your recurring bad luck and all the dead bodies than anyone else at work."

"And it had better stay that way."

She drew an invisible zipper across her lips. "Watson would

never rat out Sherlock, but I wasn't the one offered six-figures for a quasi-reality TV gig. Although, I suppose that's a non-issue now."

I nodded. "But why did someone have to die to kill the deal?"

Cloris offered me a smirk. "No pun intended?"

"None. Besides, I'd already decided I wanted no part of the TV show. No matter how much money he offered."

Cloris took another bite of her sandwich and grew thoughtful for a moment. "It's not logical that the murder had any connection to you. Someone was out to get that guy. Why? We don't know, but rotten timing gave the killer an opportunity this morning."

I sighed. "In front of my house. Seems like ever since Karl died, I'm always in the wrong place at the wrong time."

"More like the dead bodies are in the wrong place at the wrong time, but like I said, you're Joe B-t-f-s-p-l-k. Where Anastasia goes, murder and mayhem follow."

I frowned into my coffee. "I think I need a serious Karmic course correction."

"While you're waiting for Hades to freeze over, I hope you have no plans to stick your nose into this latest homicide."

"Heck, no!"

"Keep it that way. You've already used up more than nine lives, and given that you're not of the feline persuasion, you have none to spare."

"Tell me something I don't know." But as I took a bite of my tuna club, I inwardly stewed. The unspoken subtext of Cloris's comment inferred she, too, thought I had some control over the constant deluge of murder victims that found their way into my world. If only that were the case....

I heaved another huge sigh and checked my anger. Like Zack, Cloris was only looking out for me. If our roles were reversed, I would have offered her a variation of the same cautionary advice. After all, the BFF code requires us to look out for each other.

Cloris and I spent the remainder of lunch batting around ideas for the first book in the new *American Woman* crafts-through-the-decades series. Since we were supposed to be working from home today, technically, meeting up at the diner counted as a working lunch.

While I had spent yesterday in the city, she had hunkered down with the hundred and twenty back issues from the nineteen sixties. "Most of what I found sounded less than appealing, although quite popular back then. I shouldn't have a problem updating the desserts. I've already decided to feature pineapple upside-down cake. The modern twist will incorporate macadamia nuts, toasted coconut, and rum-soaked cherries instead of maraschinos."

"Sounds yummy."

"The main dishes are another story, though. Apparently, it was common back then for housewives to use an overabundance of highly processed, chemically laden, or artery-clogging ingredients. Often, all three. Our readers love to indulge themselves with the baked goods I feature, but they want nutritious, healthful dinners that won't pack on the pounds and induce coronaries."

"I don't suppose you happened to notice the featured crafts as you flipped through the pages."

She reached into her purse, pulled out a folded sheet of paper, and handed it across the table to me. "What are friends for?"

Talk about earning BFF points. Good thing I hadn't voiced my earlier thoughts.

I read down the list, scrunching my nose at some of the crafts she'd listed. "Velvet painting?"

"Apparently it was a thing back then."

"I know. Walk any flea market in the country and you'll find at least one Elvis on black velvet for sale. I just didn't know *American Woman* had once featured velvet painting."

Some of the other crafts had more potential. I could work with clothespin dolls, sock monkeys, macramé, tatting, latch hook, needlepoint, tie dye, and batik. If I set my mind to it, I could probably come up with a way to update string art, dream catchers, quilling, stone mosaics, and wood burning. However, I'd take a hard pass on velvet painting, along with crepe paper flowers and apple head dolls. I found the first two tacky and the last downright creepy.

"Each issue also featured either a knitting or crochet project," said Cloris. "But I figure you knew that."

Cloris had saved me hours of time. I refolded the paper and placed it in my purse. "I owe you."

"I'll add it to your account."

~*~

As I slowed to turn left onto my street, a line of vehicles heading toward town forced me to come to a complete stop. When the eighteen-wheeler that had blocked my street continued down the road, the car behind him allowed me to turn. I cut the wheel to begin my turn, but instead of following through, I slammed on the brakes.

SIX

Halfway down the block, four news vans filled the street. ABC, NBC, CBS, and Fox had all set up shop, their satellite dishes raised. Reporters and camera crews milled around the sidewalk in front of my house. Since the gaggle of media fell under the category of Déjà vu All Over Again, I should have expected the onslaught.

At first, I thought about driving to the next block and parking in front of my neighbor Rosalie Schneider's house. Cutting through her backyard into mine would avoid the reporters. Unless some of them had also staked out the back door.

On second thought, I continued down Central Avenue to the next block, hung two rights, and headed back into town. With the media circus camped in front of my house, I could no longer wait until this evening to speak with my sons.

Five minutes later, I parked in the lot behind Starbucks and used the rear entrance. I found Alex working the register. Farther down the counter, Sophie steamed milk at the espresso machine while a third employee prepared a swirly bright pink frozen concoction. Alex and Sophie both waved. I stepped toward the register and forced a cheery note into my voice. "When's your next break?"

"About ten minutes. Everything okay?"

"What? I can't spend some time with my son without an ulterior motive?"

His ears turned red, but he eyed me suspiciously. "Sure, Mom."

"Good. Meet me at the pond."

Before he could ask anything further, I headed for the front door. Once outside, I strode the two blocks to Trader Joe's. Instead of having a similar conversation with Nick, I zeroed in on the store manager. Having met in kindergarten, Arlo Rush and I had known each other most of our lives. I found him at the customer service desk. "Hey, Arlo, mind if I kidnap my kid for about twenty minutes?"

"No problem, Anastasia." He glanced around the store. When he spied Nick, he called out and waved him over.

Nick took one look at me, and concern filled his face. "Everything okay, Mom?"

"Sure. I just need you for a few minutes." I turned back to Arlo. "I'll return him soon."

He waved me off. "Take your time."

"Where are we going?" asked Nick as I led him toward Mindowaskin Park.

"We're meeting your brother at the pond."

Nick jumped in front of me and blocked my path. His voice trembled. "Is it grandma? Has something happened to her? Is she in the hospital?"

"Why would you think that?"

"Because she's old, and old people get sick and die."

"Don't ever let her hear you say she's old."

"It's not Zack, is it?"

"Zack is fine."

"Then what's going on, Mom? You wouldn't pull me out of work for a stroll around the pond."

I grabbed his arm and urged him forward. "I have something I need to tell you and your brother, and I'd rather do it once instead of twice."

"And it couldn't wait until we got home?"

"Afraid not."

"Now you've really got me worried. Where were you today? Don't tell me you've found another dead body."

"I was home until lunchtime, then met Cloris for lunch at the diner. I promise I'll answer all your questions as soon as we meet up with your brother." Coward that I am, I avoided his reference regarding another dead body.

Alex was waiting for us at one of the benches that circled the pond. He jumped to his feet as he saw us approach. I settled onto the center of the bench and indicated the boys should join me.

I heaved a huge sigh. "Remember the man who came to the house this morning?"

"With the flowers and candy?" asked Alex.

Nick was a bit blunter. "We're not going senile, Mom. Of course, we remember."

I blurted out the awful truth. "He was gunned down in front of our house as he walked back to his car."

Alex shot Nick a worried look before asking, "Why?"

"I have no idea."

Nick pulled his gaze from his brother and eyed me with trepidation. "Who was he?"

"The television producer from the production company that wanted to turn the podcast into a series."

"I don't get it," said Alex. "Why would someone want to kill him?"

"And why in front of our house?" asked Nick.

"I don't know, but I'm leaving that for the police to figure out."

"This is our fault for creating the podcast," said Alex.

I squeezed his hand. "No, this has nothing to do with you and the podcast."

"But if we hadn't—"

I cut him off. "Someone was out to get him. His murder had nothing to do with the podcast—or me."

His brow wrinkled with suspicion. "How do you know that, Mom?"

"Because it makes no sense."

Nick's voice filled with skepticism. "So, you're really not getting involved?"

"I promise."

"You always promise," Alex reminded me. "But then something happens, and you get pulled in."

"Not this time."

"If you say so," said Nick.

I knew neither boy believed me. I'd broken this same promise on multiple occasions, not because I wanted to. I don't go out of my way to put my life in danger, but Alex was right. Something always happens to thwart my best intentions.

I turned to Nick. "To answer your earlier question, I pulled you out of work because our street is currently crawling with reporters and TV camera crews. I didn't want you ambushed. If they're still loitering on the street when you get home, park around the corner in front of Mrs. Schneider's house and cut through her backyard."

"What about you, Mom?" asked Alex.

"I plan to follow my own advice." I stood. "Now, you'd both better get back to work."

Before we parted, they sandwiched me in a long bear hug. The seconds ticked by. I wasn't sure either of them planned to let go. Finally, they both dropped their arms and heaved simultaneous sighs before heading back to work.

I settled back onto the bench and stared out at the various waterfowl gliding across the pond. A raft of ducks, a wedge of Canada geese, and a bevy of swans shared the water. Unlike humans, none seemed the least bit interested in bumping off one another, whether their own or a differing species. Oblivious to the others, they coexisted in a peaceful kingdom. Then again, they did have to watch out for the occasional fox on the prowl. Two-footed, four-footed, or web-footed. Were any of us ever truly safe? On that morbid note, I hauled myself to my feet and returned to my car.

As I drove down Central Avenue, I slowed approaching my street. A quick glance to my left revealed the media circus still holding court halfway down the block. Their numbers appeared to have grown. I continued driving, turning left two blocks farther down the road, then hanging two additional lefts until I arrived in front of Rosalie Schneider's house.

I found my neighbor on her hands and knees, weeding the flowerbeds that lined either side of the walkway leading to her front door. When I cut the engine and stepped from the car, her face broke into a wide smile of recognition. "Anastasia, how lovely to see you."

As I approached, Rosalie removed her gardening gloves and held out her hand. "Would you mind, dear? These old bones aren't what they used to be."

After I helped her to her feet, she said, "Give me a minute to clean up. I made a fresh pitcher of iced tea and baked lemon bars this morning."

"Unfortunately, I can't stay, Rosalie."

When her face grew puzzled, I explained why I'd parked in front of her house.

She placed both palms across her chest. "Oh, dear. More crime in the neighborhood?"

"I'm afraid so." I decided not to expound on exactly what sort of crime had occurred.

"But why are there reporters on your street?" She glanced back toward her own open front door. "Was it a robbery?"

"No, nothing like that."

She offered me a knowing nod. "I see. Your mother-in-law again."

I neither confirmed nor denied her assumption. Instead, I said, "Alex will also park here later if the reporters are still loitering near the house. I didn't want you concerned over a couple of unfamiliar cars parked at your curb."

At this point, I saw no reason to worry my elderly widowed neighbor any more than necessary by filling her in on the events of this morning. The stars rarely aligned for me these days, but maybe Rosalie had better luck. Spader might catch the killer before Rosalie heard about the murder.

Besides, from all indications, Oberman was the victim of a targeted hit, not a random shooting. By now, the shooter was probably at least two states away and not prowling the neighborhood.

Then again.... "For the time being, keep your doors locked and don't open to anyone you don't know."

"Don't worry, dear. I learned my lesson after that ugly incident awhile back."

A little over a year ago, Rosalie nearly died when she tripped and tumbled down her basement stairs. Luckily, I found her in time, but the accident led to her becoming the victim of a couple of identity thieves. Thanks to me, Jane Sherman and Willow Krause, aka Virginia and Deborah Mayer, now call the Edna Mahan Correctional Facility their home.

Before Rosalie peppered me with more questions, I said, "I hate to park and run, but I'm supposed to be working from home today, and I'm on a tight deadline. I promise we'll catch up soon."

"I understand, dear. I hope that mother-in-law of yours doesn't give you any more trouble."

"That's always my hope as well." I sighed. "Unfortunately, where Lucille goes, trouble always seems to follow."

With that I waved as I headed around her house to the backyard. I held my breath as I peered over the azalea bushes that separated our two properties. The coast looked clear. I cut through a small strip of grass between two of the bushes and raced across the lawn toward my back door.

To my surprise, I found Zack brewing a pot of coffee in the kitchen. "I didn't expect you home so soon."

He met me halfway across the kitchen and drew me into his arms. "Under the circumstances, I thought it best to cut my meeting short."

I stepped out of his embrace. "You didn't have to do that."

They say a picture is worth a thousand words. The look Zack

gave me would rival the length of the Oxford English Dictionary.

From his perch atop the refrigerator, Ralph issued a squawk and proceeded to stick his beak into the conversation. *"If circumstances lead me, I will find where truth is hid. Hamlet.* Act Two, Scene Two."

I eyed Ralph, then Zack. "I'm an open book." *Unlike some.* I then changed the subject. "Were you accosted by the phalanx of press?"

"They have no idea I'm here. I parked around the corner at the Konopka house and cut through our neighbors' backyards."

"Great minds think alike. I parked in front of Rosalie's house and told Alex to do the same if the reporters are still camped outside later."

Zack flipped the switch to start the coffee brewing. "The boys know what happened?"

"A preemptive move on my part." I filled him in on my conversation with Alex and Nick. "I was worried they'd hear something before arriving home. I also didn't want them accosted by the press."

"Given the three-ring circus on our front lawn, at least half the town probably knows by now."

"True." At that moment, my phone rang. I glanced at the display, frowned, then showed Zack the screen. "And the other half will hear about it shortly."

I reluctantly answered but hit the speaker icon so Zack could hear both sides of the conversation. "Hello, Mama."

My mother jumped right in without any greeting. "What has that pinko and her Evel Knievel sidekick done now?"

"Nothing that I know of."

"Nothing? Then explain why your street is blocked by news

vans."

"Where are you, Mama?"

"On my way back home."

As far as I knew, Mama wasn't aware that I was working from home today. "It's the middle of the day. Why were you on your way to my house at this hour?"

"I wasn't. I'd gone shopping. The Uber driver turned the news on the radio, and I caught the tail end of something happening on your street. I told him to drop me off there instead."

"There's no reason for you to be here, Mama."

Of course, she immediately picked up on my slip of the tongue. "*Here?* You're not at work?"

"I'm working from home today."

"And?"

I knew she wasn't going to drop her interrogation. "Someone died."

"Oh, dear. One of your neighbors? Someone I know?"

"No. He was visiting someone."

"Visiting whom?"

I inhaled a deep breath. "Me."

"I knew it! She finally killed someone. Thank goodness it wasn't you. Maybe now they'll lock her up for good. What did she do? Club the poor soul over the head with that cane of hers? And in your house?"

I closed my eyes and mentally counted to ten, allowing Mama to gloat in her erroneous conclusion. "Outside as he was leaving."

Mama *Torquemada* wasn't satisfied with my minimal explanation, though, and continued her latest inquisition "Who was he?"

"Just someone who had come to drop something off. I can't

63

give you any other details, Mama."

"Can't or won't?"

Zack came to my rescue. "Flora, we have to go."

"Oh, hello, Zachary, dear. Were you home when the commie struck? What more can you tell me?"

"Nothing, Flora." He then reached over and disconnected the call.

Hanging up on Mama never helped. It only added fuel to her fire. "We haven't heard the end of this."

"I know. Once she gets home and turns on the local afternoon news, she'll call again."

"Except this time, she's going to be furious."

"With both of us."

"What if I don't answer the phone?"

He laughed. "This is your mother. What makes you think that will stop her?"

I hate when he's right. Knowing Mama, she'd order up another Uber. If she had to, she'd exit the vehicle on Central Avenue and march down the street, plowing her way through any reporters in her path. Then she'd use her key to enter the house.

Worse yet, she might even bat her eyelashes at a sweet-talking silver-haired reporter and invite him and his cameraman inside, killing two birds with one stone. After all, Flora Sudberry Periwinkle Ramirez Scoffield Goldberg O'Keefe Tuttnauer was currently also on the prowl for my next stepfather.

I sank onto one of the kitchen chairs. Zack poured two mugs of coffee and placed one in front of me before settling into the seat cattycorner to me. I frowned into the steaming mug. "Isn't it five o'clock somewhere?"

~*~

After we finished our coffee, Zack placed Ralph in his cage. We then slipped out of the house, locked the door behind us, and climbed the steps to the apartment above the garage. Once on the landing, I hazarded a quick glance over my shoulder toward the street but saw no one milling around on the sidewalk keeping an eye on the garage. Either they weren't aware of the apartment or figured anyone headed for it would first pull into the driveway.

I'd already wasted most of the day doing anything but what I, as a responsible career-minded adult, was supposed to be doing to earn my paycheck. Of course, I had a legitimate excuse. It's not every day someone is gunned down in front of my house. Then again, with this latest murder, it certainly looked like the dead body count intended to keep increasing rather than coming to an end any time soon.

Throughout the next few hours, I tried to focus on crafts of the nineteen-sixties, even though I'd rather indulge in a bit of hanky-panky and an early happy hour. I'm sure Zack would jump at the chance to accommodate me. However, I shoved those thoughts to the deep recesses of my gray matter and tried to access both my responsible adult and crafts editor genes. I failed miserably. The more I forced my brain to focus on macramé and tie-dye, the more my thoughts stubbornly refused to budge from homicide. Specifically, the one that occurred in front of my house.

I finally gave up, closed my laptop, and reached for the TV remote.

Zack turned from where he sat at his desk across the room. "Glutton for punishment?"

I unleased my inner Pollyanna. "Maybe Spader has already caught the killer."

Zack joined me on the sofa, checking his phone as the

Eyewitness News theme played and the logo filled the screen. "If that's the case, their onsite reporter hasn't gotten the message." Zack angled the phone screen toward me. The security footage still showed dozens of reporters and camera crews filling our lawn and sidewalk.

The news anchor announced the top story. "The formerly peaceful suburban community of Westfield, New Jersey was once again rocked by murder today when television producer and Summit resident Jared Oberman was gunned down early this morning on the street in front of a Westfield residence. Darlene Jamison is on the scene with updates. What can you tell us, Darlene?"

The screen switched to a reporter standing in front of our house. I recognized her as the same one who had reported on the body I'd found in Santa's sleigh last December. The station had probably assigned her the Anastasia Pollack beat. "At this point, we have few details, Kent, but once again, there's a bizarre twist to this story. Jared Oberman's murder took place in front of the home of Westfield resident Anastasia Pollack. Viewers may remember that Ms. Pollack has become something of a local celebrity in these parts, having aided Union County police in several other recent investigations. Some have taken to calling her the town's very own Jessica Fletcher."

"Do we know anything about her connection to the victim, Darlene?"

"We do, Kent. A little digging has revealed that Ms. Pollack is the subject of a recent true crime podcast under consideration for an upcoming TV series."

"Darlene, we're getting word that the lead detective on the case is about to make a statement. We're going to switch over to our crew outside Union County Police Headquarters."

SEVEN

The scene then switched to Detective Spader standing in front of a microphone-covered podium outside the entrance to the Ralph G. Froehlich Public Safety Building in downtown Westfield. Several other officials stood in the background on either side of Spader.

When Spader cleared his throat, the buzz of background activity, presumably from the reporters hovering off-camera, quieted. "Good afternoon. By now I'm sure you're aware that Jared Oberman, a Summit resident, was gunned down in Westfield early this morning. At this time, we have little in the way of leads other than a black Cadillac Escalade was reported at the scene of the crime. A security camera from one of the local residences captured the vehicle's New York license plates, which had recently been reported stolen from a Ford Bronco on Staten Island. Late this afternoon, the torched remains of the Escalade were located in an isolated area of Gilgo Beach on Long Island."

One of the reporters yelled out, "Do you know who the

Escalade was registered to?"

Spader shook his head. "The VINs were destroyed. So far, no one has reported a missing Escalade. At this point, we have no other leads. We're asking that anyone with any information contact the Union County Police at the number appearing at the bottom of your screen. A reward has been offered by Crimestoppers and the family of the victim for any information that leads to the capture and conviction of the person or persons responsible for this heinous crime. We'll update the press and public when we have more information, but for now we're investigating this as a targeted homicide and want to assure the residents of Westfield that we have no indication that anyone else in the community is at risk. Thank you."

As Spader stepped away from the podium, reporters began peppering him with more questions. One that rose above the din asked, "What can you tell us about Anastasia Pollack's connection to this case, given the shooting occurred in front of her home?"

Zack and I turned to look at each other. I couldn't mask the apprehension on my face. He reached for my hand as I held my breath. "Don't worry," he said. "Spader knows how to handle the press."

Spader returned to the podium, his features set in a steely glare. As he stared at the gathered mob, and they continued to shout over one another, he made no effort to answer any of them. Finally, he held up his hands to silence the crowd. "As I said, when we have more information, we'll update you." He turned and strode toward the building's entrance. The various uniformed personnel who had stood silently behing him in solidarity followed.

Zack picked up the remote and switched off the television.

Then he pulled out his phone and placed a call. When the caller answered, he said, "Anything you can do to clear the press from in front of our house and off our street?" He listened for a moment, then turned to me. "How long have they been camped here?"

"I'm not sure. At least since I returned from lunch with Cloris."

Zack returned to his call. "Probably since around one o'clock. Maybe longer." Another pause. "No, she has no intention of speaking to the media." One final pause occurred before Zack offered his thanks and ended the call.

"Spader?"

"He's sending an officer to disperse them."

"What if they refuse to leave? You know, freedom of the press and all that."

"Any news organization that doesn't honor your request to leave you alone will not be invited to the next briefing."

"Spader said that?"

"He did."

"My hero."

Zack raised an eyebrow. "Me or Spader?"

"Both, but you're required to be my hero. It comes with the marriage license. Spader could easily throw me to the wolves."

"He'd never do that. He likes you too much."

"He told you that?"

Zack answered with a wink. "In a moment of bro bonding. Now, white, red or something stronger?"

Before I could answer, my phone rang. I frowned at the display. "Definitely something stronger."

He raised an eyebrow as I answered the call. "Hello, Mama."

"Anastasia, you lied to me."

"Not exactly."

"Don't mince words with me. I raised you to tell the truth. Why did you lead me to believe the commie was responsible for that poor man's death? According to the news, she had nothing to do with it. There's an assassin loose in Westfield. How do you know he's not after you?"

"Because he targeted Jared Oberman, Mama. We just don't know why yet."

"We? I hope you're not getting involved."

"No, I'm not."

"Good. Keep it that way." After that pronouncement, she hung up.

"Mama's upset with me."

Zack handed me two fingers of Scotch. "What else is new?"

~*~

Spader wasted no time in accommodating Zack's request. By the time Alex and Nick arrived home half an hour later, our street was devoid of reporters, camera crews, and satellite-equipped news vans. While Zack concocted one of his culinary delights for dinner and Nick walked Leonard, Alex and I retrieved Zack's Boxster and my Jetta, returning them both to our driveway.

We had just finished a peaceful meal, free from any Lucille, Harriet, and Mama drama, when the doorbell rang. "That better not be a reporter," I muttered.

Zack checked the security app on his phone. "It's a woman."

"Someone we know?"

"Not anyone I recognize. She's alone. No cameraman. No press pass clipped to her shirt or dangling from a cord around her neck. Want me to handle it?"

"Let's both go."

While the boys tackled dinner cleanup, Zack and I headed for the foyer. He swung open the door to reveal a young woman standing on the other side of the threshold. Her telltale red-rimmed eyes registered confusion as they darted from me to Zack, then back to me.

"May we help you?" I asked.

"Are...are you Anastasia Pollack?"

"Yes, and you are?"

Her voice stiffened, and her eyes narrowed as she pierced me with a glare. "Aurora Oberman. Jared's wife."

I stared at the woman in front of me. She didn't look much older than the three interns I'd seen yesterday. The four of them could have passed as quadruplets, or at least siblings, right down to the magenta streaks running through her blonde hair.

Nine hours earlier, someone had murdered this woman's husband feet from my front door. Why was she now standing on my doorstep? Who makes nighttime house calls to strangers under such circumstances?

My mind detoured back a year and a half to the hours after I first learned of Karl's death. The shock, numbness, grief, and eventual anger of those first days and weeks rapidly replayed in my mind. I certainly understood some of the emotional upheaval Aurora Oberman must now be going through. What I didn't understand was why she had decided to pay me a visit. And what was up with the evil stink eye aimed at me? Did she blame me in some bizarre way for her husband's death?

I don't know how long I stood frozen, staring at her, saying nothing. Seconds? Minutes?

Zack slipped his hand into mine and squeezed, drawing me out of my stupor. Then he addressed her. "Would you like to come in?"

She nodded and stepped inside. Zack closed the door and led her into the living room. He motioned to the sofa. "Please, have a seat. Would you like something to drink?"

She emitted what sounded like a cross between a snort and an ironic laugh. "Truthfully, I'd love something to numb the pain, but I'll settle for a glass of water, please."

After Zack headed into the kitchen, she took a deep breath, exhaling in a rush, before addressing me. "You're married?"

I settled into one of the chairs opposite the sofa and nodded.

She sneered. "You're older than I expected. Nothing like Jared's usual type."

I narrowed my gaze. "Excuse me?"

"How long were you having an affair with my husband?"

At that moment, Zack returned with a glass of ice water. He and I stared at each other, dumbfounded, before he handed her the water. Then he took up a position beside the chair where I sat and rested his hand on my shoulder. I didn't know if he was offering me support or trying to keep me from erupting over the absurdity of her accusation.

She redirected her sneer from me to Zack. "You didn't know your wife was cheating on you?"

I found my voice. "I can assure you, I was not cheating on my husband, not with your husband or anyone."

She brushed my comment aside with a wave of her hand. "I'm not a naïve fool. I know Jared slept around. But he usually went for skinny blondes barely out of their teens."

Like his three interns? Or her? "Mrs. Oberman, I first met your husband yesterday afternoon when my husband, my attorney, and I had a meeting with a member of his staff. Between yesterday and this morning, I spent a total of less than an hour with him."

Her voice rose in icy anger. "Then what was he doing here this morning? A virtual stranger doesn't come calling with flowers and candy at the crack of dawn."

I opened my mouth to speak, but she cut me off. "Don't deny it. I get alerts on my phone whenever a charge is made on his credit cards. I know he stopped at Whole Foods on his way here, and I know what he purchased."

"Yes, he arrived with flowers and candy, which I'll admit was rather odd, but there was nothing remotely romantic about the gesture. I took it more as male cluelessness than anything. He didn't want to woo me into bed. He wanted to option an unauthorized podcast about me for a television series. After our meeting yesterday, I informed my attorney that I wasn't interested in pursuing the project. He arrived this morning hoping to change my mind."

"And did he?"

"He did not."

Her sneer segued into mocking disbelief. "Because you were holding out for more money?"

"No."

"Then why? Most people would jump at the chance."

Was she serious? Someone had killed her husband hours ago, and she wanted to discuss the reason I had turned down a deal to option my life for a TV show? "I am not most people. I wasn't interested in sacrificing what little privacy I have left."

I shrugged off Zack's hand and stood. "Now if you don't mind, Mrs. Oberman, I'm truly sorry for your loss. I understand your anger, but you've directed it toward the wrong person. I hope the police quickly solve your husband's murder, and that it brings you some closure. However, you and I have nothing further to discuss."

She blinked several times as she stared at me. Finally, she stood. Her earlier look of confusion returned, and her tone changed from that of an accusing spouse to an insecure teenager. "You really weren't having an affair with Jared?"

Seriously? When I'm married to Zack? I opened my mouth to answer, but the hunk in question beat me to it. "I believe my wife has already made that quite clear."

She nodded, then allowed him to escort her to the door. Once she departed, Alex and Nick poked their heads into the living room. "Wow," said Alex. "That was weird."

"Yeah," said Nick. "How could she believe you'd want to sleep with that dude when you've got Zack?"

Zack chuckled as he wrapped an arm around my waist and drew me close. "I wondered that myself."

I tilted my head to eye him and smiled. "Pretty darned sure of yourself, aren't you?"

Then I sobered. "Seriously, though, I feel sorry for her."

"Why?" asked Nick. "She was downright nasty to you, Mom."

"Sometimes grief causes people to say and do things without thinking. It doesn't appear she had the best of marriages. She needs someone to blame for her husband's death, and she chose the last person to see him alive."

"But she never even mentioned his death," said Alex, "let alone blamed you for it."

"I know, but that's probably because it's much too painful right now. I believe psychologists call it transference. It's not uncommon when people are dealing with traumas beyond their control. They lash out at the most convenient target, whether it makes sense or not. Don't judge her too harshly."

"If you say so," said Nick. "Not that it matters. I doubt we'll see her again."

With my luck? I crossed all my digits and sent out a silent plea to the celestial puppet master who constantly yanked at my strings. However, between my mother, my mother-in-law, the upheaval at work, and yet another dead body, the odds weren't in my favor. Still, after the events of today, would it be too much to ask for at least an uneventful weekend?

~*~

When the doorbell rang first thing Saturday morning, I had my answer. Once again, the gods had rolled around, laughing their tushes off at me.

Zack and I were preparing breakfast for the four of us, Lucille never having arrived home last night. With my mother-in-law spending increasingly more overnights at Harriet Kleinhample's apartment, I dared to hope she'd eventually make the arrangement permanent. Of course, that wouldn't preclude the two of them, like my mother, constantly showing up for meals at Casa Pollack. In Lucille's twisted version of communism, what's hers is hers, but what's mine is also hers.

At first, I thought Lucille had forgotten her key, but Alex returned from answering the door with Detective Spader in tow. At seven-thirty on a Saturday morning, we were all still dressed in our PJs, robes, and slippers, except for Nick who had donned sneakers, a T-shirt, and a pair of shorts to walk Leonard earlier.

If Spader noticed our bedtime attire, he gave no indication. Both his haggard face, covered in two days' worth of five o'clock shadow, and his rumpled suit in desperate need of a cleaning, indicated two things. One, Spader never made it home last night.

Two, this was not a social call. "Rough night?" I asked.

"You have no idea."

I turned to my sons. "Move the dishes to the dining room and set a place for the detective."

"Not necessary," said Spader. "I just need to ask you a few questions."

I poured a freshly brewed cup of coffee and shoved it into his hands. "What you need is a strong shot of caffeine and a hearty breakfast. I won't take no for an answer."

He grinned. "Well, if you insist."

"She insists," said Zack, adding another two eggs to the mixture he'd been whisking. "Besides, we owe you."

After nodding, Spader guzzled the coffee in one long chug. "Thanks. This sure beats the swill that passes for coffee at the station."

Without asking, Zack refilled his cup. Spader settled into one of the kitchen chairs while Zack scrambled the eggs, Alex handled toast duty, and I removed the bacon from the oven and placed the strips on a platter covered with paper towels.

Spader took his time with his second cup of java. He seemed in no hurry to ask whatever questions he needed answered. I didn't mind. Whatever it was, it couldn't be that pressing, which made me wonder if the detective had ulterior motives in arriving so early. Since my Spidey senses weren't tingling, I didn't mind the extra guest at the breakfast table.

Finally, after we'd moved to the dining room, and we all filled our plates, I allowed Spader a few mouthfuls of food before prodding him into an explanation of his early visit. "What did you need to know, Detective?"

He washed down a mouthful of egg with a swig of coffee.

"Mind telling me why you failed to mention you know Jared Oberman's wife?"

EIGHT

"She told you that?"

"She did."

"When?"

"Late last night."

"Surely, you don't think—"

He waved his fork in the air to dismiss my question. "Of course, not." But then his eyes directed a laser of annoyance at me. "At least, I hope not. Withholding evidence doesn't sit well with me, Mrs. Poll...Barnes. Or the district attorney."

I returned his glare with one of my own. "I'm well aware of—"

He cut me off and continued, "Mrs. Oberman's revelation came as quite the unwelcome surprise. Under the circumstances, I hope you understand why I need to question you."

I understood. Spader had to follow every lead. I wasn't reacting to his question so much as his attitude. He should know me better than that by now. "Point taken. But to set the record straight, none of us had ever laid eyes on Aurora Oberman until she showed up at our door last night."

Before I had a chance to say more, Nick jumped in. "She accused our mom of having an affair with the dead guy." He snorted. "Like that would ever happen."

Spader raised both his bushy salt and pepper eyebrows toward his receding hairline. "She failed to mention that."

I suspected there was much Aurora Oberman had failed to divulge to Spader about her husband. "Did she tell you I was only the most recent in a long line of his sexual conquests? Not that I was, mind you."

He nodded. "But she claimed they all occurred before she met him."

"What exactly did she tell you?" asked Zack.

"That she had arrived home from visiting you and was preparing for bed when someone fired three shots through her bedroom window."

I gasped. This wasn't the first time Spader had conveniently buried the lede, but this was definitely a whopper of an interment. "Was she hit?"

"No, but as you can see, this puts an entirely new spin on our investigation."

"How?" asked Alex.

I answered for the detective. "If someone tried to kill Mrs. Oberman, her husband wasn't the killer's only target. He wanted both the Obermans dead."

Spader nodded in agreement. "Bingo."

"Were the bullets from the same gun that killed Oberman?" I asked.

"I'm waiting on the report," said Spader. "We've got people out on vacation and several others dealing with some summer flu bug that's been going around the station. Plus, it's a weekend. Resources are stretched thin right now."

I suppose that accounted for the fact that the detective had apparently pulled an all-nighter.

"Did Mrs. Oberman offer up any names of people who might have a grudge against her and her husband?" asked Zack.

"According to her, neither of them had any problems with anyone," said Spader. "Under the circumstances, I'm finding that hard to believe."

"Except," I said, "she also claimed her husband was a serial womanizer, and she made it quite clear, she wasn't happy about his extracurricular activities. What about the women he had affairs with in the past and their former boyfriends or spouses?"

Spader shook his head. "A dead end so far. She doesn't know any names."

"Yet, she's convinced of the affairs?" asked Zack. "Sounds like she has no proof they existed."

"She jumped to the conclusion that Oberman and I were having an affair because he bought flowers and candy first thing this morning at Whole Foods."

"How would she know that?" asked Spader.

"She admitted she gets a text alert whenever he makes a credit card purchase."

Spader executed an eye roll. "That should be proof he wasn't having an affair."

"How?" asked Nick.

"Because," I said, "a man who sneaks around behind his wife's back would either have a credit card she doesn't know about or pay cash for everything."

"Oh, yeah. Right." Nick mumbled something under his breath.

I caught enough to realize his derogatory comment referred to his father. Only in my case, Karl's affair was with Lady Luck, not some homewrecking coed young enough to be his daughter.

I refrained from admonishing my son and offered up two other possible explanations. "Maybe he was utterly stupid or deliberately wanted to get caught."

Zack proposed a third possibility. "Is it possible Aurora Oberman is delusional?"

Spader shrugged. "Anything's possible, but I can't rule out even the wildest speculation at this point."

"What about surveillance footage?" I asked. "Wouldn't her security cameras have captured someone driving up to her house?"

"Sure," said Spader. "If the system worked. She said it failed a few weeks ago, and her husband hadn't gotten around to replacing it yet."

"Were you able to pull anything from the neighbors' cameras?" asked Zack.

"Nothing useful. We've got zilch in the way of leads." Spader turned to me. "That's why I'm here. I was hoping you could tell me something about her that might shed some light on possible suspects and motives."

"I wish I could, Detective. She was here less than ten minutes. All I can tell you is I sensed that Aurora Oberman is one extremely unhappy woman. Given the age disparity, am I correct in assuming she was a trophy wife?"

Spader reached inside his breast pocket and withdrew his notepad. After flipping through a few pages, he read from his notes. "Oberman's first wife divorced him ten years ago. Irreconcilable differences. They have two kids in their mid-twenties. Both in medical school, one in Chicago, the other in

Boston. Oberman never skipped out on paying child support or alimony. He's also paying full tuition for both kids. The wife remarried three years ago and moved to Florida."

"Did Aurora tell you all this?" I asked.

"Good old-fashioned police work told me."

"Have you spoken to his ex-wife and kids?" asked Zack.

"Briefly. As you can imagine, they're in shock. No one offered any information beyond stating that as far as they knew, Oberman had no enemies. Or if he did, he never mentioned anything. However, his ex-wife admitted she hasn't seen or spoken to him since their youngest kid graduated college two years ago."

"Does this mean you've ruled them out as suspects?" I asked.

Spader gnawed on the last strip of bacon. "I think it's highly unlikely either the ex-wife or his kids had anything to do with his murder. All three have seemingly airtight alibis. However, I can't rule anyone out at this point." Then he offered a conciliatory smile. "Present company excepted, of course."

"Good to know," I said. "Where do you go from here?"

Spader tried to stifle another yawn, but it nevertheless escaped. "Home to catch a few hours' sleep."

That wasn't what I had meant, and I suspected he knew it. Although, Spader had willingly divulged far more about this investigation than any of the previous ones that involved me. Not once had he uttered his standard mantra about not being able to talk about an ongoing investigation. He had arrived specifically to do just that. Not to mention, pick my brain.

He pushed himself away from the table and stood. "Once again, thank you both for your hospitality, especially so early in the morning."

"Any time," said Zack as we escorted him to the front door.

"Especially if you want to brainstorm again," I added.

Both men leveled a suspicious look at me. I held up my hands, palms outward. "Just talk, no investigating."

"I'll take your offer under advisement, Mrs. Poll...Mrs. Barnes."

~*~

Half an hour later, Zack and I had dressed and were relaxing with a second cup of coffee when the boys announced they were off to spend the day down the shore.

"Just the two of you?" I asked.

"Plus, Sophie and one of Nick's friends," said Alex.

Nick has a girlfriend? I shot him a questioning look, but his expression gave away nothing. Instead, he said, "Can you believe Sophie's never gone swimming in the ocean?"

"Not surprising," said Zack. "They don't have oceans in North Dakota."

Nick graced him with a typical teenager *duh* look.

He and Alex then sandwiched me in a hug, each kissing one of my cheeks. As they headed toward the door, I rattled off a series of standard mom commands. "Drive carefully, have a good time, and remember you're both working tomorrow morning. Don't stay out too late."

In unison, they rolled their eyes and said, "Yes, Mom."

After they left, Zack said, "Want to get away for the day?"

"What did you have in mind?"

"When was the last time you spent the day down the shore?"

I thought for a moment. "The summer before Lucille came to live with us. We rented a cottage on Long Beach Island for a week."

"I'd say you're due for some wet sand squishing between your toes."

"Overdue. But I wouldn't want the boys to think we're spying on them."

"Four teenagers down the shore? They'll head for the excitement of Point Pleasant. I was thinking someplace quieter. No arcades or amusement rides. Maybe Ocean Grove or Spring Lake?"

"Either works for me."

~*~

Once we'd walked Leonard and placed Ralph in his cage, Zack and I climbed into his Boxster, and we headed down Central Avenue toward the Garden State Parkway. With Independence Day having fallen mid-week, traffic was relatively light for a sunny Saturday morning in early July. Anyone vacationing down the shore this week was already there. However, on the downside, once we arrived in Ocean Grove, it took nearly as long to find a parking space as it had to drive the thirty-five miles from Westfield.

After parking the car, Zack opened the trunk and grabbed the backpack he'd packed with his camera and a few beach essentials. As we hiked the six blocks to the boardwalk, I inhaled deep breaths of the salty sea breeze that wafted inland from the shoreline. The closer we got to the ocean, the stronger the revitalizing, almost spa-like air grew. I sighed.

Zack squeezed my hand. "Something wrong?"

"No, I'm just reminded of how much I've missed the Jersey shore, especially the scent of the ocean. I'm glad we came, even if the place is jammed with wall-to-wall tourists and day trippers."

"Like us?"

I laughed. "Point taken, but I always considered myself one-part local day tripper, one-part semi-resident. At least back in the day."

"Meaning?"

"Like most Jersey natives, I spent many childhood summers down the shore, but unlike most of my friends, I wasn't interested in baking on the beach. My favorite times were always before the crowds descended for the season and after they departed as the weather grew cooler. We weren't considered townies, but we believed we were different from the weekend summer onslaught of people from Staten Island and Philadelphia."

"So...shore snobbery?"

I stopped walking. "Don't scoff. It's a real thing."

Zack chuckled as he shook his head. "I had no idea there was a hierarchy."

As we approached the boardwalk, we discovered the second reason for the scarcity of available parking spaces. A queue of canopy display tents lined the eastern edge of the boardwalk, completely blocking the view of the ocean. The tents stretched north nearly as far as Asbury Park and south almost to the border with Bradley Beach. Exhibitors hawked everything from skin care products to crafts to gutter guards.

"Change of plans?" asked Zack.

I scanned the sea of booths to my left and right and shook my head. "I'll pass. If you've seen one street fair, you've seen them all. The same exhibitors, no matter the town. I'd rather stroll along the water's edge with you."

Zack laced his fingers through mine and led me through the crowd of shoppers toward the kiosk selling beach tags. While he waited in line, a familiar lilac-streaked blonde caught my attention.

NINE

A few yards away, on the opposite side of the boardwalk from the rows of display tents, a woman sat with her back toward me. Strands of lilac wove through the blonde French braid that fell several inches below her nape. She sat in front of an easel where she worked on a caricature of a young girl seated on a chair in front of her. A couple, presumably the child's parents, stood off to the side, watching the artist's progression.

Surely, the artist couldn't be Ellis Cummings. What were the odds? Still, I ambled down the boardwalk for a closer look to satisfy my curiosity. The nearer I got, the more convinced I became of the ironic coincidence, especially once I was close enough to read the Cummings Caricatures sign hanging above samples of her work.

I stopped a few feet away, half hidden behind the couple to Ellis's right. As the child fidgeted, the woman encouraged her to sit still. "Just a few more minutes, honey. Then we'll get ice cream cones. Okay?"

The child's face lit up. "With sprinkles?"

"With sprinkles."

The child immediately stopped squirming.

Caricature artists are as prolific along the Jersey shore as sand flies. Most have questionable talent, their creations looking nothing like their models. I studied the samples displayed on a rack at the edge of the boardwalk. Most featured images of recognizable celebrities, thus showing off the level of the artist's talent. A smaller sign listed prices that varied by size and the number of caricatures per drawing. Ellis's skills far surpassed any caricature artists I'd ever seen at the shore, and her prices reflected her talent. Her work was nearly on a par with the late Broadway caricaturist Al Hirschfeld.

As Ellis completed the transaction and handed the wrapped artwork to the couple, she noticed me. Her face reflected surprise mixed with trepidation. She waited until the couple and their child had departed and were beyond earshot before speaking. "What are you doing here?"

"Hello, Ellis." I nodded toward her samples. "You're very talented."

"I know. It pays my tuition. And it sure beats waiting tables or pulling espresso shots."

"How are you doing?"

She glared at me. "How should I be doing? He fired me, you know. It wasn't my fault. He told us to bring him options. That's what I did."

"Apparently, he meant options as in a range of possibilities, not contracted deals."

"Then he should have said that. In film and TV production an option means something very specific."

"I don't think he was a very good communicator."

She emitted another snort. "Meaning he is now?"

I stared at her. "You don't know, do you?"

"Know what?"

"Jared Oberman is dead."

Her jaw dropped, and she reached for the back of her chair to steady herself. Her voice faltered. "H...how? Wh...when?"

I quickly explained how Oberman was gunned down yesterday. "The police haven't contacted you?"

Her eyes bugged out, and her jaw trembled. "Wh...why would they contact me? I didn't shoot him. I've been here since Thursday evening."

"Ellis, no one is accusing you of having any connection to the murder."

"Good. Because I don't. I've never even held a gun, let alone fired one. I took the first train out of Manhattan after security escorted me from the building. And let me tell you, that was one humiliating experience I'll never live down."

I couldn't tell if defiance or anger had now seeped into her voice. Possibly a combination of both. I pulled a bit of comfort from my Mom Tool Kit of Advice. "No matter how embarrassed you feel now, I can assure you, with time, you'll put the incident behind you."

Her voice rose several octaves. "Really? How clueless are you? It's already posted all over social media, thanks to that gloating tattooed skank who filmed my perp walk. My phone started blowing up with notifications before I even made it to the street."

"Where did you go?"

"Home. I live a few miles away in Neptune. I haven't been anywhere other than my parents' house and this spot on the boardwalk since hopping a train at Penn Station."

An alibi easily verified, which I suspected Spader would do once he caught twenty or thirty winks. "The police have no leads. They planned to speak with all the Flix employees."

Once again, fear creeped back into her voice. "Wh...why?"

"To see if anyone can offer information that might help them generate a list of possible suspects. A Detective Spader didn't call you?"

She shrugged. "Maybe. Everyone I know texts. Most calls are spam. If I don't recognize a caller, I block the number."

"Did you get any calls yesterday?"

She shrugged again. "Maybe. I don't know. I turned off my phone."

Certainly not usual behavior for anyone of Ellis's generation. When I raised an eyebrow, she explained. "It didn't stop pinging. The last thing I wanted was proof that I'm the newest target of a legion of online trolls."

"I'm sorry."

Ellis issued a third snort. "Like sorry will help me get another internship or a fulltime position after graduation. This is going to follow me around for the rest of my life. I'm probably a meme by now."

What could I say? I knew she was right. In junior high and high school, I had become the target of the mean girls on more than one occasion. However, those were different times. Back then, memories faded over time. Nowadays, thanks to social media, they live on forever.

I decided to change the subject. "Can you think of anything that might aid the police in their investigation? I'm happy to pass along the information if you don't want to speak with anyone."

Of course, that wouldn't prevent Spader from knocking on her door if he wanted a face-to-face with Ellis, but I didn't mention that.

"Like what?"

"Anything that could help. Like problems with a disgruntled client or vendor."

"Something that would have gotten him killed?"

"Exactly."

She shook her head. "Business owners have problems all the time. People don't get killed over them."

"Some do."

Her eyes grew wide. "Are you investigating his murder? Is that why you're here?"

"No, seeing you is pure coincidence. My husband and I came down for the day." I pointed toward the kiosk where Zack had inched his way closer to the front of the line. "He's buying beach tags for us."

I moved the discussion back to the murder investigation that I wasn't investigating. "What about Oberman?"

"What about him?"

"He told me he called you several times after he listened to the podcasts Thursday night."

"Like I said, I turned off my phone. But after the way he treated me, I would have flagged his calls as spam anyway."

"He wanted to apologize and ask you to come back to work."

She sneered. "Well, it's too late for that now, isn't it? I'm not sure I would have gone back, anyway."

"Why?"

"The guy was a total tool. He kept hitting on me, even though he was old enough to be my father. Then again, he hit on everyone at the office."

"Everyone? Even the guys?"

"What guys?"

"Are you saying no men work at Flix?"

She shook her head. "None. Except for him and his brother, the entire staff is female, blonde, and under thirty."

"What about the pastel hair streaks? Was that some weird corporate branding?"

Ellis rolled her eyes and sneered. "Jared thought so. He was always trying to act like a hipster, but he just came across as an old dude pretending to be cool."

Given Ellis's accusation that Jared hit on her, maybe Aurora Oberman wasn't delusional about her husband's extracurricular activities. I steered the conversation back in that direction. "Did any of the other staff succumb to his advances?"

"Succumb to his advances?" Her voice filled with mocking derision. "What are you, a character in a Jane Austen novel?"

"Fine. Did any of them hook up with him?"

"I don't know about the rest of the staff, but the two other interns kept score."

"They told you that?"

"They bragged about it. Like bedding the boss would give them an edge."

"And did it?"

"Not that I noticed. And truthfully, they could have been lying. We didn't get along."

Which explained the interaction I'd witnessed between Ellis and Miss Smith at Flix. "Why would they lie about something like that?"

"I don't know. Maybe they thought it would rattle me. Or

make me jealous."

"Did it?"

"Heck, no. It only made me think less of them." She then pointed across the boardwalk. "Anyway, it looks like your husband is searching for you."

I turned to find Zack scanning the area. When he looked our way, I waved, and he headed toward us.

"This is a surprise," he said.

Ellis eyed me. "Yeah, that's what your wife said." Although, she still didn't sound convinced. She waved toward her easel and addressed me. "If we're done, I need to get back to work. Unless, of course, you'd like a caricature."

Zack studied her samples, then turned to me. When I nodded, he said, "Sure. How about a sixteen-by-twenty of the two of us?"

Ellis's face lit up. Zack had chosen the most expensive option on her menu for a two-person drawing.

~*~

As she sketched, Ellis made it clear she wasn't interested in engaging in any further discussion of her firing or of Oberman's murder. As much as I'd like to learn more about the staff at Flix, I didn't blame her for clamming up. I'd leave it to Spader to earn his salary by prying any additional information from Ellis.

By the time she finished the drawing, several other people had queued up for caricatures. Segueing into a friendly but businesslike manner, Ellis wrapped the drawing, accepted payment, then thanked us as she handed the package to Zack.

Not wanting to lug the drawing with us on the beach, we first returned to the car to drop off the drawing. As we strolled down the street, I caught Zack up on my brief conversation with Ellis.

After I finished, he asked. "Did you mention there was also an attempt on his wife's life?"

"I never got the chance. Do you think it matters?"

He grew thoughtful. "I'm not sure. If someone has a grudge against Flix Entertainment, everyone who works for the company is at risk."

"Except we didn't see Aurora at the Flix office, and she never mentioned working there. Or anywhere else, for that matter. I got the impression she's a trophy wife who spends her days spending her husband's money."

"That was my impression as well. But until the police uncover a motive or motives, there isn't even any proof that the two events are connected."

I stopped short, turned, and stared at him. "Oberman was murdered yesterday morning. Someone tried to kill his wife last night. How could they not be connected?"

Zack shrugged. "I'm not suggesting they aren't, but stranger things have happened. Once Spader gets the forensics back on the bullets shot into Aurora's bedroom, he'll have a better idea of a connection. Or not."

"Or not? You're making my head spin."

"If the bullets were fired from the same gun that killed Oberman, there's a connection between the two crimes. However, if a different gun was used to shoot at Aurora, the police might still be looking for only one gunman."

"Because he used a different gun."

"Exactly."

I mulled this idea around in my head. "If so, that would indicate the police aren't dealing with a crime of passion or opportunity. No jilted lover or disgruntled client or ex-employee. The gunman might be a savvy killer who switched weapons to throw a monkey wrench into the police investigation."

"That's certainly a possibility."

"What should we do?"

"We?" Zack's brows formed a V as he narrowed his gaze at me. "*We're* not doing anything. We're letting the police handle this investigation."

"Right. Of course. But shouldn't we warn Ellis? If someone is targeting Flix employees, she's in danger. She ignored Detective Spader's calls yesterday."

"Instead of worrying her, why don't you call Spader and tell him where he can find her."

"That's an excellent idea." I whipped out my phone, hoping Spader had already finished his forty winks. I didn't want to be on the receiving end of whatever obscenities the grumpy, overworked, extremely overtired detective might hurl at me for interrupting his snooze.

The call went directly to voicemail.

By the time I finished leaving a message, Zack and I had arrived back on the boardwalk. I glanced to my left and found Ellis hard at work on another caricature. She appeared to be doing a brisk business. A growing line of people, some with and some without children in tow, waited their turn.

Zack and I made our way to the wooden steps that led to a path cutting through the protective dunes to the beach. After slipping off our sandals and slathering on sunscreen, we headed for the water's edge, serpentining through the mass of beach chairs, blankets, and umbrellas dotting the sand between the boardwalk and the ocean's edge.

We had ambled nearly to the border separating Ocean Grove from Asbury Park when Detective Spader returned my call. As usual, the detective dispensed with any telephone etiquette. Once I answered, he dove right into accusation mode.

"I thought you promised to hang up your deerstalker hat, Mrs. P...Barnes."

I placed the call on speaker so Zack could hear the full conversation. "Never owned one, detective."

"Seems to me, I remember a promise you made to your kids and husband. Why are you still sticking your nose into my investigations?"

Spader continually waffled between showing appreciation toward me and annoyance with me. It seemed he'd settled into annoyance mode lately, and I wondered if it had to do with case overload, staffing issues, lack of sleep, or all three. Part of me felt sorry for the guy, but I'm not the most patient person in the world, and my exasperation level had skyrocketed.

Which is why I chose to respond by unleashing my sarcastic side. "And here I thought you'd thank me for finding someone you wanted to question, Detective. Would you have preferred I withheld information about bumping into Ellis Cummings in Ocean Grove?"

"What are you doing in Ocean Grove?"

"Strolling on the beach with my husband."

"And you just happened to bump into Ms. Cummings on a beach filled with hundreds, if not thousands, of people?"

"No, we bumped into her on the boardwalk."

He muttered a few choice words under his breath. "So let me get this straight. In a state with a population of more than nine million people, you drove thirty-five miles south and just happened to bump into someone from New York."

"Well, put that way, it does seem highly improbable."

"You don't say."

Sarcasm was my go-to. I ignored his. "Except Ellis Cummings doesn't live in New York. She lives with her parents in Neptune, which, as I'm sure you know, is right next door to Ocean Grove. She works weekends on the boardwalk, feet away from one of the kiosks where we were purchasing our beach tags."

Spader remained silent for a long pause. I suspected a huge portion of crow was stuck in his craw. Finally, he said, "And you didn't know any of this prior to arriving down the shore?"

"I give you my word. If you don't believe me, ask my husband."

Zack didn't wait for Spader's request for confirmation of my truthfulness. "I believe you owe my wife an apology, Detective."

Spader sighed heavily. "Once again, I'm in your debt, Mrs.—" He paused, then added, "Barnes. I apologize for overreacting."

I thought about congratulating him for remembering my new name but decided against saying anything that might ruin the moment and further raise his adversarial hackles. Instead, I took the high road. "Apology accepted, Detective."

"I'm leaving for Ocean Grove now. Where will I find Ms. Cummings?"

I gave him Ellis's location. "She's set up on the west side of the boardwalk at the Main Avenue entrance."

After I hung up, I wondered if I should have asked Spader not to mention he learned of Ellis's whereabouts from me. I posed the question to Zack.

"Would it matter?"

"I doubt it. Even if Spader denied having heard from me, I don't think Ellis would believe him."

"Then, you have your answer. I wouldn't stress over it. Chances are, you'll never run into Ellis Cummings again."

"I hope you're right. I never expected to run into her this morning. I get the impression she doesn't like me very much."

"That's probably because you decided not to sign the contract."

"Maybe, but since she wasn't authorized to offer the contract in the first place, Oberman would have found a legal way to void the deal. However, I think there's more to Ellis's animosity toward me than that."

"From what I've observed and also what you've described to me, I think Ellis Cummings had more than a chip on her shoulder before the two of you ever crossed paths."

"Hmm...more like a two-by-four. In some ways she reminds me of Tessa Lisbon."

Zack raised an eyebrow in question. "Remind me who she is."

"*American Woman's* fashion editor. Both have a huge sense of entitlement. The only difference is that unlike Tessa, Ellis has actual talent."

"As a caricaturist. Judging from how she handled things at Flix, her people skills leave much to be desired. She's got a lot to learn if she wants a career in the film industry. That's a business where you need to get along with all sorts of diverse personalities if you want to succeed."

"Divas don't mix well with other divas."

"Or anyone else, for that matter." He glanced toward the boardwalk. We were parallel to the last display tent in the queue. "Hungry?"

My stomach answered for me. I was like Pavlov's dog. The mere mention of food set my tummy rumbling.

Zack glanced down at the offending body part and grinned. "I take it, that's a yes."

Ever the boy scout, Zack had come prepared. After we hiked across the sand to the spigot at the edge of the boardwalk, he whipped out a towel from his backpack. Once we rinsed off the sand, dried our feet, and slipped on our sandals, we left the boardwalk and walked the short distance into downtown Asbury Park.

Throughout the short stroll, my mind kept circling back to Ellis Cummings, and I heard Ralph chime in with his two cents of parrot wisdom. "*The lady doth protest too much, me thinks. Hamlet.* Act Three, Scene Two."

TEN

I half expected that a phone call from Detective Spader would interrupt our lunch of lobster rolls, paired with a fruity umbrella drink for me and a craft beer for Zack. My sixth sense had deserted me, though, because my phone remained silent.

Fully sated, Zack and I ambled around the shopping district for half an hour before he asked, "Up for another surf stroll?"

"Absolutely." I'd missed the Jersey shore too much to cut the day short. Besides, for those of us who don't enjoy lying on the sand, roasting to a crisp, the day couldn't be more perfect. The partly cloudy sky and gentle breeze provided Goldilocks weather. The temperature was neither too hot nor too cold, and the low humidity, the true unicorn of summer weather in New Jersey, offered the ultimate coup de grace.

An hour later, we'd strolled the waterfront from Asbury Park to Bradley Beach, then reversed direction and headed back toward Ocean Grove. After we once again rinsed the sand from our feet, I said, "If it's still in business, I know a great ice cream parlor nearby."

Zack cocked his head and grinned. "Lead the way."

Pedestrian traffic on the boardwalk had picked up considerably since we'd first arrived. As we maneuvered through the throngs of people taking in the exhibits, I was shocked to catch a glimpse of Detective Spader speaking with Ellis. I nudged Zack and tilted my head in the detective's direction. "When we spoke, Spader said he was leaving as soon as we hung up. That would have gotten him down here more than an hour ago. Do you think he's been questioning Ellis all this time?"

"Doubtful. If he'd wanted to do such an in-depth interview, he would have brought her in for questioning. Or at least spoken with her in a more private location. Maybe something delayed his departure."

Luckily, Ellis faced away from Zack and me, because at that moment, Spader and I locked eyes for a split second before Zack and I left the boardwalk.

We were crossing Ocean Avenue a few second later when my phone chimed with a text. "Spader wants to speak with us."

"What's the name of that ice cream place?"

"Day's."

Zack executed a few taps on his phone. "It's still there. Invite him to join us for ice cream."

~*~

Fifteen minutes later, a panting Detective Spader lumbered up the steps to join us at a table on the outdoor patio next to the ice cream parlor. Mixing metaphors, he looked worse than the proverbial cat that dragged itself home the morning after the night before.

Spader never looked great, but the last few months he'd made a concerted effort to take better care of himself. He'd even lost enough weight to warrant buying some new suits. The telltale odor of tobacco no longer clung to him, convincing me he'd stopped poisoning his lungs.

However, ruptured capillaries, a sign of excessive drinking, still covered his nose. I don't know if they ever heal, but at least the condition hadn't worsened, leading me to believe he'd cut back on his alcohol consumption. I'd even silently speculated that he'd found a girlfriend, although with the hours he kept, I didn't see how he'd find time for a meaningful relationship.

Currently, though, a gray pallor, dotted with beads of sweat, had replaced Spader's normally ruddy complexion. Of course, it didn't help that he wore a suit on a day when everyone around us had dressed in shorts, sundresses, or bathing suits. "Good grief, Detective. Get out of that jacket and remove your tie before you either pass out or stroke out."

He pulled a handkerchief from his pocket and swiped it across his forehead. "Can't. I'm on duty."

"Your secret is safe with us." I pointed to the opposite end of the patio. "Men's room is over there. At least splash some cold water on your face."

Spader nodded as he pushed himself away from the table. As he shuffled toward the men's room, Zack rose. "Maybe I should follow him to make sure he doesn't keel over in the bathroom."

"Good idea. I'll grab something cold for him to drink." I waved over a waitress from the restaurant that shared the patio with the ice cream parlor and ordered a large lemonade for Spader.

She returned with the lemonade as Zack and Spader arrived back at the table. Some color had returned to Spader's face. Zack must have convinced him to forego his suit jacket because it was now slung over his shoulder, conveniently concealing his holstered gun. Once Spader settled into his seat, I pushed the lemonade toward him. "Drink."

He offered me a wan smile. "Yes, ma'am."

After he'd chugged half the lemonade, I asked, "Have you eaten anything today?"

He raised an eyebrow. "Are you playing mother?"

I took a sip of my ice cream float, then frowned at him. "Apparently, someone has to."

I again waved to the waitress, then pointed to the half-empty glass. She brought another lemonade and handed Spader a menu. After a quick perusal, he ordered a club sandwich with a side salad. At least he was still watching what he ate.

Once Spader drained the first glass of lemonade, he said, "You're a good person, Mrs. Barnes."

"Not according to my mother-in-law, but nice of you to say so, Detective."

"She doesn't count." He grabbed the second lemonade, downed half of it, then continued, "I want to apologize for my gruffness the last time we spoke. You've been a huge help to me in the past. I appreciate it, but I don't want you getting hurt."

"I'm not—"

He cut me off. "We both know you've had some close calls. Don't deny it."

"I don't. However, once again, I want to assure you that I'm not investigating Jared Oberman's murder. I was as surprised as anyone to run into Ellis Cummings this morning."

"I believe you."

"Then what did you want to discuss?"

"This case."

My mouth dropped open. "Okay, who the heck are you, and

what have you done with Detective I-can't-discuss-an-ongoing-case Spader?"

He chuckled. "I suppose I deserve that. Here's the deal. I'm overworked because the department is understaffed. Crime is up, and we have nothing left in this year's budget to hire more detectives. Lately, I'm averaging three hours sleep a night, and that's only when I'm lucky. My doctor tells me I can't keep up this pace without my health suffering, and I know I can't keep up this pace without the cases suffering. Something or someone will eventually fall through the cracks. Depending on the case, that could prove deadly."

I nodded. "And you'd take the fall."

He grimaced as he scrubbed at his jaw. "Maybe it sounds selfish, but after all the years I've put in as a cop, I'd like to retire with my pension intact."

Spader currently looked like he might not make it to tomorrow, let alone those golden retirement years. "Are you asking me whether you should hand in your badge now, Detective?"

He shook his head. "No, but I'm not too proud to admit I need help, Mrs. Barnes. You have a knack for seeing things that others miss. That I've missed."

"Hold on a minute," said Zack.

Spader held up both hands, palms outward. "No worries. I'm only suggesting in a consulting capacity. No interfacing with witnesses or suspects, and no snooping of any kind. Like I said, I don't want to see your wife get hurt. And I sure as heck don't want it on my conscience if somehow, I was responsible for that happening."

He turned to me. "I'd just like to know that I can pick your brain when I'm at an impasse. Like I am with this case."

The waitress arrived with Spader's club sandwich. I turned to Zack. "What do you think?"

His jaw had tightened. For a few seconds he remained silent before he finally answered me. "It's your decision."

"No, it's our decision. Because I suspect you'll be roped into these brainstorming sessions as well." I glanced at Spader as he took a huge bite out of his sandwich. "Am I right, Detective?"

He quirked his mouth and spoke around the food. "I'll admit, you both have special talents that have previously come in handy."

I suspected Spader wasn't referring to my husband's photojournalism. As a member of law enforcement, did Spader know things about Zack that my husband deliberately hid from me? Or was my overactive imagination once again speculating up the wrong tree?

I glanced between both men. "So, this is a package deal? Two for the price of one freebie?"

Spader offered me an apologetic grin. "I don't have the budget for a paid consultant."

"I figured as much."

"Consider it a service to both your community and your favorite detective."

I raised an eyebrow. "What makes you think you're my favorite detective?"

"Call it cop intuition."

He had me there. Spader had grown to respect me, and I appreciated that he was man enough to admit it. Not many would. I turned back to Zack. "Well?"

"I have no objection as long as our involvement is limited to private conversations with the detective and nothing more."

Spader washed down another mouthful of sandwich, then emitted a huge sigh. "Thank you, both."

I nodded. "Where would you like to start?"

"What more did you learn from Ellis Cummings before you called me?"

"Speaking of which," I said, "how long were you questioning her? Before we hung up earlier, you said you were about to leave for Ocean Grove. We were surprised to see you on the boardwalk with her."

"Chalk it up to the overworked, understaffed part of my job. As I was about to leave headquarters, I got waylaid regarding another case."

"Good to know you weren't standing on the boardwalk, sweltered in the hot sun for more than an hour."

He gulped down the remains of his second lemonade and waved to the waitress for another refill. "Yeah, if that had been the case, I suspect we'd be having this conversation in my hospital room. So...back to Ms. Cummings...."

I recounted what I remembered of our conversation. "Is that what she told you?"

"Pretty much."

"But?"

"Yesterday afternoon, I drove into the city and questioned both Brooklyn Smith and Kendall Braxton, the other two interns. They told a completely different story."

"How different?" asked Zack.

"They claimed Cummings was the intern sleeping with the boss."

"If their version of the office affair is correct, that makes Ellis a prime suspect in Oberman's murder." I shook my head. "Except I don't see it."

"Why not?" asked Spader.

"For starters, how likely is it that a college kid working two jobs to pay tuition would drive a Cadillac Escalade?"

"Could be her parents' vehicle," suggested Spader. "We still have no reports of any stolen Escalades in the tristate area."

I shook my head. If Spader weren't so tired, he'd never offer up such an absurd suggestion. "Wouldn't they have noticed their car is missing?"

"Not if it's kept in the garage and they haven't had a reason to go out. For all we know, they're off on a cruise."

I rolled my eyes at him. "Neptune is a blue-collar town. How likely is it that anyone living in Neptune would own a car worth more than half the value of the average home in the area?"

Spader ran his fingers through what was left of his hair and offered up a huge sigh. "Point taken. Still, though, if Cummings was having an affair with Oberman and he fired her...a lover scorned is a strong motive for murder."

"I'll give you that, Detective, but is there any proof Ellis was having an affair with Oberman? It's her word against the other two interns. And they had time to coordinate their alibis."

"What about the other employees?" asked Zack. "Were you able to interview any of them? Did anyone else mention Oberman was having an affair with one or more of the interns?"

"No one else was at the office Friday afternoon. I'll go back Monday to interview the other staff."

I pondered this for a moment. "We didn't see anyone else at the offices Thursday afternoon, just the three interns. Don't you think it's strange that a company like that would be left for hours at a time in the hands of three college interns?"

Spader nodded. "I do. Right now, though, all I have are statements from Smith, Braxton, and Cummings. And for all I know, all three are lying."

"Or," I suggested, "Smith and Braxton threw Ellis under the bus so it wouldn't get out they were both involved with the boss, either individually or as a threesome."

"Could be. Unless we're dealing with a lying, manipulative psychopath, neither Smith nor Braxton stand out as having a motive for murder. Not that some killers need much in the way of motivation. But Cummings does have a motive. She's the one who was fired."

"Sometimes money is the only motive," said Zack.

Spader turned to him. "You think this was a murder for hire?"

Zack shrugged. "Don't you? Think about it. Broad daylight. Residential street. Strike and run. Torched vehicle. What else could it be?"

"If you want my two cents, that's what I've thought from the beginning," I added.

Spader nodded. "I'm not disagreeing. I just don't currently have any evidence pointing in that direction. Or anywhere else. Facts lead to convictions, not speculation. And I'm extremely short on facts in this case."

"But doesn't speculation often lead to uncovering facts? Isn't that why you want my input?"

He waved his fork at me. "You make a valid point, Mrs. Barnes. Speculate away."

"Have you looked at Oberman's finances?"

"We're waiting for a judge to sign off on a subpoena."

"Someone is hiding something," I said.

Spader stabbed a piece of tomato from his side salad and

scowled at it. "Someone is always hiding something, Mrs. Barnes. Maybe if my brain wasn't wrapped in a fog of exhaustion, whatever that something is would be more evident."

"Let's look at what we do know," said Zack.

As Spader polished off his club sandwich, I once again mulled over Thursday morning's murder. "Someone went to a lot of trouble to kill Jared Oberman. Whoever wanted him dead either has mad sniper skills or has connections to a certain element of New Jersey society known for making problems disappear."

"Which would involve having the money to pay for a hit," said Zack.

"Or the person who wanted Oberman dead was owed a favor," said Spader.

I came up with a third possibility. "Or had some dirt on the hitman and threatened to expose him."

"Blackmailing a hitman?" asked Spader. "Not the brightest of moves. Hitmen don't like leaving loose ends."

Ding! Ding! Ding! Bells and whistles began blaring within my gray matter. I offered Spader a huge grin. "I know who ordered the hit and why."

ELEVEN

Both Spader and Zack stared expectantly, awaiting my next pronouncement. But at that moment my phone rang. I glanced at the screen. No name had popped up, only a number I didn't recognize. I ignored the call and returned to my rapt audience.

"Only one person—"

Before I could finish my sentence, my phone rang again. Same number. Again, I ignored the call. "The one person with both money and motive—"

My phone rang a third time.

"Maybe you should answer it," said Spader. "Could be important."

I shook my head. "I don't know anyone with a six-four-zero area code. It's either a spammer or a wrong number. Anyway, as I was saying, there's only one person with both the money and motive to hire a hitman to rid her of her cheating husband— Aurora Oberman. And the fact that someone tried to kill her last night plays into your theory about hitmen not leaving loose ends.

Once she paid him, she became a loose end who could talk."

"One person that we know of at this time," said Spader, bursting my bubble. "Until I get my hands on Oberman's phone and business records, we won't know if there are others."

My phone chimed with an incoming voice message. Spammer or wrong number, I'd soon find out. I tapped the Play button. After listening to the entire message, I hit the speaker button. "You're going to want to hear this." I hit Play again.

"I know it was you who told that cop where to find me. I don't care if he denied it. You show up, then he shows up? Nothing is that coincidental. I tried to help you, and this is the thanks I get? I didn't kill Jared. Maybe it's a good thing he axed the deal because you're a lousy sleuth if you think I had anything to do with his murder. True crime, my ass. That podcast is nothing but fiction. I'll bet you've never solved so much as a crossword puzzle in your life." She then launched into a long, expletive-laden rant about my lack of character, ending with, "If I were you, I'd watch my back."

Zack addressed Spader. "That was a threat."

Spader nodded. "Excuse me for a moment." He pushed away from the table and walked down the steps to the sidewalk. Zack and I watched as he pulled out his phone and placed a call.

"You think he's arranging to haul her in for questioning?" I asked.

"I wouldn't be surprised."

I bit down on my lower lip. "Maybe I'm wrong about Aurora Oberman hiring a hitman to kill her husband."

"Any particular reason?"

"All of a sudden, I'm wondering if Ellis Cummings has friends in low places."

Zack pulled out his phone. "We'll soon find out."

"Who are you calling?"

"Tino."

I first crossed paths with Tino Martinelli when Alfred Gruenwald, Trimedia's former CEO, blackmailed me into sleuthing out his mistress's killer. At the time, Tino was wasting his talents working as Gruenwald's right-hand guy. The former Marine possessed cyber-security skills that surpassed those of most mere mortals.

"You're not going to ask him to do anything illegal, are you?" Tino believed it was perfectly acceptable to hack in the name of the greater good. He called it a gray area in the world of cyber security, but I had my doubts. Breaking the law had consequences, no matter how valid the reason. Still, I admit I had appreciated those gray areas each time they'd involved saving my butt—not to mention the rest of me.

There wasn't anything Tino wouldn't do to protect me. Although several years my junior, he'd stepped into the role of the big brother I'd always wished for, but Mama and my father had never provided. I'd grown very fond of Tino and didn't want him winding up in prison from some misguided effort to keep me safe.

Zack raised an eyebrow. "It's the weekend. Even if any of the county cyber geeks are working, given Spader's comment about staffing shortages, any request that goes through channels will take forever. Someone threatened you. I'm not willing to wait."

Tino answered after the first ring. "Yo, bro. What's up?"

Zack placed the call on speaker. "You busy?"

"Never for you and the former Mrs. P. Does it involve one of your gourmet dinners?"

"That can be arranged. We need a favor."

"Name it."

"How quickly can you dig up everything there is on an Ellis Cummings from Neptune, New Jersey? Including all known associates and relatives that might have organized crime or gang connections."

"Shouldn't take long. Mind if I ask why?"

"She just threatened my wife."

Tino muttered something indiscernible under his breath. "Give me an hour."

Before Zack hung up, he said, "Dinner's at six-thirty."

Spader returned to the table and waved the waitress over for his check. Zack reached over and beat him to it.

"I can't let you do that," said Spader. "Besides, it gets expensed."

"Consider it freeing up some funds in the county budget," said Zack.

"As well as keeping you out of the hospital," I added. "Can you imagine what it would have cost the county in medical expenses had you collapsed from heat prostration? Or worse? And who would handle all your cases? You should take the rest of the weekend off, Detective."

"Can't. Neptune police are picking up Ellis Cummings. I've got a unit heading down to transport her to Union County for additional questioning."

"She won't be happy about that," I said. "She was doing a steady business today."

"She should have thought about that before she threatened you. That rant suggests to me that she just may have killed Jared Oberman in a fit of rage over her firing."

"Or hired someone to do it for her," added Zack.

Spader nodded. "Another possibility. But for all we know,

she's an expert marksman."

"She told me she's never even held a gun, let alone fired one."

Spader's bushy eyebrows traveled toward his receding hairline. "And I'm supposed to believe her? Guilty people lie to protect themselves."

"And she's also a car thief and an arsonist with enough knowledge of vehicles to destroy VIN numbers?" I shook my head. "How did she get home after torching the Escalade on Gilgo Beach? Sorry, Detective, but I don't see it. Either she had help, or she's not your perp."

"We'll see." Spader rose and doffed an imaginary hat. "Time and a night behind bars might loosen her tongue and get us some answers."

"Hold on a second," I said. "I have no intention of filing a complaint against Ellis Cummings."

"Even if the detective finds evidence to back up the threat she made against you?" asked Zack.

I turned to Spader, "If and when you do, not that I believe you will, we'll revisit the situation at that point. For now, I don't think she meant anything by it, and I'm not willing to ruin her life because she couldn't control her temper."

"Understood," said Spader. "I'll be in touch. Thank you both, once again."

As Spader headed toward the sidewalk, I turned to Zack. "If Ellis didn't hate me before, she's certainly got good reason to now. Do you think Spader's frustration with this case is causing him to act a bit heavy-handed?"

"No, I think he's going by the book. Don't let her youth cloud your judgment. There's no minimum age requirement for committing murder."

As he often did, Zack had played the logic card. Of course, he was right. However, my gut still rebelled against the idea that Ellis Cummings had killed Jared Oberman. Unless she was a trained assassin. I suppose assassins come in all shapes and sizes, but having previously met one, I'm of the opinion that the one trait all assassins have in common is their ability to remain cool and detached under the most stressful of circumstances. Ellis Cummings was neither cool nor detached, as evidenced by her voice message rant.

Even though her attitude smacked of immaturity and entitlement, and she'd rubbed me the wrong way from the moment we met, I had given her the benefit of the doubt regarding Oberman's directive of bringing him options. Now, I wasn't so sure. But whether she'd made an honest mistake or taken a calculated risk and failed, it seemed like too huge a leap to assume the result had led her to commit murder. Unless she was a psychopath. In which case, I still didn't see her pulling the trigger, but she may have convinced someone else to do her dirty work for her.

~*~

Before heading home, we stopped at a local farmer's market for an assortment of fresh produce. Then Zack swung over to the local seafood market to pick up a few pounds of jumbo scallops for dinner.

Tino called as we exited the Parkway. "You home yet?"

"Five minutes," said Zack.

"I'll be there in ten."

Zack turned to me as he came to a stop at a traffic light on Central Avenue. "Sounds like he found something."

"I wonder if that something will amount to good news or bad

news for Ellis."

Either way, we didn't have long to wait.

After arriving home and finding the curmudgeonly commie nowhere in sight, I grabbed Leonard's leash and took him for a walk while Zack prepped dinner. By the time Leonard accomplished his doggie potty needs and we'd reversed course, Tino's black Mercedes SUV was parked at the curb in front of the house.

Once inside, Tino embraced me in a crushing bear hug before I had a chance to unclip Leonard's leash. After he'd hugged the stuffing out of me, he stepped back but held me at arm's length, his hands remaining on my shoulders. He eyed me from head to toe, then demanded, "What sort of trouble have you gotten yourself into this time?"

I glanced toward Zack, who now had his favorite member of the family perched on his shoulder. "You haven't told him?"

"Figured I'd wait until you returned."

Ralph took that as his cue and squawked, *"We wait upon your grace." Richard the Third*, Act Two, Scene One."

I offered Ralph a royal wave for which I received the parrot equivalent of the evil eye. Zack reached into his shirt pocket, presented Ralph with a sunflower seed, and was rewarded with a cheek nuzzle.

Tino roared with laughter. "Shunned by a parrot. Now I've seen everything."

I shrugged. "Fine by me as long as Zack continues to clean out the ungrateful bird's cage."

After Zack finished preparing the food we'd purchased for dinner, he poured three glasses of wine, and we gathered around the kitchen table to hear what Tino had found out about Ellis

Cummings.

He opened his phone and brought up his notes. "Nothing out of the ordinary. Typical kid. Good grades. Won some art awards and a partial scholarship to Pratt. No run-ins with the law. Not even a parking ticket. The usual oversharing on social media, heavy on the snarky commentary. Normal for someone of her generation. However, that's where I found something interesting."

When he paused for effect, I prodded him to continue. "Which was?"

"You asked for any known organized crime or gang connections. I found quite a few."

"How?"

"Some interesting names popped up on her social media feeds."

My entire body clenched. Somehow, I didn't think those *interesting names* were relatives of Monmouth County residents Bruce Springsteen or John Bon Jovi. "Are you saying Ellis has Mafia connections?"

He nodded. "I cross-referenced, dug a little deeper, and also ran facial recognition software to be sure."

When I groaned, he added, "Don't read too much into it, Mrs. B. Lots of Mafia minions live in Monmouth County. Some in Neptune. Cummings had quite a few Mafia offspring in her high school graduating class. Her social media is peppered with pictures of them. She even went to the junior prom with a Genovese cousin."

Not what I had wanted to hear. I tried not to panic. After all, I, too, had gone to school with many Mafia princes and princesses. You can't choose your father, grandfathers, or uncles but as far as I knew, none of my classmates had gone into the family business, but you never know. It's not something they'd advertise or post on a LinkedIn profile page.

However, I refused to label Ellis guilty by association. On the other hand, given her threat, I had to wonder how close she remained to that prom date. I gave myself a mental slap. I should know better than to play devil's advocate with myself. It would only drive me crazy.

Tino directed a pointed look, first at me, then Zack. "Now, which one of you is going to tell me what's going on?"

"You don't know what happened yesterday morning?" asked Zack.

He gave us a blank stare. "Something happened? I've been out of the country all week. Arrived home shortly before you called."

Tino had recently secured a job with Homeland Security. "I didn't realize your new cybersecurity position involved international travel."

"Did I say it was for business?"

"Of course not, and I'm sure if I ask, you won't tell me."

"Need to know basis, Mrs. B."

"Then it was for business?"

His silence spoke volumes.

I didn't press further. Instead, I caught him up on everything he'd missed. After I'd finished, he turned to Zack and said, "How about if we lock her up in an ivory tower?"

Zack eyed me. "Don't think I haven't considered it."

"Sure, go ahead," I said. "I'd love a vacation. You can deal with Lucille."

Zack frowned. "On second thought...."

"Look, I think you're both blowing this out of proportion. I'm not in any danger. Ellis is angry, and she's directed that anger toward me. Misguided though it is, I'm a convenient scapegoat. She made a hollow threat. That's all. She's no killer, just a self-centered, immature kid who screwed up and got fired."

"I'd feel better if we had proof of that theory," said Zack.

"Me, too," added Tino. "I'm going to do some more digging."

"Nothing illegal," I warned him. "I don't want you jeopardizing your new job on my account."

He held up both hands, palms out and shook his head. "Wouldn't think of it."

If only I believed him.

TWELVE

The remainder of the weekend passed without any further murders or attempted murders. We heard from neither Detective Spader nor Tino Martinelli. I'd received no additional rants from Ellis Cummings. I suspected Spader had released her, but that was mere speculation on my part. Either way, I convinced myself it all fell into the No News is Good News category. Hopefully, I wasn't fooling myself.

Besides, once I arrived at work Monday morning, all thoughts of the last few days shifted to the back burner of my brain. Before I had even made it to the lobby elevator, my phone dinged with a message directing me to head to the conference room.

Once I stepped out of the elevator, I speed-walked down the hallway, first dropping my tote off in my cubicle before continuing to the conference room. When I turned the corner, I spied Cloris several yards in front of me and called to her. She turned and waited for me to catch up. "Any idea what's going on?"

She shrugged. "Not a clue."

"Whatever it is, I hope there's coffee and food."

"Skipped breakfast again? I find it hard to believe that Zack doesn't wake up early every morning to fix you a gourmet breakfast."

"Only on weekends. That's why I depend on you for morning pastries."

"So, he's lolling around in bed?"

"Hardly. He rose at the crack of dawn to catch a train to D.C."

She raised an eyebrow. "Spy business?"

"Probably. Although he claimed to have a meeting at the Smithsonian."

"Do you believe him?"

Now it was my turn to shrug. That was another topic I'd relegated to the back burner of my brain. "Do I have a choice?"

We'd arrived at the conference room and entered along with several of the other editors and assistants. A few more had already entered and gathered around the credenza, helping themselves to coffee and bagels. Cloris and I joined them. We both opted for an everything bagel with cream cheese before taking seats around the table. Jeanie rushed in and grabbed the empty chair to my right a moment later.

As I sipped my coffee, I glanced around the room. Whatever the topic of the meeting, it appeared only the *American Woman* editors and assistants had been summoned. With one glaring exception. "Notice who's missing?"

Cloris scanned the room. "Tessa. She's probably waiting to make her grand entrance."

A few minutes later Naomi, accompanied by her assistant Kim and two women I didn't recognize, entered the conference room.

"Good morning, ladies," said Naomi, settling into the chair at the head of the table. The two other women took seats cattycorner to Naomi's left while Kim poured coffee for them and Naomi.

Cloris and I exchanged a quick side-eye.

After Kim had served Naomi and the newcomers and took her place cattycorner to the right of our editorial director, Naomi kicked off the meeting. "I've called this short meeting to introduce you to the two newest members of our team."

She waved her hand and smiled toward the older of the two strangers. "First, I'd like everyone to meet our new fashion editor, Sonya Richland. Sonya brings with her several decades of experience, having previously worked at *Vanity Fair*, *W*, and *Harper's Bazaar*. She's spent the last few years working as a consultant to various up-and-coming designers, assisting them in the development of fashion lines for the mature woman. As such, she'll be indispensable as we shift our focus to our key demographic."

One look at Sonya, and it was clear why Naomi had hired her. She looked to be in her late fifties or possibly early sixties, the same generation as our editorial director and our health and finance editors. With her elegant sense of style, from her precisely cut silver blunt bob to the way she'd married classic and current styles in her outfit and accessories, she came across as her own best advertisement. I suspected we'd be seeing quite a few Chanel suits and little black dresses in future issues of *American Woman* but with unique, modern twists.

While Naomi introduced each of us to Sonya, and everyone in turn offered welcoming greetings, Cloris leaned over and whispered to Jeanie and me, "Decades of experience? Talk about a refreshing change from our last two fashion editors."

"Do you think Tessa quit, or Naomi canned her?" asked Jeanie.

"I'm guessing the latter," I whispered back, "sometime after the rest of us left work Thursday. With Trimedia out of the picture, Naomi doesn't have to kowtow to a board of directors that includes Tessa's Uncle Chessie."

Once all the introductions were made, minus the one remaining new face, Naomi continued. "As you know, we transitioned on Friday. Trimedia is gone. Our new corporate name is Reynolds-Alsopp Media. Creativity Books is in the process of relocating here."

She nodded toward the younger of the two women seated to her left. "I'd like you all to meet Danica Magee, the editorial director of Creativity Books. She'll start out working on a series of special projects with Anastasia, Cloris, and Jeanie and will divide her time between here and Nebraska until everyone is resettled."

Danica returned our greetings with an eager smile that filled her freckle-sprinkled face. Either she had honed her acting chops or was genuinely happy to be working with us. Now that we'd jettisoned both Tessa and Trimedia, maybe we'd finally rid ourselves of the workplace drama that had infiltrated our offices ever since Trimedia's hostile takeover.

I pegged Danica as somewhere in her early to mid-thirties, younger than Cloris, Jeanie, and me by a decade but about the same age as our travel and beauty editors and many of the assistants. She zeroed in on the three of us. "I'm especially looking forward to working with the three of you on the retro books."

Health editor Janice Kerr turned to Naomi. "What retro books?"

Naomi had sprung the books project on us after our Thursday staff meeting. No one else knew about them yet. She explained the concept to the other editors and assistants, then added, "We have additional ideas for joint ventures with Creativity Books that will involve our other editors in the future. We'll keep you all posted." She then pushed back her chair and stood. "For now, it's time everyone got to work. Have a productive day, ladies."

As we started to leave, Danica approached Cloris, Jeanie, and me. "When would be a good time for the four of us to get together today?"

"Any time is good for me," I said.

"I've got an off-site photo shoot at one," said Jeanie. "I'll need to leave the office by twelve-thirty."

"I'm interviewing a cookie artist at three," said Cloris.

"How about now?" asked Danica.

I checked my phone. "The conference room is available all morning. How much time do you think we'll need?"

"No more than an hour," said Danica.

I tapped my phone. "I've booked the room for us."

After refilling our coffee cups, we settled back around the table and presented Danica with our various ideas for updating crafts, recipes, and decorating trends from the nineteen-sixties.

When we had finished, Danica opened a folder and passed around some cover and page mockups. "I took the liberty of having my staff come up with some layout ideas for the series, but feel free to offer suggestions."

"This is more Anastasia's area of expertise," said Cloris.

"Agreed," said Jeanie.

All three women turned to me. I took my time reviewing the mockups. The covers and interior pages differed only by the color choices and background patterns, which captured the style of each decade. The overall look was fun and inviting. I passed the pages back to Danica. "These are fabulous. I wouldn't change a thing."

She beamed. "Then, I think we're off to a great start. I'd like to schedule a weekly meeting where we discuss your progress and make sure we're keeping to the production schedule. Beyond that, I'm here to help in any way you need me, but I don't micromanage. You three have the experience and expertise. I have full confidence that we'll have a successful start to the series."

"That was refreshing," said Cloris as we headed back to our cubicles. "I think we'll work well together."

"Agreed," said Jeanie.

I was about to ditto the sentiment when my phone rang. I checked the display, quickly excused myself, and scurried to the one place that afforded me some privacy.

Once inside my models and supply closet, I closed and locked the door before answering the call. "Good morning, Detective. Do you have any news?"

"That depends."

"Meaning?"

"Ellis Cummings immediately lawyered up. The attorney advised her not to answer any questions."

"Is that so unusual? Anyone who's ever watched a cop show should have that advice seared into their brains."

"In my experience, it only happens when a suspect has something to hide."

"Does that mean you released her?"

"Had to. With you not pressing charges, I had nothing to hold her on."

"Are you suggesting this is my fault?"

"Just saying...but tell me, why are you so keen to defend this kid?"

"Because she's just a kid."

"A kid who may have committed one murder and attempted a second."

"Do you have any evidence to back that up?"

"Working on it. I'm waiting for her phone records. I'm betting we get a cell tower ping that puts her in the vicinity of Gilgo Beach Thursday."

"If I weren't so averse to gambling, I'd take you up on that bet. I seriously doubt you'll get a hit."

"We'll see."

I changed the subject. "Have you learned anything further about Jared Oberman?"

"I'm still waiting on the judge to sign off on the subpoena. I should have it later today."

"What about the ballistics report?"

He huffed out a huge sigh of frustration. "Still waiting on that as well."

"Did you work yesterday?"

Spader grunted. "No, *Mother*, I took your advice. Caught up on sleep and watched the Mets lose both games of a double-header."

"Good for you."

"Ha! At least if I'd gone to headquarters, I could have made a dent in the backlog of paperwork piled on my desk."

"Are you suggesting I'm to blame for that, as well?"

"No, just being honest and blowing off some steam. You did say you were willing to help."

"Yes, but as a sounding board, not a whipping post!"

"Feel free to reciprocate the next time you're tempted to murder your mother-in-law."

Now it was my turn to laugh. "I may take you up on that,

Detective. Meanwhile, did you ever speak with Jared Oberman's brother?"

"Not yet. Apparently, the guy was so shaken up by his brother's murder that he wound up hospitalized Thursday night. His wife thought he was having a heart attack."

"Did he?"

"She said it turned out to be a combination of stress and high blood pressure. They admitted him to run some tests."

"Hmm...."

"Before you say anything, I'll admit you were right, okay? It's the reason I took off yesterday. Even if watching those games did little to reduce my blood pressure."

"Always glad to help, Detective. You've kind of grown on me. I'd hate to lose you."

"I'd hate to lose me, too."

"So now what?"

"I hope to speak with Oberman today. He was released late yesterday afternoon."

"Based on Jared's comment when he was told his brother was on the phone, I suspect they may have had a strained relationship."

"There are always strained relationships in business, especially family-owned companies. I intend to find out what was going on between the Oberman brothers. As CFO, Devin Oberman handled the finances. People kill for a host of reasons, but money usually factors in one way or another."

I thought about all the various murders that had impacted my life since Karl permanently cashed in his chips in Las Vegas. Spader was right. Even in cases of revenge or jealousy, money had played a role. "Follow the money?"

"Always."

Before he hung up, he added, "Let me know if Ellis Cummings contacts you, even if it's only to apologize."

"I will."

Cloris popped into my cubicle the moment I returned. "What's with all the cloak and dagger? Did the police nab the killer?"

"What killer?"

We both spun around to find Danica standing at the entrance to my cubicle. I fully intended to catch Cloris up on the events of the weekend, but I didn't want everyone at the office gossiping about the latest dead body that had crossed my path.

Still, I needed to say something. I decided to keep my response as vague as possible. "A murder occurred on my street last week."

Danica's eyes grew wide. "Good grief, Anastasia! You must be freaking out."

I shrugged. "A little."

"*Only a little?* How can you stay so calm?"

"The police believe it was a targeted hit and no one else is in danger."

Danica's eyes widened. "*A targeted hit?* Where do you live? In a ghetto?"

Cloris jumped in before I could answer. "Anastasia lives in one of our many upscale suburban towns."

"Not so lovely if there are killers on the loose."

I chuckled. "Hey, this is New Jersey."

Worry swept over Danica's face. "What's that supposed to mean?"

"For one thing, we probably have more Mafia per capita than any other state in the country. Every town has its share of organized crime hiding in plain sight. Those guys don't bother with arbitration or lawsuits. They make their problems disappear. Permanently."

Danica's eyes grew so wide, I thought her eyeballs would pop out of her eye sockets. "You can't be serious!"

"Didn't you ever watch *The Sopranos*?" asked Cloris.

"But that was a TV show. It's fiction."

"Yes and no," I said. "Fiction based on lots of facts."

The trembling traveled from Danica's jaw down the length of her body. Cloris and I both reached toward her at the same moment to keep her from collapsing and settled her onto my office chair. She stared up at both of us, then lowered her head into her hands. "What have I gotten myself into?"

Cloris headed to the break room to make Danica a cup of chamomile tea to calm her nerves. I stood sentry, hoping our new hire didn't dissolve into uncontrollable tears, but she appeared more in a stupor than a woman on the verge of shrieking like a banshee.

When Cloris returned, Danica stared warily at both of us while she sipped the tea. We waited for her to speak. Finally, she inhaled a ragged breath and asked, "Is this some sorority initiation? Are you pulling my leg?"

"Not in the least," I said.

Her eyes widened again. "How do you live like that?"

"Surely you have murders in Nebraska," said Cloris.

"But not on my street or even in my neighborhood," said Danica, her voice climbing an octave. "Only in the really bad parts of the major cities. Not in places where I'd ever go."

Cloris and I exchanged a quick glance. Was Danica that naïve? Crime is everywhere. All you need to do is watch the evening news. Murder isn't confined to the underbelly of the city, no matter the state where you live. Then again, I'd heard most people Danica's age never watch the news or read a newspaper. So maybe her reaction wasn't all that surprising.

I tried to offer her some reassurance. "Statistically, New Jersey has one of the lowest murder rates in the country."

"I find that hard to believe, not when you have murders in upscale communities."

If Danica was this freaked out about a murder that occurred on my street, miles from our office, I wondered how she'd react when she learned about the murder that had taken place in the very building where we worked. However, this probably wasn't the best time to bestow such information. She'd catch the next flight back to Nebraska.

Cloris whipped out her phone and tapped the screen several times. "According to the latest statistics, the per capita homicide rate for Nebraska is not that much lower than New Jersey, only about one more murder per one hundred thousand residents in New Jersey than Nebraska."

Danica shook her head. "That can't be accurate."

Cloris stuck her phone in front of Danica's face. "See for yourself. Official government website."

"But you have about five time the number of residents," said Danica. "That's five times more dead bodies."

"You can't look at it that way," I said. "Statistically, the percentage of murders is about the same."

Danica gaped at me. "How can you speak so unemotionally about murder?"

"I'm trying to calm your fears. We really do live in a relatively safe state. One of the safest in the country. Crime happens. People die. That's true anywhere. But you don't have to worry that you've moved to Tombstone. This isn't the wild west, and you're not working at the O.K. corral."

Danica sighed. "If I knew what that meant, I might take some comfort in it."

Ouch! The woman is only about ten years younger than us. How can she be so ignorant of classic cinema? Or history?

Cloris tossed an eye roll my way. "Why do I suddenly feel like we're doddering old fogies?"

~*~

"I wonder how long Danica will last," said Cloris.

We had chosen to lunch at a soup and salad restaurant on the square in Morristown and had settled into one of the many empty booths looking out onto the square. Given the ideal weather, most of the other diners had opted for patio seating. A nearly empty dining room lessened the chance of anyone overhearing me catch Cloris up on the weekend's events.

However, before diving into that topic, as we perused the menu, we discussed our Nebraska transplant. "She's definitely a fish out of water, but she seems to know her stuff, and I like that she's not a micromanager."

"Or at least says she's not."

"Time will tell. I hope she'll acclimate. My sense is you, Jeanie, and I will work well with her."

"Assuming we don't arrive back at the office to find she's already on a flight back to Nebraska. But enough of Danica. What happened over the weekend, and why did Detective Spader call you earlier?"

After the waitress had brought glasses of water, poured our coffees, and taken our salad orders, I gave Cloris a chronological account of events since I'd last seen her on Friday.

"Seems to me, Spader has his sights set on the intern who offered you the contract."

"She's definitely a person of interest, but I'm not convinced she had anything to do with Jared Oberman's murder. It doesn't make any sense."

"Then who do you think the culprit is, Sherlock?"

I shook my head. "No clue. I'm waiting to see what Spader uncovers after he interviews Oberman's brother and gets a look at their finances."

Cloris studied me over the rim of her coffee cup. "No theories?"

"This is New Jersey. It's not inconceivable that somehow the mob is involved."

"In what way?"

I shrugged. "Maybe Flix got into financial trouble."

"You think the Obermans went to the mob for a loan?"

"It's not beyond the realm of possibilities, especially if the banks had turned them down because they were overextended. Or perhaps one of their investors is a mob shell company. Flix might be laundering mob money, either knowingly or unknowingly."

"Or Oberman had a gambling problem."

I winced. That one hit too close to home. "He wouldn't be the first."

The waitress returned with our salads. Cloris and I ate in silence for a few minutes. As I washed down a mouthful of spinach salad with a swig of coffee, I glanced out the plate-glass window and nearly choked.

THIRTEEN

Cloris gasped as I fought to stifle a fit of coughing. "Are you okay? Sip some water."

I grabbed the glass and took a tentative sip. Then another. Once the urge to continue hacking had subsided, I wiped my watery eyes and dripping nose. "I'm fine. At least physically."

"What's that supposed to mean?"

I nodded toward the window. "I can't be a hundred percent certain, but I think Ellis Cummings is standing across the street, staring at us."

Cloris turned her head to look out the window. "The blonde leaning against the tree at the curb?"

I nodded. "If it's not her, it's someone who looks very much like her."

"You think she followed you to work this morning?"

"Either that or she's been camped out in the parking lot waiting for me to leave and followed us here."

"That's creepy. Why would she do that? Especially since she

must know Spader suspects her of murder."

I worried my bottom lip. "Maybe Spader is right, and I'm wrong about her."

"Count me in Spader's camp. You said she lives in Neptune, right?"

I nodded.

"That's more than an hour from Morristown. What are the chances this is a coincidence?"

"I can't even calculate the odds."

"You need to call Spader."

I glanced at my phone but hesitated. "I'm not even sure it's her. She's not near enough for me to make a positive ID."

"Call anyway. Better safe than sorry."

I picked up my phone and placed the call.

"You okay, Mrs. Barnes?"

"Why don't you ever say hello first, Detective?"

"Saves time. Is that why you called?"

"No." I told him where I was. "I can't be a hundred percent sure because she's too far away, but I think Ellis Cummings is stalking me."

"Stay in the restaurant. I'm calling Morristown PD to check it out. Don't leave until you get the all-clear from me." With that, he hung up. No hello. No goodbye. The Spader MO.

I told Cloris what Spader had said. "We might as well order dessert and more coffee. We could be here for a while."

We didn't have long to wait, though. Within five minutes, a police car slowly cruised around the square several times. With each pass, it slowed even further as it drew in front of the woman who could be Ellis Cummings. By the third pass, it came to a complete stop, and the woman quickly scurried off in the direction of the parking garage.

"That sure looked suspicious to me," said Cloris.

"Ditto."

After another five minutes, Spader called. "The patrol officer sent me a photo she snapped. If it's not Cummings, it's her clone. The officer followed her to the parking garage where she got into an older model red Kia Rio and drove off toward Rt. 287."

"I admit, I'm rattled, Detective. I'm beginning to think you're right about Ellis Cummings. Is it safe for us to head back to the office?"

"The patrol car will follow you. Keep your eyes out for a red Kia Rio when you head home later." He rattled off the license plate number. "Call me if you spot it, with or without Cummings inside. Especially if you see it parked anywhere near your house. Also, any sightings of Cummings, if she confronts you, or if she contacts you again."

"I will."

Before he hung up, Spader offered one more piece of advice. "Keep your eyes open, Mrs. Barnes."

I again relayed his end of the conversation to Cloris. She shook her head. "Life is never dull with you around."

"I wouldn't mind a little dull in my life."

"I'll bet."

We finished our dessert, paid, and exited the restaurant. A patrol car sat idling at the curb. The officer called to me. "Mrs. Barnes, I've been asked to escort you back to your office."

"Thank you." I told her where Cloris had parked and described the make and model of her car.

"I'll follow you."

"How did she know it was you?" asked Cloris as we made our

way down the sidewalk toward the parking garage.

"I suppose Spader either texted her my photo, or she accessed my license from motor vehicle records."

When we arrived back at the office, we saw no sign of Danica, but we also heard no speculative gossip to suggest she'd hightailed it back to the land of amber waves of grain. "She's probably upstairs unpacking her office or on the phone with the rest of her staff back in Nebraska," I said.

Cloris ducked into her cubicle to prepare for her interview with the cookie artist, and I sat down at my computer.

I spent the remainder of the afternoon attempting to cross some items off my to-do list, but my mind kept wandering back to Ellis Cummings. Maybe, as Spader had suggested, she was an expert marksman and responsible for Jared Oberman's murder.

I fished my phone out of my purse and called Tino. The phone rang three times before he answered.

"Mrs. B.!"

"Are you busy?"

"Hold on a sec."

Instead of putting the call on hold, he must have held the cell against his chest because I heard some undecipherable, muffled communications before he addressed me again. "Sorry about that. I was in the middle of something. What can I do for you?"

"Have you learned anything further about Ellis Cummings?"

"Nothing to indicate she's anything more than a normal college kid. That's why I haven't called."

"She wasn't a member of the rifle club in high school? Or goes deer or duck hunting? Or skeet shooting?"

"No, and there's no record of her legally purchasing a firearm. Not her parents, either. Why?"

I told him what had happened earlier.

"Where are you now?"

"At work."

"Stay there until you hear from me."

"Why?"

"I'm going to escort you home."

"You don't have to do that, Tino."

"If I don't, your husband will kill me."

I certainly hoped that was hyperbole.

Tino called shortly before five o'clock. "I'm ten minutes away. I'll meet you in the lobby."

Talk about a classic mountain from a molehill scenario. With no indication that Ellis Cummings had ever touched a gun, let alone knew how to shoot one, I didn't see the need for such heightened caution. Then again, recent events had left me questioning my ability to read people. I offered myself an internal shrug. Better safe than sorry.

Tino was waiting for me in the lobby when I and several coworkers from some of our other magazines stepped from the elevator. I noticed two production assistants eyeing him appraisingly, telegraphing invitations through their smiles and body language. Tino ignored both young women. The ex-Marine was a man on a mission, and his training wouldn't allow for any distraction.

He placed a hand on my forearm, holding me back while the others exited the building ahead of us. While we waited, he whispered, "I checked out the parking lot. No red Rios."

Once the lobby had cleared, he escorted me from the building and walked me to my car. I found his SUV parked next to my Jetta.

Tino stood guard alongside my driver side door while I settled behind the wheel, locked myself in, secured my seatbelt, and engaged the engine. Then he slid into his own vehicle and followed me back to Westfield.

I held the steering wheel in a death grip, constantly scanning the surrounding traffic in search of a red Kia Rio. Not that I could discern one subcompact sedan from another without a make and model emblazoned across a car's trunk. However, as I crept along in bumper-to-bumper rush hour traffic, the only red vehicles I spotted were either SUVs, pickup trucks, or sports cars. After twenty minutes, I relaxed my white-knuckle grip, took several deep, calming breaths, and attempted to access my inner Zen.

The thought made me burst out laughing. When had I ever come across any inner Zen? Maybe I needed to take up yoga in my spare time. If I ever found myself with any spare time. Zen or no Zen, the laugh settled my nerves.

Forty minutes later, I pulled into my driveway behind Zack's Boxster and Alex's Jeep. Prior to leaving work, Tino had ordered me to stay in the car until he scoped out my block. "Even if no red Kia Rio is parked on the street?"

"She could have parked a few blocks away and is lying in wait to attack you."

That had sent shivers up and down my spine. We live in an older neighborhood with mature shrubs and trees that provide perfect hiding places for anyone with less than noble intentions.

I sat in my car with the engine running while Tino slowly made his way down the street and looped around the block. Finally, he returned to the house and parked at the curb. After he walked over to my car, I turned off the engine and unlocked my door.

He swung open my door as soon as the lock popped. "All clear,

Mrs. B."

"Would you like to stay for dinner?"

"Depends. Is Zack cooking?"

I stared up at Tino as I stepped from the Jetta and placed my hands on my hips. "Unlike my mother, I happen to be a fairly decent cook."

"I believe you, Mrs. B., but there's decent food, and then there's Michelin level cuisine."

He had me there.

The aromas of Michelin level cuisine greeted us the moment we stepped into the kitchen. "I rest my case," said Tino.

"About what?" asked Zack as he stepped from the stove to greet me with a kiss.

"Tino was comparing my kitchen skills to yours. I came in a distant second."

The arbiter of taste chuckled. "Don't take it personally, Mrs. B."

"I don't. Zack can cook for me any time." I turned to the chef in question. "As you can see, I brought home a dinner guest. Do we have enough food for an extra mouth?"

"More than enough, but I'm curious. Did the two of you just happen to run into each other?"

"Not exactly. Tino escorted me home from the office."

Zack's forehead furrowed as he narrowed his eyes at me first, then Tino. "That's going to require more explanation."

I sighed. "I know." I then explained how I'd noticed Ellis Cummings loitering across the street from where Cloris and I ate lunch.

"Did you call Spader?"

I nodded. "He called in the Morristown cavalry. Ellis hurried off the moment an officer pulled up in front of her. After she drove off in a red Kia Rio, the officer escorted Cloris and me back to the office."

Zack turned to Tino. "How do you fit into all this?"

"Mrs. B. called to ask if I'd found out anything more about Cummings. When she told me what happened, I insisted on following her home from work."

Zack nodded. "I owe you one."

Before Tino could reply, we heard the front door open, then close. In a loud, demanding voice that carried from the foyer, my mother-in-law announced, "Harriet is joining us for dinner."

"Of course, she is," I muttered as we heard Lucille and her commie sidekick shuffle down the hall. A moment later the TV blared from the den.

"So much for looking forward to a peaceful dinner this evening." I turned to Tino. "Still want to stay?"

"Sure, I'll arm wrestle her for seconds."

"*Brrrack!*" Ralph announced his presence from his perch atop the refrigerator. "*Sir, you have wrestled well, and overthrown more than your enemies. As You Like It.* Act One, Scene Two."

"See. No problem." Tino nodded toward Ralph as Zack reached into his shirt pocket and offered up a sunflower seed. "Even the bird agrees."

I frowned. Meals that included Harriet Kleinhample were never pleasant affairs. The woman was a ninety-eight-pound ulcer inducer. "Assuming we'll have enough for seconds, let alone firsts."

Zack winked. "We will, as long as we don't serve family style."

Tino gave us a questioning look.

"The best way to thwart gluttonous, inconsiderate commies," I said, "is to portion out meals from the kitchen."

"Devious," said Tino.

Fifteen minutes later, Zack began ladling out bowls of Boeuf Bourguignon. The boys had arrived in the kitchen. While Nick set water glasses and utensils on the table, Alex carried the bowls into the dining room.

Lucille and Harriet made their grand entrance after the rest of us had taken our seats. Lucille stopped short at the entrance to the dining room, took one look at Tino and said, "What's he doing here?"

"I was invited," said Tino.

"Unlike someone else," said Nick, looking directly at Harriet. I shot him a Mom Look.

Lucille glared at Nick as she hobbled toward the table. "If your father were alive—"

"He wouldn't let you take advantage of our mom the way you do," said Nick.

"Not helping," I muttered.

Anger suffused Lucille's face, and the veins along the side of her head began to pulse. She leaned her cane against the chair and grabbed her bowl with both hands. At first, I thought she intended to dump the contents on Nick. However, as much as Lucille resents Zack, she enjoys his cooking too much. Instead, she said, "Grab your dinner, Harriet. We're eating in the den."

However, this posed a problem Lucille hadn't considered. She needed two hands to carry her bowl without spilling the contents, but she also needed her cane to steady herself as she walks. Otherwise, she risked falling flat on her face. She frowned at us as the situation dawned on her. Then she glanced toward Harriet. But without spontaneously growing a third arm, Harriet was of no help.

Lucille continued to glare at us in stony silence. When no one volunteered to assist her, she cradled the bowl in the crook of her arm, sandwiching it against her chest. Then she grabbed her cane and slowly made her way through the living room. Harriet first lasered an evil eye at me before scooping up Lucille's utensils and following her dear leader. A minute later, the unmistakable sounds of caterwauling reality TV stars filled the house.

Zack rose, headed into the kitchen and out the back door. He returned a minute later with a bottle of wine and three glasses. After pouring, he pulled out his phone.

"What are you doing?" He knew we didn't allow phones at the dinner table.

"You'll see." A moment later, Wynton Marsalis replaced the Real Housewives.

"How'd you do that?" I asked.

Tino answered for him. "There's an app for everything, Mrs. B. You just have to know where to look."

"And she can't switch the channel back?"

Zack grinned. "Not anymore. I've blocked access to all the cable channels with the shows she watches."

"Whoa," said Nick. "Even ABC? She watches *Dancing with the Stars* and *The Bachelor*. But we watch *Monday Night Football*."

"It's not football season," said Zack. "Besides, I'll give you the passcode."

"That's a relief!" said Nick.

A few minutes later, Harriet Kleinhample marched into the dining room. "Anastasia, something is wrong with your television."

I raised an eyebrow. "Really?"

"Really. Suddenly, it switched over to one of the music

channels and won't switch back."

"On its own? How odd. Maybe one of you accidentally hit a button on the remote."

"We weren't touching the remote."

"Then it must be a cable glitch, Harriet. I guess you and Lucille will have to watch TV at your apartment."

Harriet stared at me. I could almost see the gears working in her brain as she processed my words and weighed the possibilities. Her eyes narrowed, and she began sputtering before letting loose with a torrent of insults. "This is you're doing, isn't it? You are the most inconsiderate, selfish person I've ever met."

"Look who's talking," said Nick.

This time, I didn't even bother with a Mom Look. Instead, I ignored Harriet and resumed eating my dinner. The others at the table took their cue from me and did the same. Harriet stood with hands on hips, a huge scowl across her purple-suffused face as she continued her verbal assault of my character. However, not eliciting a rise from any of us, she eventually gave up. She grabbed the two glasses of water they'd left on the table and stalked back to the den.

We were finishing up dinner when Lucille hobbled toward the front door with Harriet in tow, dragging my mother-in-law's battered secondhand suitcase. When the front door slammed behind them, I reached for my wine glass and expelled a huge sigh of relief. If by some miracle the gods had decided to cut me a break, we'd have several days of reprieve.

"Any chance she won't come back?" asked Tino.

A girl can dream, can't she?

But Alex quickly burst that wishful thinking bubble. "Not with Mom's luck. Grandmother Lucille lives to torment her."

"There's only one way she'll ever leave for good," added Nick, "Torturing us gives her too much pleasure."

"Besides," I said, "she's got it too good here. If she and Harriet pooled their Social Security and pensions, they could afford a two-bedroom apartment, but it wouldn't come with live-in help to cook, clean, and do the laundry."

Tino's eyes grew wide. "You do her laundry?"

"What choice do I have? She can't navigate the basement stairs."

Tino addressed Zack. "And there's nothing you can do?"

"Hey, man, I've offered. I'm willing to foot the cost of an apartment and a housekeeper to come in once a week. Not only has she refused, but she's accused Anastasia and me of orchestrating Karl's murder."

"Murder?" Tino turned to me. "I thought your husband died of a heart attack."

"He did. In a Las Vegas casino nearly a month before I met Zack. I thought Karl was at a sales meeting in Harrisburg, Pennsylvania. Lucille lives in her own delusional world when it comes to the son who could do no wrong in her eyes."

Tino offered a conspiratorial grin. "I know a guy who knows a guy."

I laughed. "Tino, this is New Jersey. We all know a guy who knows a guy. But I do hope you're joking."

"Of course, I'm joking, Mrs. B."

"Good to know."

Alex and Nick rose to begin clean-up duty. Alex carried a handful of dishes into the kitchen, and Nick headed toward the den to collect Lucille and Harriet's dishes. The doorbell rang as Nick approached the foyer. He hesitated, turning back toward us to ask, "Should I answer it?"

"Hold on a second," said Zack.

I watched as he tapped his phone screen several times. Given the events of the last few days, I understood Nick's hesitation. "Who is it?"

"Detective Spader."

FOURTEEN

"Have you eaten dinner?" I asked when Spader entered the dining room.

Eyeing Tino, he hesitated. "No, but I see you have company, and you've already finished."

Zack stood. "We have plenty of leftovers. Sit."

Spader took the seat across from Tino and lasered in at him. "Don't I know you from somewhere?"

"You were both at our wedding." I waved a hand in Tino's direction. "This is Tino Martinelli. He used to work at Trimedia." Then I motioned toward Spader. "Detective Samuel Spader."

The two men nodded as they commenced participating in the time-honored sizing-up ritual that takes place whenever two alpha males meet.

I broke the standoff by asking, "Still burning the candle at both ends, Detective?"

He grunted. "Like I have a choice? I was on my way home. Figured I'd get you caught up on what little I have before I finally called it a night. Assuming nothing drags me back in before tomorrow morning." He huffed out a lungful of frustration. "But the way things are going lately...." His voice trailed off as he highlighted a shrug with a scowl.

When Tino raised an eyebrow, I explained, "Detective Spader is heading up the Oberman murder case. So far, he hasn't had much success finding either a suspect or a motive."

Zack returned from the kitchen and placed a bowl of Boeuf Bourguignon, a napkin, utensils, and a glass of water in front of the detective. "I assume you're still on duty?" he asked.

Spader checked his watch. "Not as of five minutes ago."

"Want something stronger?"

"I thought you'd never ask."

Zack returned to the kitchen, returning with a wine glass. He then poured the remainder of the Merlot from the bottle we'd shared at dinner and offered Spader the glass.

As much as I wanted to hear the detective's news, no matter how minor, I allowed him first to enjoy Zack's latest culinary achievement. Especially since I suspected Spader's diet had consisted of little more than fast food since our lunch in Ocean Grove Saturday.

However, the way Spader continued to eye Tino as he ate, suggested he had second thoughts about saying anything. "You can trust Tino," I said. "He works for Homeland Security."

"I thought you said he worked with you at Trimedia."

Given Tino's recent brush with the law, I deferred the explanation to him. "Trimedia was a brief interim position," he said, "after my honorable discharge from Special Forces. My background is in cybersecurity."

"I see." But Spader still looked skeptical.

"Tino saved my life last year, Detective. He's one of the good guys."

I noticed Spader slightly raise an eyebrow toward Zack, and Zack respond with an almost imperceptible nod. Of course, that produced all sorts of questions in me, but I bit my tongue. Now was not the time to probe. However, it certainly added credence to my suspicion that Zack was more than a photojournalist, and that Spader knew things about him that Zack swore were products of my overactive imagination.

I glanced at Tino. His expression told me he, too, had observed the nearly covert interplay between Zack and Spader. He didn't seem at all surprised.

Finally, Spader settled his internal debate, finished the last of his meal, and began to speak. "I met with Devin Oberman this afternoon."

I pulled my attention away from my speculative musings. "Did you learn anything useful?"

"Not from what he said."

"Meaning?" asked Zack.

Spader polished off the last of his wine, then said, "I learned more from what he didn't say. He claimed he's worried for his own safety and that of his wife, but his delivery suggested he'd spent considerable time rehearsing his words. Plus, his body language told me he was lying."

"Someone or something must have the guy spooked," said Tino.

"Or he's hiding something," I said. "I keep circling back to Jared's comments when one of the interns told him his brother was on the phone. Something was definitely going on between the two of them."

Spader grew pensive. "Are you suggesting we could be looking at fratricide?"

"I don't think you can rule it out," I said. "It's a crime that harkens all the way back to Genesis."

"Except," said Spader, "like all other theories at this point, we don't have a single shred of evidence."

"You still don't have any forensics back?" asked Zack.

Spader grunted. "Or the subpoenas."

I pulled a scowl and punctuated it with a deep sigh. "Then we still have nothing."

"Not quite," said Spader. "We have two persons of interest who aren't telling us everything they know."

"Ellis and now Devin?"

Spader pushed back his chair and stood. "It's a start. Hopefully, those subpoenas and the ballistics reports will come through tomorrow. If so, I should be able to start making serious inroads into the case. Thank you both for the meal."

He nodded toward Tino. "Nice meeting you."

Tino nodded back. "You, too."

Alpha males still at work. I bit back a chuckle.

As Zack and I walked the detective to the door, his phone chimed an incoming text. "Maybe our luck is about to change," he said. "The judge finally signed off on the subpoenas."

"When will you execute them?" I asked.

"No time like the present. I'll head back to headquarters and scrounge up some manpower."

When we returned to the dining room after Spader left, Tino said, "I'll see what I can find out about Devin Oberman."

"He and his brother jointly owned Flix Entertainment," I said. "Those subpoenas Spader was waiting on are for their business and personal financial records along with their phones, tablets, and computers. He also requested a warrant to search Ellis Cummings's home for her tech and any guns as well as her phone records."

"What took so long?" asked Tino.

"Spader said the delay in the ballistics report is due to backlogs and staffing shortages. Too much recent crime and too many people out sick or on vacation this time of year."

"That shouldn't impact issuing subpoenas," said Tino.

"Unless the judges are also backlogged, on vacation, or dealing with the summer flu that's going around," said Zack.

Tino stood to leave. "I'll see what I can dig up. I don't like the idea of you connected to another murder, Mrs. B. Especially one with so few leads. Who knows what's really going on here?"

Tino's words sent a shiver up my spine. Not for the first time, I wondered if I had more of a connection to Jared Oberman's murder than simple coincidence. What if someone was sending me a message—again?

I gave myself a mental slap. The idea was ridiculous. Once again, I was letting my imagination run amok. I no longer had to worry about the one person who had gotten his kicks by orchestrating hits on my neighbors. Then again, I'd aided the police in apprehending several other killers since the demise of Lawrence Tuttenauer. Any one of them may have made connections from behind prison walls.

Zack placed a hand on my forearm. "What's going on?"

"Huh?" I looked up and found him and Tino staring at me.

"You zoned out there, Mrs. B."

"Did I?" After giving myself a mental kick in the keister, I offered both men a wan smile. "Just tired. I guess the last few days are catching up with me."

"I'll be off, then," said Tino. "Call if you need anything."

~*~

"What was that all about?" asked Zack as he placed Spader's plate and silverware in the dishwasher. "And don't lie to me. You're worried about something."

I finished washing the detective's wine glass and set it on the drainboard. "It suddenly occurred to me that perhaps Jared wasn't targeted, that his killing was more random. Collateral damage."

"In what way?"

"Lawrence is dead, but suppose someone else is pulling strings from a prison cell and taking a page from his playbook?"

"Someone who wants to exact revenge on you?"

I worried my lower lip as I dried my hands. "Exactly."

Zack drew me into his arms. "The other killers you had a hand in putting away have neither the connections nor the funds that enabled Lawrence to do what he did."

"As far as we know."

Although Zack was trying to comfort me, I felt a shudder course through his body. I tilted my head to look up at him. "You think it's possible?"

"I think we need to look into it. I'll make a few calls tomorrow."

"Patricia?" Zack's ex-wife worked as an assistant D.A. in Manhattan. If the Oberman brothers were suspected of shady accounting practices, or worse, her office would be investigating them.

"And Ledbetter," said Zack. "You never know who the Feds are looking into or for what."

Aloysius Ledbetter was Patricia's cousin as well as an FBI

special agent. He and Zack seemed to have more than the nodding acquaintance one would expect between an ex-spouse and his ex-wife's cousin. "Would he tell you?"

"Let's just say he knows I'd kill him if anything happened to you."

I craned my neck and offered him my best evil-eyed glower. "Very funny. Coming from the man who swears he's just a photojournalist. You're not helping your case."

Zack chuckled. "Some people just can't take a joke."

~*~

The next morning, as I sat in bumper-to-bumper rush hour traffic, listening to a traffic report telling me what I already knew because I was stuck in the middle of it, a breaking news alert came through:

"This just in. Police are on the scene of another drive-by shooting in a quiet Union County suburb. This time in Springfield. We know the victim is male and died at the scene, but other than that, details are sparse. There is currently no official statement from law enforcement or local government. However, the shooting appears connected to last week's murder of Summit resident Jared Oberman. According to our source, the unknown victim had just returned to his home off Shunpike Rd. near the Baltusrol Golf Club when the shooter pulled up in a black SUV and opened fire before speeding off. We'll have further updates as they come in."

My first thought was of Cloris and her husband Gregg. If someone was targeting people in my life, she was the only person close to me who lived in Springfield. However, her townhouse wasn't located anywhere near Shunpike Rd. or the golf course.

I loosened my white-knuckle grip on the steering wheel and called Detective Spader's direct line. When the call went straight to voice mail, I left a message. "Just heard about the murder in Springfield. Is it really connected to the Oberman case?"

My mind pinballed from one scenario to another as I inched my way toward the office. Since I knew no one who lived off Shunpike Rd., it seemed highly unlikely that someone was channeling Lawrence Tuttnauer and toying with me in the same manner.

However, if the initial report about the similar M.O. was correct, the second shooting certainly appeared connected to Jared Oberman's murder. Was there a connection between him and this unknown victim? Was the killer cleaning up loose ends?

Or were the police dealing with a copycat killer? If you wanted to eliminate someone, what better way to throw the cops off your scent than to make the killing look exactly like another that had recently occurred?

The answers to all these questions hinged on information unknown to me, though. Hopefully, the results of the subpoenas would shed light on the case, which had now morphed into two possibly related crimes, and lead to the perpetrator's quick apprehension.

Even though the logical side of my brain told me I didn't need to worry about Cloris and Gregg, I let loose a huge sigh of relief when I pulled into the parking lot and spied Cloris's car parked in her usual spot.

I still hadn't heard back from Detective Spader, but given the new murder, I wasn't surprised. He probably never made it home last night, let alone gotten any sleep, but as I entered the building, my phone dinged with a text from him. "Too soon to tell. Looking for any connections."

After taking the elevator to the third floor, I headed directly to the break room where I found Cloris making coffee. "Did you hear there was a similar shooting in Springfield early this morning?"

She nodded. "You don't know anyone who lives near the golf course, do you?"

"No one. You and Gregg are the only Springfield residents I know."

"You think the two murders are connected?"

"I hope not."

The coffee had finished brewing. Cloris poured two cups and handed one to me. Then she pulled a carton of half and half from the mini fridge. After adding some cream to her coffee, she passed me the container. "Do you know anything more than what the news reported?"

"Nothing." I added a splash of cream to my own cup and took a sip before checking the contents of the pastry box on the table. Muffins. "What flavor?"

"Lemon zucchini with pistachios."

I helped myself to one and took a bite. "I left a message on Spader's phone. He texted back to say they're looking into any possible connections between the two murders."

Cloris grabbed a muffin. "Given the similarities, doesn't it seem logical that there would be?"

"Not necessarily. It could be either coincidence or a copycat killer."

"What about the similarities? The victim was gunned down in front of his house this morning, and the killer drove off in a black SUV."

"One of tens of thousands of black SUVs on the roads in New Jersey," I said around a mouthful of muffin. "On my block alone, there are half a dozen residents who own one. Besides, no matter the make and model, black SUVs also happen to be the vehicle of choice for drug dealers and members of organized crime. Those guys don't drive around in Priuses."

"So..." Cloris grew thoughtful as she polished off her muffin. "This could have been a drug deal that went south?"

"Or a Mafia hit on a member of a rival family. A botched carjacking. A love triangle. Domestic abuse. Or any number of other scenarios. Without knowing the victim's identity and more about him, we can't do more than speculate."

"Well, I hope you and Detective Spader figure it out soon. I don't like the idea of a killer on the loose in my town. Or yours. What if it's someone we know, hiding in plain sight? That's enough to keep me up at night."

That made two of us.

~*~

I was deep into research for the first retro book, when my office phone rang later that afternoon, pulling me from the mid-twentieth century forward into the twenty-first. "You have visitors," said the receptionist.

"I'm not expecting anyone. Who is it?"

"A Mr. and Mrs. Oberman. Want me to send them up?"

"No, tell them I'll be down shortly."

I stepped across the hall to Cloris's cubicle. "Devin Oberman and his wife are downstairs."

Cloris's brows shot up under her pixie bangs. "That's odd. Why would they come here?"

"Beats me. Even if they wanted to speak with me about something—although, I can't imagine what—what would be so important that it required a face-to-face? Why not just pick up the phone and call?"

"Good point, especially since the guy's brother was murdered four days ago. You'd think he'd have more pressing matters on his mind. Want me to come downstairs with you?"

I shook my head. "No, but if I'm not back in ten minutes, call down to reception to say I'm needed in a meeting. Whatever their reason for showing up, I want no part of it."

"Will do."

After a quick detour to the ladies' room, I headed downstairs and found Devin Oberman seated in the waiting area across from the reception desk. Next to him sat not his wife but his sister-in-law, Aurora Oberman, the woman who four days ago had accused me of having an affair with her dead husband.

Oberman stood when he saw me approach and offered a polite smile that didn't quite make its way to his eyes. I noted little resemblance between him and his deceased brother. Jared had reminded me of Steve Jobs. He'd even dressed in the quintessential black short-sleeve T-shirt and black jeans of the Apple founder.

His brother wore a three-piece summer-weight ecru suit with a crisp mint green shirt and pastel paisley tie. The guy looked like he belonged sipping mint juleps on a Southern plantation. He extended his hand. "Anastasia Pollack?"

"Actually, it's Barnes," I said, as he sandwiched my hand within both of his.

His face registered confusion. He turned questioningly toward his sister-in-law. Dressed in a sleeveless ombre pastel silk sheath accessorized with a floral embellished mint green straw hat, Aurora Oberman looked like she and Devin had deliberately coordinated their outfits.

Shouldn't they both be dressed in black? And home arranging

for the funeral of his brother and her husband? Instead, they looked like they planned to attend an invitation-only dressage competition at the local equestrian center.

However, as similar as their outfits, Aurora's expression wasn't nearly as pleasant as Devin's. Her nose wrinkled and her lip curled as she nodded. "That's her, no matter what she calls herself."

I pulled my hand from his grip. Keeping my voice low to avoid the receptionist overhearing me, I confronted Aurora Oberman. "If this is about your wild accusation, I'm going to have to ask you to leave. If need be, security will escort you from the building."

"What accusation?" asked Oberman, looking even more perplexed.

I continued to stare at Aurora as I answered him. "Your sister-in-law accused me of having an affair with her husband. I can assure you that nothing is further from the truth."

I turned back to Devin Oberman. "I met your brother briefly the day before he died when my husband, my agent, and I arrived at Flix for a meeting with the person who had offered me the option on the podcast about me."

"Yes." His head bobbed eagerly up and down several times. "The podcast is why I wanted to speak with you. Jared phoned me that evening after he'd listened to all the episodes. He realized your adventures would make a great television series and insisted I listen to it."

My adventures? I stared in disbelief. He spoke as if the podcast was pure fiction rather than an account of how I had nearly lost my life on multiple occasions.

I opened my mouth to correct him, but he continued before I could utter a word. "Jared informed me about what happened at the meeting. As I'm sure he told you, Ellis Cummings, the intern, had no authority to offer a contract, no matter the amount. She's no longer with the company."

"I'm aware of that, Mr. Oberman. However, as I told your sister-in-law, I had already decided to turn down the offer. If you're here because you're worried that I might file a lawsuit, let me assure you that I have no intention of suing Flix Entertainment. If you'd like that in writing, I'm happy to oblige."

"Actually, I'm here because I'd like the opportunity to both apologize for the way things were handled and to try to change your mind."

Now it was my turn to register bewilderment. "Change my mind about suing you?"

He forced out a nervous chuckle. "No, of course not. Change your mind about accepting an option on the podcast series. I can't sign off on the obscene amount the intern offered you, but I believe I can make it quite worth your while to agree."

I crossed my arms over my chest and stared at him. "I doubt that."

He responded by offering me the smug grin of a man who always gets his way. "Why don't you let me try?"

"I'm afraid you'd be wasting your time."

"Why is that? Have you received another offer? At least give me the opportunity to counter it."

I shook my head. "You don't understand. My decision was never about the money."

"Then what? One of the other terms in the contract? That wasn't even our standard contract. I don't know where Ellis got it. She must have pulled it off some site on the Internet."

Why did he seem so desperate for the rights to the podcast? It wasn't like I was some uber-famous celebrity with tens of millions of social media followers. I didn't even have my own social media accounts, only the ones connected with *American Woman*.

This entire conversation made no sense. My inner red flags began whipping around in gale force winds of skepticism. "Suppose you cut to the chase, Mr. Oberman."

His eyes widened. "What do you mean?"

"What's really going on here?"

After a quick glance toward Aurora, he focused back on me. "We have no ulterior motive, Mrs. Barnes. I'm interested in securing the rights to the podcast because I believe we can create an Emmy-worthy production based on it. This is a win-win all around. For you. For me." He reached for Aurora's hand. "And for Aurora. With Jared gone, she now owns fifty percent of the company."

I zeroed in on their clasped hands, then locked eyes with Aurora Oberman. The look she returned told a different story. This was not a woman who wanted to do business with me. Everything about her, from the stiffness of her posture, to the tight set of her mouth, to her evil-eyed glare, told me she still thought I had succumbed to her husband's animal magnetism.

Frankly, if he'd had any, I hadn't noticed. Why would anyone choose cafeteria mystery meat over fillet mignon?

Across the lobby, the receptionist's phone rang. Shortly after she answered it, she called over to me. "Anastasia, you're wanted at a meeting in the conference room."

Cloris to the rescue. "Tell them I'm on my way."

I turned back to the two Obermans. "Feel free to contact my agent. Perhaps she can convince you that this deal is never going to happen."

I then spun on my heels and marched toward the elevator.

FIFTEEN

"Well, that was beyond odd," I said, stepping into Cloris's cubicle. I crossed the short distance and dropped into her guest chair.

She swiveled away from her computer screen to face me. "In what way?"

"For starters, it wasn't Devin Oberman and his wife. It was Devin Oberman and his sister-in-law."

Her eyes widened in disbelief. "The dead guy's wife?"

"And it gets even weirder than that."

Cloris placed a finger to her lips and stood. "Best to head to your supply closet. You never know who might be listening."

"Good idea."

We checked to make sure the hallway was clear before scurrying toward the supply closet. Once I had locked the door behind us, I related the conversation I'd had with Devin Oberman. I also mentioned Aurora Oberman's continuing hostility toward me. "The entire situation was odd. If Oberman wanted to sweet talk me into changing my mind, why bring someone incapable of masking her unwarranted animosity toward me?"

"It makes no sense."

"Exactly. By the way, thanks for the rescue. The timing couldn't have been better. I owe you."

"I'll add it to your tab. What now?"

"I promised Detective Spader I'd notify him if I noticed Ellis or her car anywhere. I can't imagine he wouldn't want to hear about what just happened. Something is up with those two. Maybe once the police dive into Flix's finances, it will all make more sense."

Cloris furrowed her brow. "Not that I want to talk you into it, but Devin might be right about the potential of a series based on the podcast."

I shrugged. "I know very little about the industry, but according to Zack's agent Ibba, a very small percentage of optioned books ever make it to TV or movie screens. That's why you want as large an option as possible. Even if the show is never made, you get to keep the option money. She said the odds grow exponentially worse when the production company is a recent start-up, like Flix Entertainment."

"Why is that?"

"Because they have neither a track record of successes, nor deep enough pockets to compete against well-established, successful companies."

"Still, depending on how desperate they are...."

I slumped against the door. "I suppose anything is possible. I had hoped by now, Spader would have established a money trail connected to Jared Oberman's murder. If so, that might explain his desperation last Friday morning before he was gunned down, as well as his brother taking over the arm-twisting today."

Cloris tilted her head toward me. "What sort of angle?"

"Who knows?" I hugged my chest and blew air from my cheeks. "One possibility that comes to mind is that they borrowed money from a mob-connected loan shark to keep the company afloat. They're leasing an entire floor in Midtown Manhattan. It's in an older building, but—"

Cloris finished my sentence for me. "These days, even rents in older buildings don't come cheap, no matter where in Manhattan they're located."

"Exactly. And this was no dive. The building looked recently renovated, even though the offices were furnished courtesy of Ikea."

"But killing the guys who owe you money doesn't get you paid. Wouldn't they first do something less drastic, like break kneecaps?"

"If the brothers had missed or come up short on multiple payments, someone may have decided to bypass the kneecaps and head straight to the ultimate strongarming tactic."

"Which is?"

"Kill one of the partners to scare the surviving one into coming up with the money. That could certainly explain their eagerness to get me to sign on the dotted line."

"Except, even if you weren't paid a dime, wouldn't they first have to spend a huge sum of money in the hopes of making money?"

"Not if they lined up additional backers behind a new project, but instead of producing the project, the money goes to the loan shark to pay off the debt and keep Devin from becoming the next victim."

"You think they're trying to pull off a Ponzi scheme? What happens when the investors realize there is no project?"

I offered her a wicked grin. "Maybe Devin and Aurora are planning a Bialystock and Bloom."

"Like in the plot of *The Producers*?"

I nodded. "Raise the money, then flee the country. Preferably to a location without an extradition treaty with the U.S."

She grew thoughtful for a moment. "You think Devin and Aurora are planning to use the podcast about you as bait to scam investors?"

"My gut is telling me they have an ulterior motive for showing up today. Whether they're being squeezed by the mob, want to scam investors, or both, is anyone's guess. Maybe it's something entirely different. Until we learn more, right now, one theory is as good as another."

Cloris pulled one of the large plastic tubs from the lowest shelf and dropped onto it. She struck a thoughtful pose with one arm draped around her midsection and her opposite hand cupping her chin. "True crime podcasts are all the rage. But the one about you is unique. They're probably thinking they could parade you and your family around to prospective investors."

"Which is another reason I'd never agree, even if they're not planning on scamming investors." My body let off an involuntary shudder. "I don't want my family dangled as a PR stunt to give investors the added cachet of rubbing elbows with the actual sleuth and the kids who came up with the idea for the podcast."

Cloris rolled her eyes. "Talk about a PR bonanza, though."

"Which it won't be because I'd never agree to it."

"Devin Oberman doesn't know that." She wrinkled her nose. "He sounds like a man who believes everyone has a price. If he's listened to the podcasts, he knows you're swimming in debt. He's feeling you out to learn your price."

"Then he didn't listen very carefully. I'd never do anything that placed my kids under the scrutiny of a public microscope. I've done everything I could to protect them. They still don't know half of what Karl did and never will know if I have any say about it."

Cloris gaped at me. "Seriously? What more did he do? Don't tell me he killed someone!"

I inhaled sharply, staring at her in stony silence. Even my BFF didn't know Karl had tried to kill his mother. And never would.

She held up her hands. "Okay, I won't press. Let's backtrack. If they are planning to scam investors, it's right out of the Unscrupulous Stockbroker's Playbook. Max Bialystock. Bernie Madoff. The only difference is the industry."

"Except," I reminded her, "Max Bialystock is a fictional character."

"But Bernie Madoff wasn't," she said, "and he pulled off his con for years before he was finally caught."

"Because his arrogance convinced him he'd never get caught. If Devin and Aurora jet off to a Caribbean Island without an extradition treaty with the U.S., chances are they'll get away with the scam."

"As long as one of them doesn't run off, leaving the other to take the fall."

I nodded. "I can certainly see Aurora Oberman leaving Devin to deal with the mob, the Feds, or both. She strikes me as cold and calculating. But perhaps Devin is just as ruthless and only a better actor."

"Truth is often stranger than fiction."

"Good point." I unlocked the door. "You'd better get back to work in case someone comes looking for one of us."

Cloris rose and returned the storage bin to the shelf. "What about you?"

"I'm going to call Detective Spader from here. Given that he's now juggling two murders, I shouldn't be long. Assuming he even takes my call."

Before leaving, Cloris wrapped her arms around me. "I'm sorry. I didn't mean to pry, but if you ever need an ear—"

"I know." I hugged her back. "Thanks."

Once she stepped out into the hallway, I relocked the storage closet door and placed a call to Detective Spader.

"Any chance this can wait?" he asked, once again dispensing with any greeting.

"You tell me. Devin and Aurora Oberman showed up at my office a few minutes ago."

A string of muttered expletives traversed the connection, followed by, "This day just keeps getting better and better." He huffed a huge breath, then asked, "Are you worried for your safety, Mrs. Barnes?"

"If you're asking, was I threatened, no. Quite the opposite."

"Meaning?"

"Devin Oberman tried to convince me to accept an option on the podcast."

"Not what I expected to hear."

"Nor I, Detective. The entire exchange was surreal, not to mention the way the two of them were dressed."

"What was strange about that?"

"Nothing if they were attending a fancy equestrian soiree in Bedminster. But maybe I'm not up on the latest mourning fashions. Any idea if pastels are the new black?"

He snorted. "You're asking me?"

"If you'd like, I'll see if I can get our security guy to pull a photo and send it to you."

"Sure. I could use a good laugh today. I assume you have some theories?"

"Regarding their apparel choices? No. But maybe a few possible motives regarding the offer."

"Can this conversation wait? I get off at six, assuming no additional shoes drop between now and then."

"How many have already dropped?"

"Enough to furnish a shoe store."

"Dinner is at six-thirty."

"I can't let you keep feeding me, Mrs. Barnes. It doesn't look right."

"And who's going to know, Detective? I consider it my civic duty, not only to help you figure out this case but to keep you healthy. Besides, I have an ulterior motive. When you come for dinner, my mother-in-law and her minions make themselves scarce."

He let loose with a loud guffaw. "So, you're using me?"

"Not exactly the way I'd put it. Consider it more a quid pro quo."

"I'll see you at six-thirty, Mother."

Instead of returning to my cubicle, I headed for the break room for an infusion of caffeine. I found Cloris making a fresh pot. "Anything to report?"

I settled into one of the plastic molded chairs and shook my head. "Nothing you don't already know except Spader is apparently having a really bad day."

"No news on the case?"

"None that he mentioned but he's coming to the house after he gets off this evening."

I picked up my phone. "I'd better text Zack to let him know."

He responded immediately: *Everything OK?*

I answered with a shrug emoji. *Nothing bad. Don't worry.*

Then why the shrug?

Doesn't look like there's any good news yet. I then changed the subject. *Will you be home early enough to make dinner, or should we plan on bringing something in?*

I'll take care of it.

You're a prince among men.

Only a prince?

Actually, an emperor but I don't want you getting a swelled ego.

He ended the exchange with a kiss emoji.

I looked up to find Cloris watching me. "Everything okay?"

"My husband is an emperor among men."

She laughed. "What else is new?"

~*~

When I turned onto my street, I noticed Detective Spader's unmarked car already parked at the curb in front my house. With Harriet Kleinnhample's VW minibus nowhere in sight, my home was most likely free of Daughters of the October Revolution—with the possible exception of their fearless leader. I mentally crossed all digits, hoping Lucille was off fomenting revolution with her minions.

Upon entering the house, I found Detective Spader sitting in the living room with Zack, both men enjoying a beer. Instead of the blaring of reality TV emanating from the den, Jon Batiste played in the background. If only I came home to such a calm setting every night....

Zack and Spader rose to greet me, but only one did so with a kiss. I've grown fond of Detective Spader, and I know the feeling is mutual, his irascibility notwithstanding. However, some lines should never be crossed, especially between a police detective and the married reluctant amateur sleuth helping him. Physical contact heads that list. I was quite happy the detective was a man who observed boundaries.

As I hung up my purse and tote in the hall closet, I suddenly realized no mouth-watering aromas wafted through the house. I glanced toward the dining room and saw the table set for dinner. "Do you need help cooking?" I asked Zack.

"The boys are picking up dinner. I ordered an Asian smorgasbord. Everyone's favorites."

On cue, the back door opened, and Nick yelled, "Dinner's here, and we're starving."

Five minutes later, we had all gathered at the table and were passing around a feast of Miso Sea Bass, Seafood Delight, Blue Crab Rangoon, Pad Thai, Shanghai noodles, spring rolls, spareribs, steamed dumplings, and Himalayan red rice. As we ate, we engaged in nothing more than small talk, refraining from any mention of the Oberman murder.

Once we'd stuffed ourselves to the proverbial gills, the boys took charge of cleanup while Spader, Zack, and I retreated to the apartment above the garage. I didn't want Alex and Nick overhearing our conversation, and I also had no idea when Lucille would return. Call me a coward, but I'd rather not put up with another one of her tirades if she came home to find Spader sitting in the living room.

Inside the apartment, Zack and I settled onto the couch with

Spader taking the chair on the opposite side of the coffee table. The detective raised a bushy salt and pepper eyebrow as he faced me. "Let's hear it, Mrs. Barnes."

I started by filling both men in on my strange visit from Devin and Aurora Oberman. When I'd finished, Spader said, "You stated earlier on the phone that you have a few theories."

"Two, actually." I began by mentioning the possible involvement of a loan shark who had run out of patience. "That's Theory A."

"Tried and true," said Spader, "if not hackneyed."

"But not beyond the realm of possibilities," I pointed out, reminding him, "After all, this is New Jersey."

"What's your connection to Theory A?" he asked. "Can't be Tuttnauer anymore."

"Hopefully, none. Theory A is all about opportunity. The killer was following Jared that morning and waited for the perfect opening to take his shot. Jared's murder in front of my home was pure coincidence."

"Assuming we can accept coincidence where you're concerned," said Spader.

I bit down on my tongue as Zack asked, "And Theory B?"

"A Bialystok and Bloom-type investor scam."

Spader's brow wrinkled as his expression grew thoughtful and he massaged the bridge of his nose. I could almost see the wheels turning while he searched his cop brain for the reference.

Zack helped him out. "Are you familiar with Mel Brooks, Detective?"

"Of course. *Blazing Saddles* is a classic." He began rattling off some of the Brooks' oeuvre. "*Young Frankenstein, Spaceballs...*" Finally, the lightbulb in his brain sparked megawatts. "*The*

Producers."

"Exactly," I said. "Theory B involves me."

Now it was Zack's turn to wrinkle his brow. "How?"

"It's the only way Devin and Aurora's visit makes sense. They want to use the podcast, me, and the kids as bait to lure in investors."

"Are you suggesting," asked Zack, "that they have no real intention of turning the podcast into a TV series?"

I nodded. "That's the Bialystok and Bloom connection. Once they have the money, they hire a private plane to fly them somewhere without an extradition treaty with the U.S. It's also possible that Theory A and Theory B are connected. If so, maybe they plan to pay off the loan shark before they abscond with the rest of the cash. Or maybe not. My guess is not."

Another thought then occurred to me. I turned to Detective Spader. "Do you know if Jared Oberman had life insurance?"

"He did. A two-million-dollar policy."

"Between that and scamming investors out of a few million, they could amass quite a tidy nest egg," said Zack.

Spader nodded. "Agreed. Except there's one major problem with your wife's theories."

SIXTEEN

I thought my theories made perfect sense, but Spader completely dismissed them without so much as a few seconds of consideration. I glared at him. "What's the problem with my theories?"

"Flix Entertainment is solvent. The subpoenas turned up no evidence of financial irregularities or malfeasance. The company is completely in the black and has been since its inception."

"What about the brothers' personal finances?" I asked.

"Same. We found no outstanding loans, and both have healthy bank accounts."

"Isn't it unusual for a business not to have a running line of credit?" asked Zack. "Don't most companies rely on them for cash flow purposes? My agent mentioned the company is so new that none of their projects have aired yet."

"Cash flow isn't a problem for trust fund babies." Spader's expression telegraphed exactly how he felt about those born with a platinum spoon in their mouths. "Between them, the brothers have enough money to buy a small country."

My jaw dropped. "Seriously?"

He grunted. "Turns out their great-great-grandfather made a fortune during the Depression by investing in undervalued stocks and real estate."

I found it difficult to restrain my sarcasm. "How nice for them. And yet, Jared balked at the sum Ellis offered me for the rights to my story. Even though that figure was huge by my standards, it's mere pocket change for two guys who can afford to buy their own country."

Spader shrugged. "Call it fiscal responsibility. I suspect that's what caused the tension between the brothers. Jared was the creative arm of the company. As CFO, Devin handled the books. My guess is that's like oil and water in the business world. Although they self-financed the startup, that's as far as they went with their own money. Once their first project won a few awards at film festivals, investors began lining up."

I rolled my eyes as I suggested one giant incongruity. "Why would people who lease expensive Manhattan real estate to impress investors furnish their offices with cheap pressboard furniture from Ikea?"

Zack chuckled. "She raises a good point, Detective."

"She usually does," muttered Spader. Then turning to me, he said, "I'll admit, it makes little sense, Mrs. Barnes. After all, what's another ten or twenty grand to guys like that? Then again, so far, little about this case makes sense. But I doubt their taste in office furnishings has anything to do with Jared Oberman's murder."

Score one point for the detective. "Fine. What about gambling debts or drug problems?"

"We found no large cash withdrawals from any of their

accounts that might indicate payments connected to anything shady."

"Like to loan sharks?" I asked.

"Loan sharks, drug dealers, blackmailers. No evidence, past or present, that would suggest any sort of addiction problems. No indication of gambling debts. No stays at tony rehab facilities. No prior lawsuits for anything from slip and falls to sexual harassment. Also, no brushes with the law."

"Unless they paid to make their problems go away," I suggested.

Spader shrugged. "Always a possibility when you've got unlimited funds and greedy people willing to look the other way. However, aside from the interns' accusations, from what I've found so far, those two are—and apparently always have been—squeaky clean."

I lobbed another eye roll his way. "I wouldn't call a man who repeatedly cheats on his wife squeaky clean. Aurora Oberman's accusations lend credence to those of the interns."

"Except for the opposing stories the three interns tell," said Zack. "Either Ellis is lying, or the other two are."

"Besides," said Spader. "There's a difference between legally squeaky clean and morally squeaky clean. I'm investigating a crime. I'm not a priest taking confession."

"But doesn't moral turpitude often lead to criminal activity?" I asked.

Spader nodded. "Often but not always. You wouldn't believe how many sleazeballs I've known who've consistently tiptoed right up to the line but never crossed it."

In my book, there's little difference between the two. Illegal activity and moral depravity are both dishonest. But this wasn't the time for a philosophical discussion.

Instead, I refocused on my theories. "We can't necessarily rule out a mob connection just because the brothers have plenty of money."

"It rules out owing a loan shark," said Spader.

"Yes, but what if the mob was squeezing them for a piece of the business? Isn't the Mafia always trying to stretch their tentacles into various legitimate businesses?"

"It's not that much of a stretch," said Zack. "They've infiltrated all sorts of commercial enterprises."

Spader glanced between the two of us as he mulled over the suggestion. "I suppose it's as good a theory as any. Nothing else is panning out. But where's the proof?"

"What about the other employees?" I asked. "Did you ever interview them?"

"The few that exist. Turns out they only employ a handful of people."

Zack and I both stared at him. "How is that possible?" I asked. "Who's doing all the work?" I rattled off a host of jobs that came to mind. "Writing the scripts? Auditioning talent? Securing location sites. Costume design and creation? Directing? Filming? Editing? Promoting? And a million other jobs involved in producing a movie or TV show. Have you ever sat through the credits at the end of a film? It doesn't take a village; it takes the population of an entire city."

He shrugged again. "According to the interns, they mostly use independent contractors, hiring out for specific jobs. They subcontract to other companies for everything else. Turns out Flix is more a general contractor than an in-house production company."

"Which saves on salaries and benefits." Zack's expression

telegraphed what he thought of Devin Oberman's *fiscally responsible* management tactics. "Pander to the investors and screw the worker bees."

Spader agreed. "Exactly. And those few salaried employees mostly work from home, remotely tying into the company servers. They come into the office only when needed."

"Like when Flix wants to parade the talent in front of prospective investors?" I asked.

"That and have lots of those worker bees scurrying around looking busy. At least according to the employees and interns."

I wrinkled my nose. "Seems more like a smoke and mirrors operation run by con men."

"You'd think so," said Spader, "except there's no proof of that, either. From everything I've discovered so far, this is a startup on its way to becoming quite successful. I spent some time surfing the web and discovered there's a lot of buzz about the productions they've completed so far."

I stood and began to pace around the room. "If money wasn't a motive, why were Jared and Devin so desperate to get the rights to the podcast?"

"Maybe," suggested Zack, "it's as simple as recognizing huge potential and not wanting a competitor to beat them to it."

"Could be," Spader said.

I thought about that for a moment. "I suppose. After all, Jared admitted that Ellis was right about the podcast. He even said he'd tried calling her to apologize and wanted to take her back. Ellis told me she never answered any of the calls. I'm not even sure she listened to any of the messages he left her before she blocked his number."

However, even though I had nothing more to offer, the needle of my skept-o-meter continued to hover close to the red zone. I stopped pacing and returned to the couch. We were back to Square One. Why was Jared Oberman killed? And by whom?

I turned to Spader. "That leaves us with nothing but the shoes. Care to share?"

Zack executed a quick double-take first toward me, then Spader. "What do shoes have to do with anything?"

"Detective Spader told me he was having a bad day," I said. "Lots of shoes dropping. Isn't that how you voiced it, Detective?"

His face grew tight. He curled his right hand into a fist and began a rhythmic pounding of the sofa cushion. "Too many cases. Too few resources and staff. This case is driving me nuts. And now I either have another murder connected to it or a copycat on the loose."

When Zack and I both cast worried glances his way, he stopped pounding and stared at his fist. Then he shook his head and sighed. "Sorry. I apologize if I'm sounding like a broken record. I've had better days."

"Anything specific to the Oberman case?" asked Zack.

The detective's frown deepened into a grimace. "Just that along with not turning up anything in their finances, none of the subpoenas produced any evidence at all. Nothing on the computers at Flix. Nothing on Oberman's home computer or his phone. And nothing from the search of Ellis Cummings's residence."

"What about your interviews of those other employees?" asked Zack.

"All goose eggs. Since they're rarely in the office, they had little to offer about either man. All claimed they never saw anything unusual, including any evidence of Jared having a drug or alcohol problem. They all said they enjoyed working for the company, were paid well, and hoped Devin planned to keep Flix open."

"What about Ellis's phone?" I asked. "Did you get a cell tower ping from anywhere near Gilgo Beach?"

Spader huffed as he ran his fingers through what was left of his hair. "Once again, Mrs. Barnes, you were right. Ellis Cummings may just be an immature kid. We did find a few selfies with the victim but nothing remotely compromising that would suggest an affair."

I refrained from gloating as he pulled up a series of photos on his phone and showed them to Zack and me. The snapshots featured all three interns with the Oberman brothers. They sat around a large circular table in a Mexican-themed restaurant. Dishes of nachos, taquitos, guacamole, salsa, a huge basket of tortilla chips, and bottles of Dos Equis filled the table.

Along with the selfie of Ellis with Jared Oberman, she'd also snapped a selfie with his brother and several with the other two interns. There were also non-selfie photos, both individually and in various groupings. Everyone looked like they were having a great time. Maybe too great, considering both men were married, and the festivities didn't include their wives. "This looks like a celebration."

"It was," said Spader. "I checked with Devin Oberman. The brothers had taken their new interns out to dinner to celebrate their first day at Flix."

I handed the phone back to Spader. "What about the ballistics report? Has that finally come in?"

He blew a wave of frustration out his cheeks. "It did, but the results aren't helpful. The bullets from the murder scene don't match the bullets fired into the Oberman bedroom Friday night.

Either we're dealing with two unconnected incidents, or the perp was smart enough to use two different guns."

"It stretches credulity to think there's no connection between the two shootings," I said.

"Yeah, most likely, there's a connection. Maybe it's staring me right in the face, but I'll be damned if I can see it."

Before either Zack or I could comment, Detective Spader's phone chimed with an incoming email. He glanced at his phone. "Hmm, we may have a lead." But after tapping his screen, his eyes grew wide, and his jaw dropped.

"What is it?" I asked.

Spader held up his index finger in the universal signal for hold on a moment. Then he placed a call. "Eastman, did you just send me an email?"

The volume on Spader's phone was turned up high enough that Eastman's response filled the room. "No, sir, why?"

The detective let loose with more than a few choice words before explaining. "I just received an email from you. The subject line reads, *Break in Oberman Case*."

"It didn't come from me, sir."

"Good thing because the photo that popped up is grounds for dismissal, not to mention criminal charges. Anyone from tech still at HQ?"

"DeFrancisco is about to leave."

"Tell her to stay put. I'll be back shortly. I need her to find out who sent this email. I don't care if it takes her all night."

"Yes, sir."

Zack and I exchanged a quick glance. Whatever was on that photo must be explosive. And it might just be the break Spader needed to crack this case, no matter who sent it. I just hoped Tino had nothing to do with it.

Spader ended his call and turned his attention to me. "Mrs. Barnes, I hope you don't mind, but I'd like to speak with your husband in private."

I gaped at Spader. "Seriously?"

Zack jumped to my defense. "Anything you have to say to me, Detective, you can say in front of my wife."

Spader's face reddened but not with anger. His entire body, from the way he wouldn't meet my eyes to his fidgeting fingers and the nervous bounce of his leg, projected embarrassment. "I don't think so. No offense, ma'am. Not before running this by your husband first. I wouldn't feel comfortable."

I threw my arms in the air. "For heaven's sake, Detective, I'm no shrinking violet. Given what I've experienced the last year and a half, do you really think there's anything I can't handle, no matter how offensive, disgusting, or lewd?"

"What makes you think—?"

"Because that's the pachyderm in the room and the source of your discomfort, isn't it?"

"Not sure what you mean," he mumbled, still averting his gaze.

He knew. I'd bet my last nickel on it. "The image on your phone. It's pornographic, isn't it?"

Spader's eyes registered guilt, even though his mouth formed an expression of surprise. "What makes you think that?"

"Oh, I don't know, Detective. Could it be the way you're acting? Or how you threatened to charge Officer Eastman if the photo came from him?"

Spader glanced down at his phone once more, his face set in a grim scowl. "You're right, Mrs. Barnes. It's porn, and it's revolting."

"Fine. Pull the Protecting the Little Lady card and show Zack first. But then you're showing me. I can assure you, I'm a big girl. No need to bring out the smelling salts. I won't swoon."

Zack rose and walked around the coffee table to Spader's chair. He quickly glanced at the screen, then nodded for Spader to show me the image before he returned to sit beside me.

Spader reached across the coffee table and handed me his phone. My breath caught in my throat, and I wrinkled my nose. "Ugh!"

Back in college, some of the male students often deliberately left copies of *Hustler* in the student lounge, hoping to shock some of the more innocent coeds. I once worked up the nerve to see what all the fuss was about. As offensive as some of the photos were, none rose to the raunchy level of the image on Spader's phone. I certainly would have remembered.

However, guys only focus on one thing when it comes to pornography. I noticed something else. "Detective, would you mind pulling up the photos from Ellis's phone?"

"Why?"

I passed the phone back to him. "You'll see in a moment."

After he tapped the screen and returned the phone to me, I scrolled to the photos Ellis had taken of the two other interns at the Mexican restaurant. In all fairness, both young women wore less-revealing blouses than they had last Thursday. Little of their tattoos peeked out above their necklines. That also may have been the case when Spader interviewed them. Additionally, neither yet sported the pastel streaks in their hair.

Spader was an excellent detective. I'd give him the benefit of the doubt when it came to the tattoos. But my photojournalist husband? He should have noticed immediately. I held the phone in front of his face. "You really don't see what I see?"

"Of course, I see it."

"Why didn't you say something?"

His eyes twinkled as he grinned at me. "I wanted to give you the pleasure of pointing it out."

Spader cleared his throat. "What the heck is going on?"

I handed the phone back to him. "Look closely, Detective. Notice anything?"

Spader studied the restaurant photos, enlarging the images and squinting at them for several long seconds. He then returned to the new photo and enlarged that one. His jaw dropped. "I'll be damned."

"Your porn isn't just any porn lifted off the Internet. Those are images of Kendall Braxton and Brooklyn Smith, most likely with Jared Oberman."

The photo showed two women and a man partaking in what I assumed was Marquis de Sade-type carnality. All three wore masks obscuring their faces, but Kendall and Brooklyn were easily identified by their tattoos. The man's shaved head suggested Jared Oberman completed the ménage à trois.

"At least we now know Ellis told the truth about the other two interns," I said.

"Not quite," said Spader. "She failed to mention the threesome was a foursome. I'm guessing Cummings took the photo."

"Or not," said Zack. "Jared may have set up a hidden camera. That still image could be pulled from a video."

Spader shook his head. "We found no evidence of a hidden camera when we searched his home. And no porn on either his or Ellis's computer."

"Wait a minute," I said. "What makes you think they're in

Jared's home?" The image was too closely cropped to show anything other than the bodies on the bed. "Isn't it more likely they're in a hotel room or the apartment of one of the women?"

"Another good point, Mrs. Barnes."

From his tone, I couldn't tell if Spader was annoyed with me or appreciative of my observation. What I did know was that the guy needed a decent night's sleep. Normally he'd never make such a rookie mistake. Given that he planned to return to headquarters tonight, I suspected he'd once again miss his rendezvous with Mr. Sandman.

I kept those thoughts to myself, though. Something else had occurred to me. "You didn't have a subpoena for either Kendall or Brooklyn's phones and computers, did you?"

He shook his head again. "The judge would never have issued one. I had no probable cause for seizing their tech. Only those of Cummings and the victim."

"Because Ellis threatened me?"

He nodded.

"Maybe one of the other interns hid the camera," said Zack, "and removed it afterwards."

"To blackmail Oberman?" Spader mulled that thought around for a minute before he stood. "Looks like I need to haul those two in for more questioning."

~*~

After Detective Spader departed, Zack and I returned to the house. We found Nick clipping a leash on Leonard for his evening walk. I held my hand out for the leash. "I'll walk him tonight. I need some exercise."

Nick eyed me suspiciously. "Since when do you exercise, Mom?"

"Whenever I walk the dog, smartie."

He handed me the leash and a plastic bag, which I hoped I wouldn't need. Picking up doggie poop is one of my least favorite chores and why I rarely walk Leonard.

"Whatever you say, Mom. Enjoy your walk."

As Zack and I headed back outside, I passed him the bag.

He laughed. "I knew that was coming."

With a full moon lighting the way, we strolled hand-in-hand for several blocks, waiting for Leonard to sniff out the perfect spot to make his evening's deposit. The sounds of traffic along Central Avenue, the occasional car that zipped past us down the street, and the chirping of crickets filled the air.

Leonard finally found the ideal tree and raised his leg. We waited, but he seemed satisfied with his performance, reversed course, and tugged on his leash. We were halfway back to the house when both my phone and Zack's dinged with an incoming text from Tino: *Found something you should see. Can't text or email. In city all day tomorrow. Any chance we can meet?*

"Whatever he's found, it sounds urgent," I said. "Why wouldn't he contact Detective Spader?"

Zack quirked his mouth. "You really need me to answer that, Nancy Drew?"

I grimaced. "I was hoping you'd have a less sketchy suggestion, something that didn't smack of an illegal hack." I mentioned my concern that Tino had sent Spader the email, covering his tracks to make it look like it had come from Officer Eastman.

"The thought had occurred to me, as well. I hope Tino is smarter than that and won't do anything to jeopardize his job with Homeland Security. He wanted that position too badly."

"I hope you're right."

"However, whatever Tino found, if he won't or can't share it electronically, it doesn't sound like he discovered it through a simple Google search."

I was afraid of that. I also knew that any evidence Tino uncovered, either in less-than-legitimate or quasi-legitimate ways, wouldn't be admissible in court. If it was as explosive as his text suggested, we'd have to find some way of pointing Detective Spader in the right direction without exposing ourselves or Tino. Unless Tino had already taken care of that thorny issue by sending Spader the email.

And what was the likelihood of two different explosive pieces of evidence showing up at nearly the same time? One thing was certain. This internal pinball debate was causing me neural whiplash. I sent up a plea to whichever god looked out for guys with good hearts who sometimes leaped without looking.

SEVENTEEN

Luckily, whatever spy or photographic business Zack had in D.C. last Friday and Monday, he still hadn't jetted off on another assignment, and I had the perfect excuse for mixing business, pleasure, and sleuthing. In addition to monthly craft projects in *American Woman*, each issue included an article about some aspect or history of crafting or an interview with a crafter. A few times a year, I also featured writeups on crafts museums located around the country. I had yet to do one on the Museum of Arts and Design. Located on Columbus Circle in Midtown Manhattan, the museum was not far from The Essex House, where Tino was attending a daylong cybersecurity symposium.

Before hopping the train into the city, I dashed off an email to both Naomi and Human Resources to let them know of my plans to visit the museum today. Not wanting Cloris to worry that I'd once again fallen victim to kidnappers—or worse—I also shot her a quick text.

Tino had said he was free until ten o'clock and suggested

meeting for breakfast at a diner on Eighth Avenue. We found him waiting for us at a booth located at the very back of the restaurant.

After the waitress had poured our coffees, taken our orders, and departed, he removed a folded sheet of paper from the inside breast pocket of his suit jacket. Before he handed it across the table to Zack, he said, "Hold this on your lap under the table before you open it. Keep it out of view."

Zack did as instructed. We both took a quick look at the unfolded sheet before Zack refolded the paper and handed it back to Tino.

"You don't look surprised," he said.

"That's because we've already seen it," said Zack.

Tino's eyebrows shot up, and his eyes grew wide. "How?"

"Someone sent a copy to Detective Spader last night," I said. "I'm hoping it wasn't you."

"Heck no!" He crossed his heart. "Marine's honor."

I let loose a sigh of relief. Keeping my voice to not much more than a whisper, I said, "I was worried. Whoever sent it, made it look like it came from one of the county law enforcement officers. You're the only person I know with mad hacking skills, and you said you were digging around."

"Even though I know how to mask my footprint, nothing is a hundred percent foolproof, Mrs. B. I'd never risk something like that tracing back to me. I'd lose my job."

And yet, he had crossed the line in the past. I decided not to remind him. "Are you saying you didn't hack one of the intern's phones?"

"No hacking involved."

"Then how did you come by the photo?" asked Zack.

"It popped up on the dark web during an ongoing

investigation. I recognized the tattoos when I did a search of Flix Entertainment employees and checked out their social media accounts. Both Brooklyn Smith and Kendall Braxton are quite active on Instagram and TikTok. Smith even documents each time she visits her favorite inker for a new tat."

I didn't care about Brooklyn Smith's obsession with body art. Instead, I zeroed in on something else Tino had said. "An investigation of whom?"

Tino shook his head. "Afraid I can't divulge that, Mrs. B, but what I can tell you is that the photo isn't real."

"It was Photoshopped?"

"Worse."

"A.I.?" asked Zack.

"Nearly perfect A.I.," said Tino.

"Are you suggesting artificial intelligence created that image?" I asked. "It looked so real."

"How did you view it?" asked Tino.

"On Spader's phone."

"Not surprising then. When the image is enlarged, the imperfections become evident. Artificial Intelligence is getting better every day, and many deep fakes are hard to spot. The technology isn't perfect yet, but it's headed that way and at breakneck speed. However, right now a well-trained eye can still spot them." He paused for a moment before adding. "Most of the time."

I pulled a frown. "Looks like I was wrong about Ellis Cummings."

"What makes you think it was her?" asked Tino.

"She's the intern who told both Detective Spader and me that Brooklyn and Kendall were engaged in a ménage à trois with Jared

Oberman."

"Here's the problem," said Tino. "You can't tell the detective about this. He's going to want to know your source, and you can't tie this back to me. It might jeopardize our investigation."

"That won't be a problem," said Zack. "He already suspects Cummings."

"How?"

"The latest theory is that the ménage à trois was a ménage à quatre," I said. "He's bringing Cummings in for questioning and also getting subpoenas for the personal computers and phones of the other two interns."

The waitress arrived with our omelets and topped off our coffees. Once she left, I said, "If Ellis made the A.I. image, wouldn't there be evidence of it on her phone or computer?"

"Most likely," said Tino.

But as I savored a forkful of my mushroom, spinach, and feta omelet, I realized something didn't add up. "Spader found no evidence connecting Ellis to any criminal activity. Not on her phone, her computer, nor any tech found at her parents' home. Same for the Flix computers and all personal tech owned by the Oberman brothers."

Furthermore, did Ellis even have the skills needed to create a near-perfect image using A.I.? Skills as a caricaturist wouldn't necessarily translate into A.I. skills. After all, I excelled in drawing and painting, but I was never able to master a potter's wheel. Having one artistic skill didn't mean I—or Ellis—had proficiency in all artistic disciplines. I pointed this out to Zack and Tino.

Tino shook his head. "It no longer takes time, money, skill, or even much effort to create A.I. Middle school kids are getting in on the act. Already some estimates put A.I. generated media online as high as twenty percent."

I shuddered at the frightening implications of that but also realized something else. "Even if A.I. never crossed Ellis's mind, someone else may have suggested it or created it for her. A classmate or boyfriend, perhaps. She attends Pratt Institute. They offer courses in interactive technology, video graphics, and special effects."

"That's how we raise the subject of A.I. with Detective Spader," said Zack, "assuming his tech expert hasn't already realized the photo is a fake."

Tino spoke around a mouthful of his Western omelet. "Not following you."

I took another swig of coffee before explaining. "Either someone created the A.I. for Ellis and posted it on the dark web, or someone created it and sent it to one or both interns."

Tino nodded. "As blackmail."

"Exactly, why would they create such an incriminating image of themselves and post it on the dark web? It had to be someone else doing it to blackmail them or perhaps, just out of spite, which goes back to someone doing it for Ellis. If Spader cross-references their phone contacts, he may find the person who created the image."

"Or not," said Tino. "The culprit might be an Internet troll with little or no connection to either intern or the murder vic. He may just be some random creep who trolls Instagram and gets his kicks shaking down social media posters."

"Because he can?" I asked.

"Tino's right," said Zack. "This could be some guy working out of a troll farm in China, Russia, or Iran."

"But if that's the case," I asked, "who sent the photo to

Detective Spader?"

Tino offered me an eye roll. "The same person who created it. Only takes a Google search of the interns' names." He pulled out his phone, typed for a few seconds, then passed the phone across the table to me. Links to various social media sites as well as dozens of articles about the Oberman murder appeared on the screen, including a video of Spader's press conference.

As far as I was concerned, this was yet another reason to stay off social media. "If someone was blackmailing one of the interns, wouldn't she have a copy of the photo on her phone?"

Tino shook his head. "Not necessarily. Unless her Wi-Fi signal is very weak, a multimedia message would automatically open the photo with the text message, but a text message with a link wouldn't show the photo until she clicked on the link."

Under Tino's theory, none of us was safe from the machinations of an army of evil bullies with A.I. skills. I handed the phone back to him. "Thanks, I now have one more worry to keep me up at night."

"Sorry about that, Mrs. B."

I stared at him for a moment, wishing I could read his mind. I was convinced Tino knew more than he was saying. "Is this cyber creep the subject of your investigation?"

He waved my question away. "We're after far bigger fish."

"Is he connected to your fish?"

"No."

I refused to let up. "Then how did you come across the photo?"

"It was under one of the many rocks we turned over."

"Then how is it not connected?"

Tino glanced up at the ceiling as if searching for an appropriate answer. A moment later, he lowered his chin and locked eyes with me. "Think of it this way: Law enforcement raids a home they suspect contains a stolen painting. They find the painting, but there are also other paintings in the home, all of which were purchased legally. Those other paintings have no connection to their case and aren't seized as evidence."

I stared down at my half-eaten omelet and sighed. I'd suddenly lost my appetite. "For the time being, let's assume this creep is someone known to one of the interns, because that might help us help Detective Spader solve this case. The question then becomes why did he do it? Was it to help someone, to frame someone, or both?"

"And how does it relate to Jared Oberman's murder?" asked Zack. "If it even does."

Tino waved his fork at us. "True. You could be dealing with two separate crimes by two individuals with no connection to each other."

"At least two," I corrected. "We still don't know if there's a connection between Jared's murder and the attempt on Aurora's life Friday night. Not to mention, the second murder yesterday. Is it connected to Jared's murder? Or is it a copycat crime?"

None of us knew the answers to any of those question. Not even the various law enforcement working the case—or cases. Spader's frustration was so palpable yesterday that it had practically emanated from every pore in his body.

In comparison, my life as a magazine crafts editor was relatively stress-free, albeit not as well-paid as a Union County detective. Unlike Spader, I wasn't entitled to hazard pay since my job didn't include putting my life in jeopardy. Or at least it hadn't prior to Karl bequeathing me his loan shark. Since then, the dead bodies continue to pile up, both in and out of the office.

With the Trimedia tightwads having fled our Morris County cornfield, perhaps I could convince Naomi to institute a hazard pay policy. A ten thousand dollar bonus every time I discovered a murder victim. Another ten thousand for solving the murder. At the rate I stumble over dead bodies, I might be debt free before I hit fifty. Couldn't hurt to ask.

The waitress dropped the check at our table and began to clear the plates while Tino and Zack tussled over who would pick up the tab. They finally settled their alpha male battle by each handing her a credit card and telling her to split the bill.

She placed the credit cards and check in her apron pocket, turned to me, and pointed to the remaining half of my omelet. "You want a box for that?"

Was she kidding? Carry around half an omelet in ninety-degree July heat for several hours? Not wanting to risk food poisoning, I judiciously declined.

A few minutes later, we stood on the sidewalk outside the diner. Tino turned to Zack. "Keep me in the loop, and keep Mrs. B. safe."

"Always," said Zack. "Thanks for your help."

Tino slapped Zack on the back. "Hey, man, I was totally redundant this time. You beat me to it."

"Only because Detective Spader received the emailed photo while at our house," I said. "But your knowledge of all things cyber is invaluable, Tino. I learned a lot this morning." Not all of which thrilled me, but I kept that to myself.

"Always happy to help, Mrs. B."

At that point, Tino headed to his symposium. Sidestepping neck-craning tourists, Zack and I made our way toward Columbus Circle and the museum.

~*~

Since the museum didn't open until ten o'clock, I hadn't been able to call ahead to set up an appointment with the director. Luckily, she was available when we arrived. Not surprisingly, she immediately recognized Zack, was familiar with his work, and assumed he'd come to speak with her.

Zack quickly disabused her of that notion but in a friendly way and with a promise to have his agent contact her about a future gallery exhibit. He then introduced me.

I explained my idea for a write-up in *American Woman*, showing her several past issues where I'd featured other museums. I had no clue whether she really loved the idea on its own merit or feigned exuberance for a better chance of lining up Zack at some future date. If the latter, unlike me, she had no discernable tells. However, she insisted on giving us a personal tour of not only the galleries but the inner sanctum.

Nearly four hours later, I had more than enough information for my future article as well as dozens of photos, courtesy of Zack. Mission accomplished.

When we stepped back onto the street, we discovered that while we had toured the museum, a cold front had blown in, bringing with it the trifecta of a July weather unicorn—cooler temperatures, lower humidity, and a light breeze. "How do you feel about forgoing the subway and walking back to Penn Station?" asked Zack.

Even if the temperature hadn't dipped below stifling, I would have opted for walking. Summer in the city turns the subway into an underground oven, easily twenty degrees hotter than whatever the thermometer reads above ground. "I'm game."

However, I'd only eaten half an omelet since early this

morning. By the time we arrived in the Garment District, my stomach erupted in a credible impersonation of Audrey II, the man-eating plant from *Little Shop of Horrors*. In grumbles I feared loud enough to make heads turn, my tummy demanded, "Feed me!"

Zack choked back a laugh as he pulled out his phone and searched for a place to appease the beast. Five minutes later, we settled into a booth in a dimly lit Italian bistro on Eighth Avenue.

A dark mahogany bar ran the length of one wall. Every conceivable potent potable filled a series of glass shelves that covered the back mirrored wall of the bar. A row of booths occupied the opposite wall. Small bistro tables for two dotted the center aisle, leaving just enough room for people to pass on either side. The long, narrow room looked so familiar that I was certain it had been used on multiple occasions to film scenes from the various *Law & Order* franchises.

When we first entered, half a dozen people, mostly men, stood at the bar. A few of the booths were also occupied. I ordered a glass of Riesling, Zack a craft beer, and we decided to split an antipasto. As we sipped and ate, several other people wandered into the bistro, either for a late lunch or an extremely early happy hour.

A few minutes later, my padded banquette seat rocked slightly as someone dropped into the booth behind me. They must have placed their orders at the bar because a moment later I heard the waitress delivering a pitcher of beer and glasses to their table.

Once the waitress departed, conversation commenced, and I found myself hanging on every word. In a trembling voice that sounded vaguely familiar, a woman asked, "What are we going to do?"

"Not much you can do," said a male voice, also vaguely familiar.

"My father will kill me if he ever discovers that photo," said a second woman. "Or it will kill him."

"Only if he surfs the dark web," offered the man.

The second woman sneered. "What makes you think someone won't download it and post it all over social media? Or that it hasn't already happened? We should do a reverse image search."

The first woman gasped. "Who would do such a thing?"

"Seriously?" asked the second woman. "Just about every jerk on the planet. Not to mention a certain former coworker who comes to mind. From the very first day, she made it crystal clear she'd do anything to secure the permanent position at Flix."

"I don't know," said the man. "Does she have the skills to pull off something like that?"

"Who knows?" asked the first woman. "Maybe she hired someone. But Brooklyn's right. It's got to be her. Who else would it be?"

A line from Casablanca suddenly sprang to mind. *Of all the gin joints in all the towns, in all the world....*

EIGHTEEN

What were the odds? Even though the bistro was situated not far from Flix Entertainment, it was one of dozens of such establishments within walking distance to the production company. Besides, what CFO closes shop to go day-drinking with his interns in the middle of a workday?

I was so intent on eavesdropping that I didn't realize I sat frozen, staring vacantly at a speared artichoke heart hovering halfway between my plate and mouth, until Zack cleared his throat.

I blinked and pulled my gaze away from the artichoke heart. Across the table, Zack stared at me, a look of concern filling his face. "Everything okay?"

I placed a finger to my lips, then grabbed my phone and shot him a text: *OMG! Don't look now, but I think Brooklyn Smith, Kendall Braxton, and Devin Oberman are seated in the booth behind me.*

Zack's phone pinged the incoming text. After reading the

message, he placed his forearms on the table, leaned forward, and quietly asked, "What makes you think so?"

I responded with another text: *They're talking about the threesome photo, and it sounds like they may know it's a fake. I'm guessing Spader came into the city to interview them earlier.*

Zack glanced toward the bar, then texted back: *The bottles are blocking the mirror. I can't get a bead on them. Are you sure? Did they mention Spader by name?"*

I turned my attention back to the people behind me in time to hear the first woman say, "Maybe that detective is trying to trick us."

"Trick you into what?" asked the man. "Admit that the two you were having a kinky affair with my brother?"

"We weren't!" said the second woman. "How could you think such a thing?"

His voice filled with derision. "I know—knew—my brother. Jared had some less than mainstream predilections."

"Well, I don't," said the first woman.

"And neither do I," said the second. "Besides, you're forgetting the detective said the photo was created using A.I."

I shot back a reply: *Trust me. It's them. One of the women is named Brooklyn. She said the detective told them the photo was A.I. generated. Plus, the guy just referred to his brother Jared in the past tense.*

Zack nodded and texted back: *Keep listening.*

I forked some Caprese salad onto my plate and cut the mozzarella, tomato, and basil into bite-sized pieces. As I ate in silence while continuing to eavesdrop, two thoughts tied my insides up in knots.

First, I hoped the Flix contingent had only stopped in for a quick drink. Otherwise, Zack and I might be stuck in the bistro for hours. Leaving meant walking directly past their table, and chances were good that one of them would notice us.

Secondly, I crossed my fingers that none of them would need to use the restroom, which was situated at the far end of the bistro. To get to it meant walking directly past our booth. Unless they had their heads buried in their phones, there was no way they wouldn't notice us.

I doubted Kendall Braxton would recognize either Zack or me. She'd only popped her head into the conference room for a few seconds Thursday, and her attention was completely focused on Jared. However, I was certain Brooklyn would remember both of us, and Devin would certainly remember me after he and Aurora showed up at the magazine yesterday.

I sent up a plea to the bladder gods that if anyone needed to go potty, it would be Kendall Braxton and neither of the other two.

The chances of that grew slimmer as Devin Oberman called over the waitress and ordered another pitcher of beer for the table. I frowned.

Zack raised an eyebrow and mouthed, "What?"

I reached for my phone: *They ordered another pitcher of beer. Looks like we're stuck here for a while.*

He offered a shrug before typing: *Not the worst thing.*

I texted back: *As long as no one needs to use the restroom.*

Zack twisted in his seat and glanced toward the rear of the restaurant. He then replied: *We can leave out the back through the kitchen.*

I nodded. The sooner we skedaddled, the less likely we'd be spotted. I polished off the last slice of bruschetta while Zack flagged down the waitress for our check. After briefly glancing at the slip of paper, he handed her a fifty. "Keep the change."

Her eyes widened with delight as she pocketed Ulysses S. Grant. "Thank you, sir. I hope we'll see you and your wife again soon."

I'll bet she did. As she headed back to the kitchen, Zack and I scooted from the booth and followed several steps behind her.

On the other side of the swinging kitchen door, we were greeted by a cacophony of clattering cookware, dishes, and the voices of kitchen staff, shouting to be heard over the other noises. The waitress yelled an order to the cook before turning right to pick up food for another table.

Zack and I race-walked straight toward the back door. Either the waitress never noticed us following her or hadn't cared. No one else in the kitchen stopped us. A moment later, we exited into a back alley.

"Odd that everyone in the kitchen ignored us," I said as we made our way around a Dumpster and headed for the street.

"I suspect we aren't the first customers to duck out through the kitchen," said Zack.

"To avoid paying? Even more reason to stop us," I said.

He laughed. "I wasn't thinking of deadbeats."

"Then what?"

"I'm pretty sure I recognized a couple of the guys hanging at the bar."

I didn't think he meant fellow photojournalists. I gave myself a mental head slap. That hole-in-the-wall bistro was exactly the sort of establishment favored by certain New York crime families. "Gambino?"

"Bonanno."

"Really? I should have taken a closer look. I went to school with a few Bonannos." I had never given it much thought before and until recently never made the connection between some of my Italian classmates and the Five Families. New Jersey had a huge Italian population. Not everyone with an Italian surname had mob connections. Then again, as I've since learned, many do, and some of them were my former classmates.

Zack wrapped an arm around my shoulders as we turned left onto Eighth Avenue. "I'm glad you didn't. I think you've crossed paths with enough mob guys for several lifetimes."

"Probably. But they keep multiplying. Exponentially."

"Like rabbits?"

"Too cuddly. More like rats."

We arrived at Penn Station to find the train to Westfield already boarding. After racing downstairs to the platform and walking through several cars, we finally found two empty seats. By the time we settled into them, the train was pulling out of the station.

I whipped out my phone and shot off a text to Detective Spader: *Did you meet with Smith, Braxton, and Oberman in the city this afternoon?"*

My phone rang a moment later, and Detective Spader's name popped up on the screen. When I answered, he asked, "Why do you ask?"

After telling him of the coincidence at the bistro, he said. "Are you still in Midtown?"

"On the train back to Westfield."

"Which car?"

"Why?"

"Because I'm on the train back to Westfield."

I glanced up at the front of the car and rattled off the number.

A moment later, I saw Spader rise from a seat in the front row and walk toward us.

"Small world," I said.

He offered a skeptical squint, first toward me, then Zack. "Is it? What were you two doing in the city?"

I decided not to mention breakfast with Tino, instead jumping right to my meeting at the museum, then asked, "What are you doing in the city?"

Spader cocked his head. "Exactly what you thought I was doing, but how did you know?"

Before I could answer, Zack said, "I think this is a conversation for a more private location."

"Agreed," said Spader. "I'll meet you back at your house." Without uttering another word, he turned and lumbered toward his seat.

~*~

Forty minutes later, the train pulled into the Westfield station. Spader had parked his unmarked car in a dedicated law enforcement spot near the building that housed the station waiting room. When Zack and I continued down the path that led to the South Avenue crosswalk, he called out to us, "Did you walk?"

We both nodded. Spader aimed his key fob at the car and beeped the locks open. "Hop in."

In less time than it would have taken us to reach the intersection and cross the street, we arrived back at the house. We entered to find that thirteen Daughters of the October Revolution had commandeered my living room and dining room. My mother-in-law took one look at Detective Spader, speared him with an evil eye, and declared, "We've done nothing wrong."

Hardly. My living room and dining room resembled a war zone with papers, envelopes, and rolls of stamps strewn across my dining room table. Dirty dishes and glasses covered the remaining horizontal surfaces of both rooms. Picket signs declaring STAND UP FOR YOUR RIGHT TO FROWN lined the walls.

Did I even want to know what that meant?

All work on their cause du jour had come to a halt as the Daughters of the October Revolution, all with either hands on hips or arms crossed, silently glared at us. I quickly executed a mental count to a hundred in search of some hidden inner Zen. As usual, I failed to find any. I inhaled a deep breath and as calmly as possible, said, "Lucille, you and your rabble-rousers have thirty minutes to clean up this mess and return my home to the way it looked when I left the house this morning. I will scoop up anything remaining at that point and toss it in the trash and recycling bins."

"You can't do that!" yelled head minion Harriet Kleinhample.

The other women screeched and bellowed in agreement.

I raised my voice to be heard over them. "I most certainly can, and I will. This is my house. And don't think any of you are staying for dinner this evening. You're not welcome."

Lucille pointed an arthritic finger at Spader. "This is your doing, isn't it? I'm filing a complaint with the county sheriff's office."

Spader smirked. "Feel free, ma'am. After all, the sheriff is such a fan of yours."

The jaws of all thirteen Daughters of the October Revolution dropped open, then snapped shut. If looks could kill, Spader, Zack, and I would now be toast. I set a timer on my phone and flipped the screen around to show the commies. "Time's ticking, ladies." I then walked through the living room and dining room toward the kitchen.

Zack reached for my arm as I stopped short at the entrance and surveyed the aftermath of the Bolshevik tornado that had struck. Empty food containers and dirty dishes covered the counters and kitchen table. I yanked open the refrigerator door to find all my perishables—cheese, fruit, vegetables, lunchmeat, eggs, milk, and orange juice—gone. I checked the pantry. Not a single slice of bread or box of crackers or cookies remained.

I gritted my teeth. Forget counting to a hundred this time. Counting to a hundred *thousand* wouldn't prevent me from losing my cool. "I. Am. Going. To. Kill. Them."

"Probably not the best statement to make with a homicide detective in the room," said Zack.

I turned to Spader. "Think I could get off on a justifiable homicide defense?"

He held up his hands. "For what? I didn't hear a thing."

But I did hear something. A pathetic doggie whimper coming from the direction of the back door. I stepped into the mud room and found Leonard, pawing the back door and looking like he was about to burst. Had Lucille bothered to walk her dog at all today? I clipped on his leash and made it outside without a second to spare.

Zack had grabbed Ralph from his cage, and after Leonard had relieved himself, we all climbed the steps to the apartment above the garage. Ralph immediately spread his wings and took flight, swooping around the room several times before settling onto Zack's shoulder to await a sunflower seed. Leonard curled up on one end of the sofa and proceeded to fall asleep.

As the room filled with the sound of doggie snores, Zack and I squeezed onto the remainder of the sofa, and Detective Spader dropped into the chair across from the coffee table.

Despite my best efforts, my curiosity about the picket signs had gotten the better of me. Before I filled Detective Spader in on what I'd overheard in the bistro, I asked, "Any chance you have a clue about my mother-in-law's latest wacky cause?"

Spader rolled his eyes and barked out a guffaw. "I'm guessing it has something to do with one of the weird laws still on the books in New Jersey."

I raised an eyebrow. "One of them concerns frowning?"

He nodded. "Under state law, it's technically illegal to frown at a police officer. I'm guessing one of those women was recently involved in a confrontation with an officer, and he issued her a warning."

I gaped at him. "Cop humor, Detective? Come on. You can't be serious."

He held up a hand. "It's the absolute truth, Mrs. Barnes."

"I don't believe you." I turned to Zack. "He's pulling my leg, right?"

Spader placed his raised hand over his heart. "On my saintly mother's honor. You can look it up."

"If so," said Zack, "Can we assume it's one of those laws rarely enforced?"

I laughed. "If not, the Daughters of the October Revolution would be permanent residents of the Edna Mahan Correctional Facility."

Spader shook his head. "Maximum fine is a thousand dollars and up to six months in jail."

I'd settle for a six-month reprieve from Lucille and her minions. "How on earth do you happen to know about such an arcane law? I can't imagine it comes up often in homicide investigations."

He held up his phone. "I Googled it while you surveyed the kitchen disaster. But get this: although it's illegal to frown, grimace, or make gestures of facial contempt or derision at an officer, giving a middle finger salute is protected under the First Amendment."

I scoffed. "That makes no sense."

Spader shrugged. "The law often makes no sense."

"Don't tell my mother-in-law about that First Amendment protection." I pictured Lucille and her minions flipping the bird at the wrong person. No matter how I felt about my mother-in-law, I didn't want some hothead causing her harm. Or worse.

Spader crossed his heart. "Wouldn't think of it. Now, let's change the subject and talk about how you knew I was conducting interviews at Flix today."

I explained what I'd overheard. When I finished, I asked, "From what they said, I take it you showed them the photo?"

"I did. During my individual questioning of them. Neither woman reacted well when they viewed the photo."

"What do you mean?"

"They were both horrified. One of them unleashed a torrent of tears. The other went almost catatonic, kept staring off in the distance, shaking her head, and whimpering."

"They didn't accuse each other?" I asked.

"No."

"Is it possible one of them was acting?" asked Zack.

Spader shook his head. "I doubt it. I've had to deliver dreadful news to too many relatives of victims over the years. Based on my experience, their reactions were genuine."

From everything Spader had gleaned from his interviews of Kendall and Brooklyn, it appeared he had ruled both out as suspects, at least for the A.I. photo. The only other likely culprit was Ellis Cummings, especially since she'd claimed Kendall and Brooklyn were both doing the horizontal tango with Jared before the photo ever showed up on Spader's phone.

"It's not looking good for Ellis Cummings," said Zack.

Spader nodded.

"What about Devin Oberman?" I asked.

"What about him?" asked Spader. "Are you suggesting he created and sent the photo?"

"No, but I was wondering how he reacted when you showed it to him."

"That's where it gets interesting," said Spader. "He dismissed it with a shrug. Said his brother was into some kinky stuff and that he'd probably filmed the three of them. That was before I told him the photo was A.I. generated."

"And after?" asked Zack.

"He suggested that even without A.I., Jared had the computer skills to create such an image."

NINETEEN

"Wow!" Talk about a mic drop. "I didn't see that coming."

Spader leaned back in his chair and muttered, "You're not the only one, Mrs. Barnes."

"But Jared is dead," I reminded him. "He couldn't have sent you the photo."

"True."

I played dumb and asked, "Was the photo really generated by artificial intelligence, or did you just tell them it was?"

"According to our computer guru, it's definitely A.I. She knows her stuff. Once she pointed certain things out to me, it became obvious. However, the average person probably wouldn't notice any discrepancies without a thorough study of the image. And maybe not even then."

"Was she able to trace who sent the email?" asked Zack.

Spader's jaw clenched. "No, whoever sent that image knew how to mask a digital footprint."

I chewed on my lower lip as an idea formed. "Let's assume for a minute that Jared Oberman created the image. What's the likelihood that it was the first such image he created?"

"Where are you going with this?" asked Zack.

"Whoever killed Jared may have been one of his digital victims. Maybe he was creating them to blackmail people."

"What would be his motive?" asked Zack. "Certainly not money."

I shrugged. "Power? Kicks? Revenge? And don't forget, for some people, no matter how much money they have, it's never enough." I turned to Spader. "I know you said you found nothing incriminating on any of the office or personal tech you searched, but is it possible Jared kept another computer and maybe even a second phone somewhere other than his house or office?"

"Like where?"

I offered another shrug. "A vacation home? A storage locker? Aurora is convinced he cheated on her, even though she's offered no proof. Maybe he kept a laptop at a girlfriend's home and logged on through her account."

Spader scrubbed his jaw. "Except we turned up no evidence to indicate any of that. How would he pay for it? We ran his financials. Nothing popped up."

"It wouldn't if everything was in someone else's name."

Spader narrowed his eyes at me. "Come on, Mrs. Barnes. You're not suggesting a fictitious girlfriend was paying for his porn obsession, are you?"

"If it was a mutual obsession? Or a shakedown scheme? Why not? But what makes you think he didn't reimburse her?"

"Because, as I said, we found nothing to indicate questionable payments to anyone."

"Maybe you did and don't realize it."

Spader leaned forward and stared at me for several long seconds. I stared back, daring him to think outside the box. Finally, the lightbulb in his brain lit up. His eyes widened. "One of the subcontractors?"

I smiled in acknowledgement of his Henry Higgins moment. "By George, he's got it."

"You think Jared Oberman masked reimbursements to an accomplice by funneling them through Flix as subcontracting payments?"

"It's a theory. You said Devin handled all the finances, but I doubt he'd investigate every subcontractor his brother hired or verified every dollar spent. If the expenses appeared legitimate, my guess is that he'd authorize payment, no questions asked."

Spader grew thoughtful, stroking his chin as he digested my words. "You could be right, Mrs. Barnes. I'll certainly explore that avenue if and when I rule out Ellis Cummings."

I huffed out my frustration. I don't know why I continued to defend Ellis so vociferously, but my Nancy Drew instincts told me Spader was wasting his time and should look elsewhere. "You've found no evidence connecting her to any aspect of this investigation."

"Not yet. But with her art school background and now the A.I. monkey wrench thrown into the investigation, she still tops my suspects list."

Rather than argue with him, I took another tack. "I know your resources are currently stretched thin, Detective. However, while you're traveling down that dead end, may I suggest you also investigate Aurora Oberman's claims about her husband's affairs? My gut tells me she's hiding something."

He sighed as he offered me a slight smile. "I'm not discounting your theory, Mrs. Barnes. I've made it clear that I value your input. Admittedly, Mrs. Oberman hasn't been very forthcoming. For both those reasons, I'll assign an officer to dig deeper. Maybe we can find someone who knows more and is willing to talk."

At that moment, the alarm on my phone sounded. "Any chance they complied?" asked Spader.

"I wouldn't bet money on it."

"From where I sit, Mrs. Barnes, you have the patience of a saint."

I stood. "This saint is quickly running out of patience, Detective."

Zack reached for my hand. "Why don't you stay here? Let me handle it."

I debated, then declined. "The devil in me needs the satisfaction of tossing the commies out of the house and dumping their protest paraphernalia."

He rose from the sofa, held his arms akimbo, and grinned at me. "I'd never deny you any satisfaction."

Spader forced a cough. He lowered his head and stared at his shoes, but he couldn't hide the flush that coursed up his neck and spread to his cheeks. Under his breath he muttered something that sounded like, "TMI."

I bit back a chuckle. The man's cell phone contained a lurid piece of evidence, but he blushed at a mild double-entendre. In some ways, I found that endearing.

I roused Leonard while Zack held out his arm and whistled for Ralph. Once we'd wrangled both animals, we headed back to the house. Sure enough, nothing had changed in the kitchen. I stepped through the archway to survey both the dining room and living room. The dirty dishes remained, but the protest materials had disappeared. As had every member of the commie brigade and their fearless leader.

I muttered under my breath as Zack and I began stacking dishes to carry into the kitchen. Spader scooped up silverware.

"You don't have to do that," I said as the three of us made our way from the dining room into the kitchen.

"Consider it partial payment for all your help, Mrs. Barnes." He placed the silverware in the sink, then grabbed some of the empty food wrappers scattered across the counter and kitchen table and dumped them in the trash can. "Does this happen often?"

"Lucille Pollack is the unwanted gift that keeps on giving," said Zack as he loaded the dishwasher. "She and her cohorts live to spite my wife."

I sighed. "And with every day it gets progressively worse."

"*Brrrack!*" Ralph flapped his wings from where he'd perched atop the refrigerator and proclaimed, "*Still thus, and thus; still worse! Measure for Measure.* Scene Three, Act Two."

Truer words were never squawked.

As we continued to clean up the mess the commies had left, something nagged at me, something that had begun niggling at the edges of my brain since yesterday when Devin and Aurora showed up at the magazine. Their visit felt off in so many ways. The more I tried to reconcile the disparities, the more questions it raised.

I hadn't realized how deeply into my thoughts I'd retreated until Zack said, "Watch that frown, Sweetheart. Spader might arrest you."

Maybe that was the impetus my brain needed to land on the problem, because the thought suddenly took shape. I turned to Spader. "You said the Oberman brothers were squeaky clean. Yet what Devin claims his brother was into is anything but squeaky clean. Wouldn't something like that have popped up when you looked into their backgrounds?"

Spader stacked more dishes into the sink. "You'd think so. But not necessarily. Some people are really good at hiding their degenerate behavior."

"Until they get caught," said Zack.

"Except some never get caught," said Spader. "Or not for decades. Often because others are complicit in covering up their crimes. And don't forget, it's not a crime if it's consensual."

I snorted. "The Harvey Weinstein defense? Come on, Detective."

He held up his hands, palms outward. "Hey, I'm not saying that's the case with Oberman. We only have his brother's accusation. Not a shred of proof other than a fake photo."

"Maybe you have no proof because there's nothing to find," I said. When both men stopped and stared at me, I continued, "What if Devin Oberman has an ulterior motive for painting his brother in a pornographic light?"

"But why?" asked Spader. "What's his motive?"

"That's what we need to unearth," I said. "Along with what's going on between him and his sister-in-law. They certainly didn't behave like a grieving spouse and sibling yesterday."

I thought back to the way Devin had reached for Aurora's hand when he told me she now owned half the company. If he'd placed a comforting hand on her forearm or shoulder, I would have taken it as a gesture of sympathy. But intertwining his fingers with hers to clasp hands? That telegraphed an entirely different statement. "What if Devin and Aurora are having an affair?"

My mind now raced as pieces began to fall into place, and the most obvious guilty parties came into focus. For the most obvious of reasons. "What if Devin and Aurora are responsible for Jared's death?"

Spader shook his head. "Both have alibis for the morning of Jared's murder."

"We both know alibis can be bought. Besides, I'm not suggesting either pulled the trigger. However, they certainly have the money to hire someone to do their dirty work for them."

Spader dropped onto one of the kitchen chairs. He placed his elbows on the table and leaned his chin on his fisted hands, his forehead furrowed as he mentally chewed on my words. Finally, he looked up and said, "Why didn't I think of that?"

"Probably because you're in desperate need of a vacation," I said.

Spader scowled. "Or at least a good night's sleep."

Zack closed the dishwasher door and pressed the start button. "Haven't there been several recent cases around the country of women arrested for hiring hit men to kill their husbands? There was that case in the Bahamas that made national headlines."

"And several wives who resorted to poison," I added. "Wasn't one a doctor or pharmacist? And the romance author who wrote *How to Murder Your Husband*. She's in prison for doing just that."

"All the more reason I should have focused on Devin and Aurora Oberman from the start," said Spader. "Murder 101, the spouse is usually the prime suspect."

Zack patted Spader on the back. "Don't beat yourself up, man. We all can't be as smart as my wife."

Spader chuckled. "At least I did one thing right. I asked for her help." He stood. "But now I need to prove this latest theory. As much sense as it makes, I can't make an arrest without evidence.

I'd better get back to headquarters and figure out how I'm going to get the proof I need."

"Not before you have a decent meal," I said.

Spader glanced around the kitchen. "If you're inviting me to stay for dinner, Mrs. Barnes, may I remind you that you're all out of food?"

"But I know how to make dinner reservations," said Zack, holding up his phone.

"Only if you let me pay," said Spader.

"Isn't that against regulations?" I asked.

"Not if I don't expense it. This one's on me, not the force."

~*~

Not wanting to run the risk of bumping into anyone he worked with, Detective Spader suggested we steer clear of local Westfield restaurants. "Avoids having to explain," he said.

"What do you suggest?" asked Zack.

"Legal Sea Foods."

I shook my head. "On a detective's salary?" Even as a senior detective, I doubted Spader made more than a hundred grand a year. Although, with all the overtime he clocked, maybe he was pulling in twice that amount. Still, dinner for three with drinks would easily set him back several hundred dollars.

"We can't let you pick up the tab for that," said Zack.

"Consider it payback for all the meals and drinks I've mooched off you lately."

I seriously doubted I'd served him three hundred dollars' worth of food and booze in the year since we'd met. "How about Cheesecake Factory?" I suggested.

Spader crossed his arms over his chest, set his jaw, and shook his head. "Legal Sea Foods. I won't take no for an answer."

Zack and I looked at each other and shrugged. "Legal Sea Foods it is," said Zack. "But I'm covering the tip."

After Spader reluctantly agreed, he offered to drive to avoid taking two cars.

Zack rode shotgun while I settled into the back seat of Spader's unmarked car. At least it didn't have a prisoner partition separating us.

I pulled out my phone and sent the boys a text. They had texted earlier to say they were going out for burgers and a movie after work. I didn't want them to grow concerned if they arrived home before us and found both cars in the driveway but no sign of either Zack or me.

As we drove through Westfield toward Summit, I noticed Spader continually frowning into his rearview mirror. Likewise, Zack kept turning his head toward the passenger side mirror. I twisted in my seat to glance out the back window and found a dark SUV keeping pace with us. "Are we being followed?"

"Could be," said Spader. "I'm about to find out."

He stepped on the gas and sped through a yellow light just as it turned red. Horns blared, and brakes screeched as the car behind us followed.

"Sorry, folks, we might be a little late for our reservation." Spader called for backup, giving a description of the vehicle behind us, along with a plate number. "Pull him over for running a red light at South and Central."

I sighed. And here I thought we were about to enjoy a peaceful dinner.

We had driven through Watchung Reservation and entered Summit when Detective Spader received a call. "Whatcha got for me?"

Nice to know I wasn't the only person who was the recipient of his terrible telephone manners. The one-sided conversation revealed little, mostly Spader muttering quite a few choice words under his breath as he listened to the person on the other end of the call.

"Get that gun down to Hamilton pronto."

The person following us had a gun?

Spader paused for a moment. "Yes, tonight. Call ahead to let them know you're on your way. I don't care how backed up they are. Tell them this takes priority. I want answers tonight. If they've got a problem with that, they can take it up with me. Understood?"

Spader continued, "Have someone prepare a warrant. I want it in front of the judge the moment we have a match. And Eastman, have DeFrancisco comb through Cummings's tech and social media feeds to see if there's a connection between the two of them."

After Spader hung up, he said, "They brought him in for questioning."

"Is that normal for a moving violation?" I asked.

"It is when there's an open can of beer in the cupholder and a Glock on the passenger seat."

"That explains Hamilton," said Zack.

"Who's Hamilton?" I asked.

"Not a who," said Spader. "A what. State Police Headquarters. It's where the forensics center is located."

I stared at the back of Zack's head. *Why would a photojournalist who claims he's not a spy know this?*

"Bad enough," continued Spader, "but he also lives in Neptune and is the same age as Cummings. Worst case scenario, he's doing her dirty work. Best case scenario, he gets scared straight when he's faced with jail time for the beer and weapons violation. Even if he's a licensed gun owner, he can't drive around with a weapon out in the open. By state law, it's got to be locked up somewhere other than the passenger compartment."

Was this another nail in Ellis's coffin? Maybe I wasn't such a good judge of character, after all. If Detective Spader kept connecting dots in this manner, the only caricatures Ellis Cummings would be drawing for years to come were of prison staff and inmates.

However, just because the driver hailed from Neptune, it didn't mean he and Ellis were friends. They may not even know each other. For Ellis's sake, I hoped that was the case, but it was yet one more piece of circumstantial evidence. Gather enough circumstantial evidence, and it was eventually bound to lead to some hard, irrefutable facts.

Besides, all of that failed to take into consideration that the kid with the gun had been tailing us. How likely was it that we weren't his intended target?

"So, this kid," I said, "does he have a name?"

Spader glanced up into his rearview mirror and locked eyes with me. "Mario Cappitani. Mean anything?"

"Never heard of him."

"Does he have any priors?" asked Zack.

"None, but his father is a Genovese soldier. He's currently serving time for armed robbery and drug trafficking. Looks like the rotten apple didn't fall far from the tree, even if there's no connection to Cummings."

"But you think there is?" I asked.

"We'll soon find out."

"How soon?"

"The forensics center can normally run ballistics in less than forty-eight hours."

"But you think you'll have a report tonight?" I asked.

"A partial report. Shouldn't take them long to fire off some test rounds and compare the casings with the ones from the three other crime scenes. Every firearm leaves a unique fingerprint on the rounds as they pass through the chamber."

"We already know a different gun was used at Aurora Oberman's home," I reminded him.

"Also in the second murder," he said, "but I'm betting Cappitani's gun was used in one of the murders or the attempt on Oberman's wife. I doubt the Glock is his only firearm. Not with his family background. It's also probably not registered. Bottom line? I wouldn't be surprised to learn he's responsible for all three crimes."

~*~

After a dinner of stuffed lobster tails with coleslaw and roasted broccoli, Zack, Spader, and I were indulging our sweet tooths with slices of Boston cream pie when Spader's phone rang. He glanced at the screen. Before answering, he peered across the table at Zack and me. "Looks like we may have some answers."

I held my breath.

Spader jabbed his screen. "Did DeFrancisco find something?"

TWENTY

After another brief pause, Spader said, "Pick her up."

"Ellis?" I asked when he ended the call.

He nodded. "She and Cappitani are Facebook friends. He also follows her on Instagram and TikTok. They've known each other since kindergarten."

"That doesn't mean the two of them conspired to kill Jared Oberman."

Spader's tone grew sympathetic. "I know you've been giving Cummings the benefit of the doubt at every turn, Mrs. Barnes, even when she threatened you, but it's not looking good for her. We'll know more when I get the results of the ballistics test."

I didn't know why I kept championing Ellis Cummings in the face of everything I'd learned about her. Still, I refused to let go of the slim hope that I was right, and she was nothing more than an immature kid who lashed out because she was angry and scared.

Maybe she hadn't even been stalking me. What if she had a legitimate reason for being in Morristown Friday and was as surprised to see me as I was to see her? Had she stood across the street from the restaurant debating whether to approach me?

I gave myself a mental head slap. I wasn't looking at the situation through the eyes of Nancy Drew, Miss Marple, or Jessica Fletcher. Some sleuth!

I'd allowed emotion and Pollyanna naïveté to hinder my objectivity. You'd think with everything I'd gone through the past year and a half, my cynical genes would have killed off any remaining eternally optimistic genes. Good thing no one had approached me lately with a deal to purchase the Brooklyn Bridge.

Zack placed his hand over mine. "You need to brace yourself for the worst, Sweetheart."

I sighed. "I know." If Mario Cappitani had killed Jared Oberman, Ellis Cummings was either a willing participant to the murder or had abetted it, knowingly or unwittingly. I didn't see a jury letting her off with a suspended sentence.

We also still didn't know who created the A.I. image. "Have you found any evidence that Ellis created the A.I. or knows anyone with A.I. skills?" I asked Spader.

"I checked her curriculum at Pratt, both prior years and present. She took one computer illustration course last year. Got a C for the semester. Her advisor said she hated it and prefers to draw the old-fashioned way."

"And she's not friends with anyone majoring in the tech side of design?"

"Not that we've discovered."

Hopefully, that ruled Ellis out as having anything to do with the A.I. image. I'd hate to think she had such anger control issues that she'd stoop to doing something so heinous, no matter how much she claimed Brooklyn and Kendall had bullied her.

But that alone didn't clear Ellis. She could still find herself in legal trouble, and someone who hustled the way she does to earn tuition money, doesn't have the funds to hire a shark of a defense attorney. More than likely, she was in for a fashion makeover that would reduce her wardrobe to nothing but orange jumpsuits for at least the foreseeable future.

~*~

Spader received another call as we headed back to Westfield. "Have they finished?" He listened for a minute, then said, "I'll be there in twenty minutes."

He ended the call, glanced over at Zack, then into the rearview mirror. I stared back at him. "The Glock wasn't used to kill Oberman or the victim in Springfield."

I breathed a sigh of relief. Maybe Ellis Cummings had dodged a bullet—no pun intended—and the state wouldn't be fitting her for an orange jumpsuit after all. "Then Ellis knowing Cappitani means nothing. It's just coincidence."

Spader once again stared at me from the rearview mirror, his eyes narrowed. "Afraid not. The ballistics report shows that the shots fired into Aurora Oberman's house Friday night came from Cappitani's Glock. Right now, he's facing attempted murder, among various lesser charges. Most likely, with more to come."

Which could include two murder charges. It now seemed highly likely that Mario Cappitani had killed Jared Oberman, but with a different gun, and possibly the second murder victim with a third gun. "What happens now?" I asked.

"I'll drop the two of you back at your house, then return to headquarters. I need to get the judge to sign off on a search warrant for Cappitani's home. Hopefully, we'll find those other guns before anyone gets wise and makes them disappear."

"Has he been allowed his one phone call?" asked Zack. "If so, they may already have disappeared."

"We've got that covered," said Spader. "Since we haven't questioned him yet, no one's read him his rights."

"Wouldn't he know to demand his phone call immediately," I asked, "given his family connections?"

Spader slowed for a red light and glanced back at me. "Quite the opposite. I'm sure he's been drilled from an early age on how to act if he's ever picked up. He's playing it cool, waiting for us to make the first move. Right now, he hasn't been booked on any charges. No one has even suggested he might be."

That made no sense to me. "Surely, he must know he's in trouble for the DUI and firearms violation."

"He's arrogant. With no priors, he probably figures he'll walk once the mob lawyer arrives. Right now, he's cooling his heels in an unlocked interrogation room with an officer posted outside the door. They've told him they're waiting for a detective to come in to speak with him. That would be me. If everything goes to plan, I won't step into that room until the search is executed."

A few minutes later, Spader pulled up to the curb in front of our house. Alex's Jeep was in the driveway. Harriet Kleinhample's VW minibus was nowhere in sight. "Thank you for dinner," I said as Zack and I stepped from the car. "You really didn't have to do that."

"It was my pleasure," said Spader. "Maybe next time we can do it without any drama."

"Or guns," I said.

"That, too."

"Except next time," said Zack, "I'm paying."

"I'll arm wrestle you for it," said Spader.

I laughed. "Then you'd better catch up on your sleep, Detective."

"Unfortunately, that's going to have to wait until some other night, Mrs. Barnes."

~*~

Our doorbell rang at six-forty-five the next morning. Zack checked his phone. "Spader."

"This early? Something's up."

We had both just finished dressing. Together we made our way from the bedroom. When Zack swung open the front door, we found Detective Spader, dressed in the same suit, shirt, and tie he'd worn last night, although far more rumpled and dotted with several coffee stains. He cradled a box of donuts against his chest and offered us a bleary-eyed grin. "I'll trade you donuts and information for a decent cup of coffee."

Zack waved him inside. He followed us into the kitchen where he collapsed onto a chair. After scrubbing at the stubble on his jaw, he yawned and rubbed his bloodshot eyes.

I bit back the admonition on the tip of my tongue, then turned to Zack as he poured beans into the coffee grinder, "Better make that a double strength pot."

Then I returned to assessing Spader. "I'm guessing you've been up all night."

He tried—unsuccessfully—to stifle another yawn as he opened the box and grabbed a glazed donut. After taking a huge bite, he said, "I'm on my way home but thought you'd want to know what happened after I dropped you off last night."

As much as I wanted to hear what Spader had to say, the mama bear in me had other ideas. The man looked awful. He needed a decent breakfast. And that meant protein, not deep-fried sugar.

I held up a finger. "First things first."

After Spader had dropped us off last night, Zack and I had run to the supermarket to restock the kitchen. I grabbed a carton of eggs, a zucchini, and a package of ham from the refrigerator and a large ripe tomato from the basket on the counter. Zack set a frying pan to heat on the stove, then began cracking eggs into a bowl while I chopped the veggies.

We worked with the speed of short-order cooks. Not long after the coffee had finished dripping, I placed three plates of loaded scrambled eggs on the table.

Spader wolfed down half his breakfast, afterwards taking a long swig of coffee before he spoke. "We've booked Cappitani for the attempted murder of Aurora Oberman."

I raised an eyebrow. "That's all?"

"Along with a host of other offenses."

"But not the two murders?" asked Zack.

"As of now, we have no evidence to tie him to either murder. None of the weapons we found at his apartment match those used at the other crime scenes."

When he paused to take another mouthful of egg, I studied his haggard face. Besides looking exhausted, he appeared royally peeved. Who could blame him? "Are you suggesting he got rid of two of the guns used in the crimes but kept the third? That makes no sense."

"And that's the problem in a nutshell. If we can't tie Cappitani to the murder weapons, we can't charge him. However, it's looking more and more like we're dealing with two unconnected murders."

"Why?" asked Zack.

Spader polished off the remainder of his eggs before answering.

"We haven't found any connection between the Springfield victim and Oberman or Flix Entertainment. According to his wife, they'd just moved from Utah days ago. He was about to start a residency at St. Barnabas. They have no connection to anyone in New York or New Jersey, and as far as we can tell, Oberman never stepped foot in Utah."

"Then why would someone want to kill the guy?" I asked.

"Chances are it was a carjacking that went south. Maybe the gun went off accidentally. The perp panicked and took off."

I rose to clear the dishes and returned with the coffee pot. As I poured refills, I tried not to sound mocking. "You really believe that, Detective? An early morning carjacking in a residential area near the golf course? What are the odds?"

He grabbed an apple fritter from the box, taking bites between sentences. "No, I don't, but I also don't have any leads. He had just returned from the gym. Security cameras didn't show an altercation or anyone else leaving the parking lot at the same time. The only other scenario that makes sense is a road rage incident that occurred on his way home. The shooter may have followed him and gunned him down as he stepped from his car. Either way, it looks like the Springfield victim is dead because he was in the wrong place at the wrong time."

"What about Ellis?" I asked. "Are you still holding her?"

Spader washed down his fritter before answering. "Either that kid is a damned good actress, or she's completely innocent. She claims she hasn't spoken to Cappitani in years, and even then, rarely. Said he had a huge crush on her back in high school, but she always thought he was a creep and never wanted to have anything to do with him."

"Then why was she Facebook friends with him?" I asked.

"It's all about numbers and likes with these kids. Someone sends a friend request, you click accept. The larger your following, the more popular you are. Same for her other social media accounts."

I thought back to Saturday when I spoke with Ellis in Ocean Grove. "She was extremely distraught when she heard someone had murdered Jared Oberman."

Spader nodded. "She told me. Apparently, she'd posted that she'd been unjustly fired and was contemplating a lawsuit. Cappitani may have thought he'd score points with her if he got rid of Oberman."

"But Jared was gunned down Friday morning," said Zack. "Aurora was targeted Friday night."

Spader nodded. "We think Cappitani didn't know Oberman was already dead. He drove to the Oberman home late Friday night, saw a shadow behind the drapes, and opened fire."

I tilted my head and narrowed my eyes at Spader. "Except something's not adding up."

"What's that?"

"Do you know when Ellis posted on social media?"

"Does it matter?"

"It might. She told me Brooklyn Smith had filmed security escorting her from the building. She said her phone started blowing up with notifications before she stepped onto the street. She became so upset that she turned off her phone."

Spader raised an eyebrow. "Are you stepping into my camp, Mrs. Barnes?"

"That depends on the timeline, Detective."

"She may have posted after Oberman fired her and before she was escorted from the building," said Zack.

Spader pulled out his phone. "I'm texting DeFrancisco."

A moment later his phone chimed. Spader glanced at the screen, then nodded toward Zack. "You're right. Cummings posted before Smith filmed her."

"Then my answer to your question, Detective, is no, I'm not stepping into your camp. I still believe Ellis is innocent and had nothing to do with Oberman's murder."

He attempted to choke back another yawn and failed. "Except Mrs. Oberman was nearly killed because of Cumming's Facebook post."

I'd concede that. To a point. "Which is something Ellis will have to live with the remainder of her life, but she wasn't asking anyone to avenge her, was she?"

When he shook his head, I continued, "Besides, she can't be held responsible for an unhinged ex-classmate. John Hinckley, Jr. shot Ronald Reagan to impress Jodie Foster. Does that make the actress culpable in an attempted assassination?"

Spader scowled into his empty coffee mug. "Point taken, Mrs. Barnes."

A few minutes later, Alex and Nick entered the kitchen, took one look at Spader, and simultaneously asked, "What's up?"

I glanced across the room to the clock on the stove and jumped to my feet. "Yikes! I'm late."

"Has something happened?" asked Nick, as both he and his brother speared me with looks of concern.

"Nothing to worry about," said Zack. He gave me a quick peck on the lips, then said, "Go. I'll explain."

With that, I gave my sons a hurried hug, waved to Spader, and rushed to the hall closet to grab my purse and tote. A minute later, I had pulled out of the driveway and was on my way to work.

~*~

The traffic gods had seen fit to smile upon me with no backups impeding my trip to the Morristown cornfield home of our offices. I glanced at the dashboard clock as I pulled into the parking lot and discovered I was only ten minutes late. In other words, on time. More or less.

Still, when I entered the building, the receptionist stopped me as I headed for the elevator. "Anastasia?"

When I veered toward her desk, she pointed across the entry to the seating area. "That woman has been waiting for you. She said her name was Sabrina and that you knew her."

I couldn't remember ever meeting anyone named Sabrina. Glancing over my shoulder, I spied a woman I didn't recognize sitting in one of the chairs. I knew I had no vendor meetings scheduled for today, but salespeople often showed up unannounced to hawk manufacturers' new products. However, I saw no briefcase or samples case on the end table next to her nor at her feet.

When she noticed me staring at her, she stood and walked toward me. She appeared to be about my age with shoulder length light brown waves. She wore a pair of white linen trousers with a cerulean blue and white pin dot boatneck silk T-shirt. A gold chain with three names written in script, most likely her children, hung from her neck She wasn't pudgy but not exactly thin, which let me to speculate, like me, she still carried remnants of baby weight from long ago pregnancies.

"Anastasia Pollack?"

"Yes?"

She held out her hand. "I'm Sabrina Oberman, Devin's wife." She glanced toward the receptionist's desk. "May we speak somewhere in private?"

Although she appeared nervous, worrying the shoulder strap of her handbag, I didn't feel threatened by her. But with a killer on the loose, I wasn't taking any chances. I led her back to the seating area. Once we'd both settled into chairs, I asked, "What can I do for you, Mrs. Oberman?"

She clenched her hands in her lap and said, "I'm sure you're wondering why I'm here."

"The thought had crossed my mind. I'm assuming it has something to do with your brother-in-law's murder."

She lowered her head and stared at her hands. "It does."

When she didn't offer anything further, I prompted her. "And?"

She raised her chin. Tears floated in her eyes. "I think Devin might have something to do with Jared's murder."

TWENTY-ONE

Holy guacamole! Maybe I wasn't such a bad amateur sleuth after all. Hadn't I pondered the possibility of Devin's involvement more than once over the last few days?

But why come to me with this information? Why not contact Spader? She must have a reason for not wanting to go to the police, but I decided not to ask. At least, not yet. Instead, I forced a combination of surprise and concern into my voice. "Come with me. We have a conference room upstairs."

Before she rose, she opened her purse and pulled out a tissue, patting her eyes and blowing her nose. She didn't say a word as she followed me to the elevator or on the short ride to the third floor. Once we exited onto the floor, I asked, "Would you like a cup of coffee?"

"Yes, thank you. That would be lovely."

Cloris was exiting the break room as we approached. She held a coffee mug in one hand, a muffin in the other. She eyed Sabrina before shifting her gaze to me, then back to Sabrina. "Welcome,

I'm food editor Cloris McWerther. And you are?"

Sabrina hesitated for a moment. "Sabrina Oberman."

Cloris is a much better actress than I am. She didn't miss a beat, hiding her surprise as she said, "Nice to meet you, Sabrina. Help yourself to a lemon blueberry muffin before they're all gone."

I stepped aside to allow Sabrina to precede me into the break room. As soon as her back was turned to us, Cloris raised an eyebrow and mouthed, "You okay?"

I nodded. "We'll be in the conference room if anyone is looking for me."

Once I'd poured two coffees and we each grabbed a muffin, I ushered Sabrina down the hall to the conference room. I hadn't thought to check the app, but luckily, I found the room unoccupied.

After we took seats at the table, I smiled to put her at her ease and took a sip of coffee before asking, "What makes you think your husband had anything to do with his brother's death, Mrs. Oberman?"

"I had suspected for some time that Devin was cheating on me."

"Still, it's a cavernous leap from cheating to murder."

Her features hardened, and her eyes grew steely. "He's having an affair with his brother's wife."

I had seen evidence of that when Devin and Aurora showed up at the magazine on Tuesday. Nice to have conformation that my instincts hadn't gone rusty. "But why not file for divorce? Many marriages don't work out. Few people resort to murder."

"Because Devin and Aurora want total control of the company."

"Do you have any proof of this, Mrs. Oberman?"

"I was hoping you could find that proof."

"Why me?"

"The police will brush me off as nothing more than an angry wife with an axe to grind against her philandering husband and his slutty lover. I overheard Devin on the phone with someone, talking about the importance of securing the rights to the Sleuth Sayer podcast. I'm certain it was Aurora."

"Why is the podcast so important to them?"

"They have nothing in the pipeline. If they don't come up with another project to keep investor money flowing, they'll be forced to shut down and admit failure, like so many other startups before them."

That seemed odd to me. "Isn't Hollywood overrun with screenwriters trying to sell their scripts? And what about all the bestsellers on bookstore shelves?"

She shrugged. "Their option offers keep getting rejected. They're desperate. Jared had grand dreams of success, but Devin keeps a tight control on the purse strings."

"I thought they both inherited a fortune."

She eyed me skeptically. "How did you learn that?"

"It's no secret, is it?"

"No, I suppose not. They wanted to succeed by their talent. The industry has a long history of trust fund babies who never succeed because they believe all it takes is money."

She sighed before continuing. "Anyway, after overhearing the phone conversation, I decided to listen to the Sleuth Sayer podcast to see what was so special about it. I have no idea if it would make a successful TV show, but I realized, with your experience, you could help me prove Devin and Aurora had killed Jared."

"How do you propose I do that?"

She stood and began pacing. Frustration filled her voice as she flung her arms in the air. "I don't know. You're the sleuth."

Common sense told me I should decline and escort her from the building, but my instincts told me if I dug a little, I might uncover a clue that would break this case wide open for Spader. "Have a seat, Mrs. Oberman."

She stopped pacing and stared at me. "Why?"

"What can you tell me about your sister-in-law?"

Her features tightened. "Aside from the fact that she's a husband-stealing, gold-digger?"

"I want to know everything you know about her."

She plopped back onto the chair, threw her head back, and exhaled forcefully. "Where would you like me to begin?"

"How did she and Jared meet?"

"They both worked for the same production company in L.A. Jared was head of project development. She started out as an intern and slept her way up the ladder until she became his assistant."

"How long ago was that?"

"When she became his assistant?"

"Yes."

She thought for a moment. "Nearly five years ago."

Assuming Aurora hadn't scurried up those ladder rails at the speed of light, that would make her older than I originally thought, most likely early to mid-thirties. It also meant she might be responsible for the breakup of Jared's marriage. Spader had said Jared and his first wife had divorced ten years ago. Still, not wanting to divulge what I already knew, I asked, "Was Jared married at the time?"

She shook her head. "Jared's wife had divorced him before he began his affair with Aurora. She wasn't his first conquest. There were quite a few before her, but brains and treachery are a powerful combination. Once she set her sights on Jared, it wasn't long before she sported an enormous diamond and had set a wedding date."

"When did Jared and Devin start Flix?"

"My husband and his brother always dreamed of becoming movie moguls. The company was secretly in the planning stages from the time they both started working in Hollywood."

"Why leave? Isn't L.A. the heart of the industry?"

Before answering, she took a sip of coffee. Her hand shook slightly. "Yes, but more and more companies are setting up shop on the East Coast and other locales. They also had an eighteen-month non-compete clause in their contracts. Flix officially opened three years ago."

Even though I knew enough about the industry to understand timelines, I played dumb to try to tease out more information. "Three years? Why haven't any of their projects released yet?"

She waved away the question. "That's not unusual in the film industry. It takes years to develop a movie or TV series. They have several finished projects in the can and scheduled for release this year."

To me, "in the can" meant the trash can, but thanks to Zack, I knew she referred to film cannisters. However, again I projected ignorance. "In the can?"

"That's what it's called when a project is completed but not yet released."

"I see. Are you part of the film industry as well?"

She released a nervous chuckle. "No, I've gleaned all my lingo and knowledge through the osmosis of marriage. I teach high

243

school English."

"What about your sister-in-law? What's her role at Flix?"

She sneered. "Aurora is a dilettante with dreams of becoming a female Steven Spielberg. Devin claimed she was always getting in the way. He convinced Jared to set her up in her own off-site office where she could play all day on her computer. As far as I know, nothing ever came of her efforts. I now suspect it was Devin's way of creating a little love nest for them and hiding it from both Jared and me."

Spader hadn't mentioned Flix having another location. I wondered if his investigators had slipped up. "Do you have an address for this property?"

"I didn't for the longest time. It wasn't like I planned to visit her there."

"But?"

"I recently hired a private investigator. If, as I suspect, Devin plans to divorce me to marry her, I need to become proactive to protect myself and my children." She pulled an envelope from her purse. "She rents an office in this building. The P.I. said it's under the name Inspired Ideas. These are contact sheets of the photos he took of the two of them together."

I opened the envelope and briefly scanned the damning photos. Placing them back in the envelope, I wondered if Inspired Ideas was one of the independent contractors that really isn't an independent contractor. Easy enough to find out. But I was curious about something else. "Why come to me if you already have a private investigator?"

She looked at me as if I didn't understand what a P.I. does. "He works through a divorce attorney and only investigates cheating husbands."

"Kind of a niche business model, isn't it?"

She shrugged. "I have no idea. You'd have to ask him. He came highly recommended by several friends who had divorced their husbands and walked away with huge settlements. They said he was extremely thorough and very discreet. He was." She pointed to the envelope. "I have the photos to prove it."

"Have you filed for divorce yet?"

"I had an appointment but postponed it after Jared was killed." Her voice quaked. "If Devin is involved, I could be his next victim."

I leaned forward, placing my elbows on the table and steepling my hands. "Mrs. Oberman, I happen to know the detective investigating Jared's murder. I believe this information will be extremely helpful to him."

Her face brightened. "Will you contact him for me, please? I'm terrified Devin will learn I spoke with you."

"I will."

She breathed a sigh of relief. "Thank you."

"Keep in mind, this still may come to nothing. You haven't provided me with any proof that your husband and sister-in-law had anything to do with Jared's death. Having an affair is immoral, but it's not a criminal act."

"I'm aware of that."

"However, you've opened the door to a new lead. Law enforcement will have to see if it turns up anything."

"That's all I ask."

When I rose, she followed my lead. I escorted her from the conference room and down the hall. As we waited for the elevator, I asked her one final question. "What will you do if your suspicions result in your husband's arrest and conviction?"

She grew thoughtful. "I hadn't allowed myself to contemplate that yet. Part of me hopes it's not true. It will be devastating for our children."

"And you?"

"Of course, no matter what he's done, he's still my husband and the father of my children." She inhaled a shuddering breath. "I suppose I'll take comfort in knowing I did the right thing, then get on with my life and help my kids get on with theirs."

Had Karl lived, I might have wound up in similar circumstances. After all, as I'd learned after his death, he'd tried to kill his mother. However, even if Devin Oberman is found guilty of murdering his brother, his wife and kids will likely gain control of his enormous trust fund, not massive debt. Those millions should go a long way in cushioning the blow.

~*~

Cloris stopped me as I returned from the elevator. "What was that all about?"

"I'll tell you shortly. First, I need to call Detective Spader." I started to head toward my supply closet but stopped and turned back toward her. "Has anyone been looking for me?"

"Not yet, but Danica wants to schedule a meeting for later today."

"Good. That took much longer than I had anticipated, and I may be on the phone with Spader for a bit."

Cloris raised an eyebrow. "The plot thickens, Sherlock?"

"Indubitably, Watson. But truthfully, I saw this one coming. I even suggested it previously to Spader. I'll catch you up once I'm off the phone."

My biggest dilemma now was whether to phone or text Detective Spader. If he had fallen asleep, I didn't want to wake him. Not after he'd pulled an all-nighter. If he was still awake, he'd head back to the office. I didn't want to be responsible for the man collapsing from exhaustion, but I also didn't want to impede an investigation by not letting him know what I'd learned. I opted for a text: *Devin Oberman's wife was waiting for me when I arrived at work. Call for details.*

When he failed to respond within five minutes, I figured the Sandman had worked his magic. Spader really needed forty winks. And then some.

Before finally starting my day's work, I popped into Cloris's cubicle to fill her in on what I'd learned from Sabrina Oberman.

"At least all the cop shows get one thing right," she said. "The spouse is usually the killer."

"Or hires the killer. I don't see Aurora Oberman pulling the trigger. She might break a nail."

Cloris rolled her eyes. "Perish the thought."

I waved before stepping across the hall to my own cubicle.

Ten minutes later, I received a call from Detective Spader. So much for those forty winks. "What did she want?"

"Didn't your mother ever teach you telephone manners, Detective?"

"Is that what Devin Oberman's wife wanted to know?"

"Of course not."

"Then?"

I gave up, reminding myself that you can't teach an old dog new tricks. "Hold on while I duck into someplace private." Once I'd returned to my supply closet, which was quickly becoming my second home, I said, "She thinks her husband and Aurora were in cahoots to eliminate Jared and take control of Flix."

"Does she have any proof?"

"No, but I know where you might find some."

"I'm all ears, Mrs. Barnes."

"Can I assume you didn't have a subpoena for Aurora Oberman's computer and phone?"

"The judge said we had no probable cause for seizing her phone. We only found one computer at the house."

"Are you aware that her husband set her up in an off-site office?"

"There was nothing on the books about any off-site locations."

"Look again. See if Inspired Ideas is listed under independent contractors."

"Are you saying a multi-million-dollar trust fund wasn't enough for him? He created a no-show job for his wife?"

"According to Sabrina Oberman, it was set up to get Aurora out of their hair. At Devin Overman's urging." I related what Sabrina had told me. "Jared thought his wife was working on screenplays. You might find some attempts on her computer, but I won't be surprised if you also find A.I. software and proof she created the image of her husband with the other two interns."

"Does Sabrina Oberman know about the A.I. photo?"

"Not from me. I played dumb throughout the conversation. Just kept asking questions."

"Why would Aurora create that image?"

"Not sure. To blackmail her husband, perhaps, if he learned of her affair?"

"What affair?"

"She's having an affair with her brother-in-law."

Spader released a string of expletives. "How the heck do you know that? We found no evidence of texts or emails on Devin's phone to suggest an affair with his sister-in-law."

"You wouldn't if they were using an encrypted app to communicate."

Frustration colored Spader's next words as he spit out, "Damn technology."

"There's more. Sabrina hired a private investigator. She's got photographic evidence of the affair. I have copies for you."

"Why didn't she come directly to me?"

"Because she's worried that she's living with a killer and might be his next victim. She asked me to pass the information along to you."

"You wouldn't happen to know where this office is located, would you?"

"As a matter of fact,....." I rattled off the address.

~*~

On my way home from work, I decided to exit Route 78 in Summit rather than Scotch Plains. The slight detour took me along the street of Aurora Oberman's office cum love nest. The building wasn't hard to locate. Several police vehicles, Detective Spader's unmarked car, and a crime scene unit van were parked in front of the building.

Stopping for a red light placed me in the middle of the block, directly in front of the building, and gave me an unobstructed view between two of the police cruisers. Aurora, flanked by a couple of uniformed officers, stood on the sidewalk. She held her arms crossed, her mouth pulled into a tight line, as she glowered at Detective Spader standing in front of her.

As members of the crime scene unit exited the building and placed armloads of boxes into the van, she shot them the same contemptable evil-eyed glare she'd previously directed toward me. Maybe that was her go-to expression for everyone she deemed inferior to her.

The driver behind me leaned on his horn. Aurora pulled her attention from the parade of evidence and toward the street. When our eyes briefly met, hers widened in recognition, then narrowed with rage. I quickly averted my gaze and stepped on the gas.

TWENTY-TWO

Throughout the remainder of the drive home, I ruminated over the hate-filled glare Aurora Oberman had directed toward me. I'd like to believe I was imagining or exaggerating the brief eye contact, but I doubted that was the case. I knew hate when I saw it.

But why? Did she still believe I'd had an affair with her husband? If so, talk about the height of hypocrisy!

Or was it a case of guilt by association? Did she now blame me for the subpoena to seize her phone and computer simply because I happened to drive down the street while the search of her office took place? How would she know her sister-in-law had sought me out and that I had contacted the police?

Had Sabrina told her?

Or had Aurora followed Sabrina this morning?

The former made no sense, given Sabrina's antipathy toward her sister-in-law and worry about her husband finding out she knew of the affair. The latter, although unlikely, made more sense.

But again, if so, why?

If Spader had gotten any background information on Aurora Oberman, he hadn't shared it with me. Under the circumstances, I found that highly unlikely. That left three options: A) He hadn't yet assigned the task to someone. B) The designated person hadn't begun his investigation. Or C) The search had turned up nothing of relevance.

I couldn't call Spader. He'd be up to his bushy eyebrows with the search of Aurora's office, and I certainly didn't want to risk Aurora noticing my name popping up on his phone. I'd see what I could find out about her on my own. If I struck out, I'd once again ask Tino to put his computer sleuthing skills to work for me.

~*~

I arrived home to find both Zack's Boxster and Alex's Jeep missing from the driveway. The boys were working late shifts this evening and wouldn't arrive home until after eight o'clock. I sent Zack a quick text that he'd find me in the apartment.

After taking Leonard for a walk, I released Ralph from his cage and brought both animals with me. Leonard immediately curled up with a chew toy under the coffee table. Ralph stretched his wings for a few turns around the apartment before taking up a position on his perch in the corner. I handed him a sunflower seed from Zack's stash and settled in at my computer.

Even if Devin Oberman had killed his brother, as his wife feared, I couldn't help but wonder if his lover had played some role in her husband's murder. Aurora Oberman was an enigma I needed to crack. I hoped the all-knowing Google gods would smile down on me and shed some light on her.

When I typed in her name, the Flix Entertainment website popped up first. The only mention I found of her was as an intern who had worked on one of the projects awaiting release.

The second link brought me to the Inspired Ideas website where she listed herself as a screenwriter and the award-winning assistant producer of the first Flix film.

Given the disparity, I clicked back to the Flix website to see if I'd missed something. I hadn't. Sabrina claimed Aurora had slept her way up the company ladder until she became assistant creative director under Jared. Had someone scrubbed the website after Devin convinced Jared to edge out Aurora, or had she embellished her credentials on her own website?

The bare-bones personal information on Inspired Ideas stated she had graduated from UCLA with a double major in Film and Computer Science. Before diving down the rabbit hole of alumni, I clicked on a link for the *L.A. Times*. It brought me to a wedding announcement for Jared Oberman and Aurora Woods.

Since what happens in cyberspace, stays forever in cyberspace, I decided to narrow my search to Aurora's maiden name. Even though Woods was a common surname, Aurora was not a common given name. With any luck, I wouldn't get thousands of hits. Twenty minutes later, I hit paydirt.

As I shot Detective Spader a text, I heard Zack climbing the staircase to the apartment. When the door opened, I said, "You'll never guess what I found."

"Try me."

I spun around to find Aurora Oberman standing in the doorway, a gun pointed at me. "Stand up slowly. Put your hands on your head, and get down on your knees."

From my Google search, I'd learned enough about her to know I wouldn't be able to talk my way out of this situation. I had no choice but to comply. However, as I stared at the gun in her right hand and a roll of duct tape in her left hand, I realized I had a fighting chance. To secure me, Aurora would need to use both hands.

"Now, on your stomach."

I lowered my elbows to the floor and walked them forward until my stomach hit the floor. Then I stretched out my legs. Aurora dropped to the floor and leaned one knee onto my lower spine. She grabbed one of my wrists and twisted my arm behind my back. I held my breath, waiting for the sound of the gun being placed on the hardwood floor.

The room had grown silent the moment Aurora entered the apartment. Leonard had stopped gnawing his chew toy. I glanced toward the corner of the room and spied Ralph staring at me. The moment Aurora placed the gun on the floor, he took flight. Emitting an ear-splitting squawk, he flew directly toward her head.

Aurora screamed. Her one-armed attempt to fend off Ralph failing, she released my wrist. As she flailed both arms, I pushed myself up, flipping her off me. She landed on her back, her head hitting the floor with a thud. Ralph landed on her face and dug his talons into her cheeks as his beak pecked at her hands.

Aurora's body bucked like a mechanical bull. I held on for dear life, keeping her shoulders pinned to the floor. At the same time, I twisted my neck, frantically searching for the gun.

Finally, out of the corner of my eye, I spotted the weapon a few feet from my right foot. I shifted my weight to position my left knee into her groin. Then I swept my right leg across the floor, hooked the gun with my foot, sending the deadly weapon skittering across the floor.

That's when Leonard pounced, sinking his canines into

Aurora's thigh. She let loose one final blood-curdling scream before passing out. Once she no longer posed a threat, he released his grip on her.

A moment later, I heard Zack racing up the stairs. He threw open the door with enough force that it banged against the wall. After he stepped inside and assessed the situation, he holstered his gun. "I see you, Leonard, and Ralph have everything under control."

"Not quite." As much as I hated guns, once again I was glad the man who claimed he wasn't a spy now kept his with him most of the time. Not that I had needed a knight in shining armor to come to my rescue this time. I'd gotten lucky. But the situation could have ended quite differently.

I held out a shaky arm. The adrenaline that had coursed through my body and enabled me to thwart Aurora Oberman had plunged as quickly as it had surged, leaving me suddenly weak, exhausted, and afraid to move. "Think you can help me up?"

Zack strode across the room and pulled me into his arms. Ralph and Leonard continued to restrain Aurora. When she moaned, Ralph squawked, and Leonard growled menacingly.

Zack glanced down at her. "We'd better secure her before she wakes up."

He lowered me to the floor. With a shaky hand, I began tearing off strips of Aurora's duct tape. After I helped Zack bind her arms and legs, I convinced Leonard to release her. "She's not going anywhere, boy. You did good."

"*Brrrack!*" Ralph flapped his wings. I stroked his beak. "You, too, Ralph."

Zack called for an ambulance and notified Detective Spader. Then he held out his arm and whistled. Ralph released his grip on

Aurora's face and flew to him.

Zack helped me over to the sofa and lowered me onto the cushions. I scanned the room. "Her gun is somewhere, but I don't see it. I kicked it out of the way. I don't know where it landed."

He switched on all the lights and searched the room, eventually finding the gun in the far corner under his desk. Grabbing a towel, he retrieved the gun and placed it on the kitchen counter. Then he poured me a shot of bourbon and joined me on the sofa. "Want to tell me what happened?"

I took a sip of the bourbon. "She did it."

"Killed Oberman? Did she confess?"

"She didn't have to. I'm sure of it."

He raised an eyebrow. "That's going to be a tough sell to a jury, Sweetheart."

"Spader will figure it out. I've found the missing puzzle pieces for him." I heard sirens in the distance growing closer. "Sounds like he's on his way."

~*~

The EMTs and Detective Spader arrived a few minutes later. After Aurora was loaded onto a gurney, handcuffed to the railing, and removed, Spader insisted I go to the hospital to be checked out.

"I'm fine. She never fired the gun, and thanks to my attack dog and attack parrot, I don't have so much as a scratch on me."

After some back and forth, he finally capitulated and settled into the chair across from the coffee table. He pulled out his notepad and began firing off questions. "First, before you tell me what you found, I want to know why she was here."

"I don't know, but I have a theory."

He waved his pen at me. "Go on."

"I think she either followed Sabrina this morning or had

planted a tracker in Sabrina's car."

Zack turned to me. "What happened this morning?"

"Devin Oberman's wife showed up at my office."

"And why don't I know this?"

"Because I haven't had a chance to tell you." I then filled him in on the visit.

After I'd finished bringing Zack up to speed, Spader asked, "Why would Aurora stalk Sabrina?"

"To keep track of her."

"Why?"

"I don't know, Detective. Maybe she found out Sabrina had hired a private investigator and knew about the affair. If she kept tabs on Sabrina, she and Devin wouldn't need to worry about any surprise visits."

"Hmm, so you suspect she knew Sabrina met with you this morning."

"It makes perfect sense. Then, when she saw me this afternoon—"

"Exactly what were you doing at my crime scene, Mrs. Barnes?"

Zack pounced. "You were at a crime scene?"

I winced. "Not exactly."

Technically, was it a crime scene? The police were executing a search for evidence that might connect to a crime, not investigating a crime that had taken place on the premises.

However, since I didn't think this was the time to debate semantics, I explained how I'd driven past Aurora's office on my way home from work. "I didn't expect to find the street crawling with police and Aurora under guard on the sidewalk. I guess when she saw me stopped at the red light, she put two and two together and decided to confront me."

"With a gun and a roll of duct tape," said Zack. "I think she had something else in mind besides a polite chat."

"Yeah, I figured that out by myself. By the way," I said, turning to Spader, "how did she have a gun? You had a search warrant."

He grimaced. "For her computer and phone. We found both in the office. Had we found a gun while executing the search, we would have seized it. We never checked her car because we had already found the items stipulated in the warrant."

Zack shook his head. "With each passing day, that ivory tower is looking better and better."

"Just make sure it has good wi-fi."

"Before you do that," said Spader, "I want two and two defined. What did you find, Mrs. Barnes?"

"Thanks to Google, I discovered that not only does Aurora Oberman have enough skills to create credible A.I. images, but she was also a member of her high school and college rifle teams. She nearly made the cut for the U.S. Olympic team. Two plus two equals prime suspect in both her husband's murder and as the porn poster."

Spader flipped his notepad closed. "All circumstantial, Mrs. Barnes."

"Let's see what happens once you start interrogating her, Detective. Oh, and one other thing...."

"Yes?"

"Ask her why she changed her maiden name."

"How do you know she changed her name?"

I smiled at him. "Google told me."

He huffed and opened his notepad again. "I'll bite. What was her maiden name, and what did she change it to?"

"She changed her name to Woods after she moved to L.A. for

college."

"And prior to that?"

"*Boschi*. Italian for Woods."

Both Zack and Spader stared at me, their eyes wide, their mouths agape. Spader found his voice first. "Are you saying she's related to Carmine Boschi?"

I nodded. "He's her father."

Ralph squawked. "*Thou art thy father's daughter; there's enough. As You Like It.* Act One, Scene Three."

Spader whistled under his breath. "If what you're claiming is true, the apple didn't fall far from the tree."

"And it would explain quite a bit that your team hasn't yet figured out, like the stolen Escalade that wound up torched on Gilgo Beach. Mafia princesses have connections in all sorts of low places."

He grunted as he stood, then stifled a yawn. "Looks like I've got another long night ahead of me. You know the drill, Mrs. Barnes. I'll need you to come to headquarters to make a statement. I'm assuming this time you'll agree to press charges."

"Definitely. See you after dinner, Detective. I'll be the one bringing you a doggie bag."

Spader's eyes twinkled as he placed his hand over his heart.

~*~

After a late dinner an hour and a half later, we pulled into a guest parking space at county police headquarters and sat in the car, watching as two officers escorted Devin Oberman inside.

TWENTY-THREE

I would have loved to stand on the other side of a two-way mirror and observe Detective Spader interrogating Devin Oberman. Zack speared me with a look that needed no interpretation. He thought it was a terrible idea. As a matter of fact, he thought it such a terrible idea that he pulled out his phone and shot Spader a text, saying I'd provide my statement first thing the next morning.

"What if I forget something important?"

"Write it down tonight. Bring it with you tomorrow."

I held up the doggie bag. "What about Spader's dinner?"

He took the bag from me. "I'll leave it at the front desk for him. Stay in the car, and keep it locked."

I was too tired to argue further.

~*~

The next morning, Zack insisted on accompanying me to police headquarters. I could almost see the gears turning in his brain as the architectural blueprints for that ivory tower took shape. I suppose I couldn't blame him. Even when I made a concerted effort to distance myself from murder and mayhem, I still found myself smack in the middle of it.

I had expected that Detective Spader would take my statement, but he'd assigned the task to another detective. According to him, Spader first left headquarters a few hours earlier. I hoped he'd sleep all day, but knowing Spader, he'd probably set his alarm to wake him in a few hours.

After I'd finished at headquarters, Zack refused to allow me to drive myself to work. When I protested, he said, "Humor me."

I humored him. Once we arrived, he even insisted on escorting me upstairs, where he popped into Cloris's cubicle and said, "Do me a favor, Cloris?"

She shot me a quick side-eye before answering, "Sure, Zack. What do you need?"

"Don't let Nancy Drew out of your sight today."

"Uhm...okay?"

"Thanks. I'm sure she'll explain everything." He then planted a quick kiss on my lips and said, "I'll pick you up at five."

After Zack left, Cloris asked, "Does this have anything to do with your visitor yesterday?"

"Probably. I still don't know the entire story, but I'll fill you in while I grab a cup of caffeine." After the events of last evening, I had a feeling today was going to be a minimum four-cup day. I had earlier refused a cup of the sludge that passed for coffee at the police station.

We headed to the break room. The normal buzz of magazine activity was nearly nonexistent today. Many of my coworkers horded their vacation days, using them on Fridays throughout the summer. I felt comfortable we could speak freely today without having to hide out in my supply closet, but I still closed the break room door after we entered.

As Cloris made a fresh pot of coffee, I dipped into the bakery box on the table and helped myself to a chocolate and raspberry mini croissant. I caught her up as I made short work of the croissant. "Can you believe it was only a week ago today that Jared Oberman was gunned down in front of my house?"

"It must feel like a year."

"Or two."

When I'd finished filling her in, she shook her head and said, "Typical male."

"Who? Zack?"

Cloris chortled. "Zack is anything but typical. I'm talking about Detective Spader. You were suspicious of Jared Oberman's wife from the start, but he set his sights on that intern who offered you the contract."

I drained my mug and stood to help myself to a refill. "Ellis Cummings."

"Right. Her. The man asked for your advice, then proceeded to ignore it."

I returned to the table and helped myself to another croissant. "In all fairness, I never suspected Aurora of killing her husband, at least not at first. Just of hiding something."

"She certainly did that. In spades. What about the brother? Is he complicit or just a clueless pawn with a wandering eye?"

"I don't know yet. Spader brought him in for questioning last night. So far, I haven't heard anything, but for the sake of his wife and kids, I hope he's only guilty of cheating."

"What about the murder of that poor doctor in Springfield? Do the cops still believe it was a road rage incident?"

"I have nothing new on that, either, other than a theory."

LOIS WINSTON

"Which is?"

"I think Aurora killed him to lead the police on a wild goose chase, looking for a serial killer. I suspect she planned at least one more murder to insure they redirected their resources in that direction."

Cloris stared wide-eyed at me. "Make that two more. Sounds like she planned to get rid of you, as well."

"Or possibly three. She may also have planned to get rid of her sister-in-law."

Cloris shook her head. "Sometimes I think you've missed your calling. Your talents are wasted as a crafts editor."

"Thanks, but no thanks. I don't have the stomach for a steady diet of murder investigations."

"And yet, you're constantly knee-deep in them."

"Reluctantly."

She shrugged. "If you say so, but admit it, you secretly get a rush from figuring out whodunit and proving the police wrong."

Did I? "Are you saying I'm really an adrenaline junkie masquerading as a mild-mannered crafts editor?"

Cloris smirked. "If the shoe fits...."

"I certainly hope you're wrong." I sighed and rose to leave.

However, as I opened the door, I nearly collided with Danica. How long had she been standing there, and what had she overheard? Her expression told me too long and too much.

"It's true, then?" she asked.

I decided to play dumb. "Is what true?"

"Rumor has it you're something of an amateur sleuth."

"Reluctant amateur sleuth," I said.

"Does it matter?"

"To Anastasia it does," said Cloris.

It's always nice when your BFF comes to your defense, but Danica was correct. It really didn't matter whether I searched out murder victims or simply stumbled across them. I still wound up, as Cloris so aptly put it, knee-deep in dead bodies.

Danica kept pressing. "I heard there was a murder right here at *American Woman.*" She hugged her arms around her torso and shuddered. "Is it true?"

I nodded. "About a year and a half ago. A former fashion editor." I didn't mention the body Cloris and I found a few months later. Technically, Philomena, the one-named rapper-turned-entrepreneur, wasn't killed in the building, only transported here in a trade show display case.

Danica's eyes widened, not in fear, but with excitement. "Have you seen any ghosts? I've always wanted to see a real ghost."

Cloris and I exchanged a quick look. Not what either of us expected to hear from the woman who freaked out about living in the land of Tony Soprano. Dead bodies were not okay, but the ghosts of death bodies were? She looked downright disappointed when we both told her we'd never come across a ghost haunting the halls of *American Woman.*

"If I ever come across one," I assured her, "you'll be the first to know,"

Cloris took that as the cue to change the subject. "Is there something you need, Danica?"

"Uhm...no. I was just on my way to meet with Naomi and thought I'd grab a cup of coffee first." She then waved before scurrying down the hall, sans coffee.

"What was that all about?" asked Cloris after Danica was out of earshot.

"Not sure, but it's obvious that someone in the office is

gossiping about me."

Cloris patted my shoulder. "It was bound to happen eventually, given the numerous times you've been mentioned on the news and in the newspaper."

"I suppose."

"And I'm sure it will happen again."

"Thanks for reminding me."

~*~

Spader called later that afternoon. Instead of answering with a friendly hello, I pulled a chapter from his playbook and said, "Have you made arrests?"

He roared with laughter. "Touché, Mrs. Barnes. I'll trade you information for one of your husband's gourmet dinners this evening."

"Is this a celebratory dinner?"

"Definitely."

"You're on, Detective." After hanging up, I texted Zack.

EPILOGUE

Spader arrived at six-thirty. I glanced questioningly at the bakery box cradled in one arm and the bottle of wine in his other hand. He cocked his head toward the bounty. "Least I can do since I can't pay you for your help. I know you like wine, and I hear you consider chocolate one of the major food groups."

"Doesn't everyone?" When he chuckled, I added, "Thank you, Detective. It's always nice to be appreciated."

He looked down his nose at me. "Try not to gloat too much, Mrs. Barnes."

"Wouldn't think of it. I'm happy I was able to assist you in apprehending a killer."

At that moment, my mother-in-law rounded the hallway and stopped short. Her features darkened, and she struck a combatant pose. "What's he doing here?"

"Having dinner with us."

She furrowed her forehead, drawing her brows into a V and hurling an evil-eyed glare at him. "I'll have my dinner in the den this evening." Then she did an about-face and lumbered off in the direction she'd come.

Fine by me. I'd take a little Zen wherever and whenever I could get it. I ushered Spader into the living room. Zack joined us a moment later. "Dinner's ready. I thought we'd eat out on the patio."

"Lovely. The commie took one look at Detective Spader and opted for a tray table in the den."

Zack had grilled filets and a veggie assortment with potatoes and mushrooms. After we entered the kitchen, I poured a glass of water for Lucille while Zack filled a plate for her. With a wide grin and a twinkle in his eyes, he asked Spader, "Would you care to do the honors?"

Spader grinned back, accepting the plate, a napkin, and utensils from Zack. "She'll love that."

I stared at both men. "Nothing like flirting with danger."

I then scooted out of the kitchen ahead of Spader. I had no desire to be in the same room when she saw him enter with her dinner. I just hoped she didn't throw the plate at him.

I passed Spader in the foyer on my return. "Chicken," he said.

"And proud of it."

A minute later, he was back in the kitchen, his suit in the same condition as before he entered the den. I guess Lucille was too hungry to waste a good filet.

"No boys tonight?" Spader asked as we settled around the picnic table.

"They're out with friends." Thankfully. I knew I'd have to explain what had happened, but I'd prefer to provide the mom version of events rather than have them hear the official police version.

Spader opened the wine and poured three glasses of Merlot. After we filled our plates, he began to relate the events that had transpired since we last saw him. "Once again, your instincts were on the nose, Mrs. Barnes. Ellis Cummings is just an immature kid with a short fuse. She had nothing to do with anything that occurred."

I was tempted to say I told you so but held my tongue. After all, there were times during the past week that I'd questioned my instincts. Instead, I asked, "What about Devin Oberman?"

Spader pulled a face. "A horndog under the spell of a much younger woman."

"He wasn't in any way complicit in his brother's death?" asked Zack.

Spader took a swig of his wine. "He claims he had no idea that Aurora was plotting to kill Jared."

"But?" I asked.

"When pressed, he admitted it had crossed his mind after Jared's murder."

"Let me get this straight," I said. "The man believed his sister-in-law may have murdered his brother, yet he never mentioned his suspicions to you?" I scrunched up my nose. "Call me highly skeptical, Detective."

Spader chuckled. "You're not alone, Mrs. Barnes. At the time of his initial statement, he had no idea we'd uncovered enough evidence on Aurora's computer to charge him as an accessory."

"Have you arrested him?" asked Zack.

"We never released him last night."

Spader turned to me. "You were right about something else, Mrs. Barnes. Aurora was tracking her sister-in-law. We found an AirTag containing Devin's fingerprint hidden under the carpet in the trunk of his wife's car."

"He planted the tracker?" I asked.

"Something else he at first denied."

"Then, Aurora knew Sabrina had visited me at the magazine yesterday."

"That's probably why she showed up here after noticing you in Summit," said Zack.

I frowned. "You're probably right. She knew about the podcast and probably worried I'd figure out her role in Jared's murder. I became a loose end she needed to eliminate. Even if she hadn't spotted me in Summit, she would have come after me."

"Chances are, Sabrina was next on Aurora's hit list," said Spader.

Something I'd earlier suggested to Cloris. "Do you have any proof of that?"

"No, but it makes sense. Luckily, we arrested her and Devin before she murdered anyone else."

I shuddered at the thought of how much worse things might have gotten. "What about the second murder?" I asked. "Did Aurora also kill that doctor in Springfield to misdirect the investigation?"

Spader nodded. "Her phone puts her in the vicinity of your house last Friday and in Springfield on Tuesday. The gun from yesterday is the same one used to kill both her husband and the doctor."

"So much for her ironclad alibi," I said.

"Has she confessed?" asked Zack.

Spader's face tightened. "As you might imagine, she's lawyered up and isn't talking. However, between the gun and the evidence found on her computer, we had more than enough to charge her.

The D.A. believes he has a solid case. Ultimately, it will be up to a jury to decide their fates unless one of them flips and tries to cop a plea."

"Any chance of that?" I asked.

Spader shrugged. "I hope not. I'd like to see them both put away for the remainder of their lives."

I chewed on my lower lip. Zack noticed. "I know that look. What's churning around in your mind?"

"I still don't understand Aurora's attitude toward me, but maybe it was all part of the script she created."

"Script?" asked Spader.

"To get away with murder. Did you find any screenplays on her computer?"

"A few."

"Has anyone read through them?"

"Not yet. We were more concerned with finding evidence of a crime."

"If I'm correct, you'll find Aurora laid out her plans in one of those screenplays."

Spader's face scrunched up in puzzlement. "Why would —?" Then it dawned on him. "Like that romance author you mentioned. The one who wrote a book about how to get away with murdering her husband."

"Exactly. And that's not all."

He raised an eyebrow. "There's more?"

"I believe so. The more I think about it, the more I doubt Jared Oberman was the womanizing creep his wife and brother claimed."

"Explain," said Zack.

I turned to Detective Spader. "Did you uncover anyone else

271

who admitted to having an affair with Jared or suspected him of having affairs with other staff members?"

He shook his head. "None except the three interns, Aurora, and Devin."

"But the three interns accused each other, and all denied the accusations. Other than a fake photograph, there's no evidence of any of them having an affair with Jared."

"Are you suggesting they lied?" asked Spader.

"I'm suggesting that catty mean girls will stoop to anything to attain their goals. In this case, the goal was a permanent position at Flix Entertainment. Ellis claimed Brooklyn and Kendall bragged about sleeping with Jared, but they claimed Ellis was the one having an affair with him. Given that no one else corroborated the accusations, perhaps all three were lying."

Spader scrubbed at his jaw as he digested my words. "But you said Ellis claimed Jared hit on her and everyone else in the office."

I shrugged. "Maybe he did. Or maybe he didn't. Remember, she was angry he'd fired her. She was talking about filing a lawsuit. Adding charges of sexual harassment strengthened her claim."

"Since he's not here to defend himself," said Zack, "and there were no witnesses, we'll never know if those accusations are true."

"What about Aurora's accusations of Jared's cheating?" asked Spader.

"Did his ex-wife mention he'd cheated on her?"

"No, she claimed they had an amicable divorce. She never mentioned adultery."

Spader reached for his phone and placed a call. "Get someone to read through the screenplays on Aurora Oberman's computer. I want to know the plots of all of them."

~*~

An hour later, Zack and I walked Spader to the door. The detective had thanked us for dinner and was about to leave when he paused. His hand on the doorknob, he turned back to face us. "I forgot to mention, I'm taking a much-needed vacation next week."

I smiled at him. "Good for you, Detective. Much needed and well-deserved. Have a restful time."

"Do me a favor, will you, Mrs. Barnes?"

"Of course."

"Try not to find any dead bodies while I'm gone."

"I'll do my best, Detective."

Zack draped his arm across my shoulders and drew me to his side. "She won't have a chance, Detective. I've finalized plans for that ivory tower."

Good thing I knew Zack was joking. *Or was he?*

ANASTASIA'S MACRAMÉ TIPS

Macramé is the decorative art of knotting. It's a craft that dates to Arabian weavers in the thirteenth century. From Asia, the craft traveled to Europe and saw a resurgence in Victorian times. The popularity of macrame soared when Hippies and Baby Boomers discovered it in the late 1960s. Just ask **Flora Sudberry Periwinkle Ramirez Scoffield Goldberg O'Keefe Tuttnauer.** Mama still has a few macramé plant hangers in her condo.

Other popular macramé items include jewelry, wall-hangings, belts, tote bags, vests, table runners, curtains, and even hammocks and chairs.

One of the charms of macramé is that it takes very little skill. If you remember your basic knots from scouting or summer camp, you can do macramé. If you don't remember or never learned how to tie basic knots, there are plenty of tutorials online.

All you really need is cord made from cotton, linen, jute, or hemp, a pair of scissors, a measuring tape or yardstick, and a little practice. Depending on the project, you may also need metal or wooden hoops and rings, purse handles, and belt buckles. Once you've mastered the art of knotting, you might want to branch out using thin strips of leather. You can also incorporate decorative beads as embellishments.

Most home décor projects are made with 4-6mm cord. Use a 2mm elasticized cord for jewelry. For outdoor projects like hammocks or chairs, you'll want to use polypropylene rope.

As with any craft, work in an area with good lighting. Small projects can be worked on a flat surface. For wall-hangings, it's best to work vertically from a clothing bar or shower rod.

The most common knots used in macramé are the Mounting Knot (also known as the Lark's Head Knot or Cow Hitch Knot), Square Knot, Clove Hitch Knot (also known as a Double Half Hitch), Spiral Stitch (also called a Half Knot Sinnet or Half Knot Spiral), Overhand Knot, and Gathering Knot (also called a Wrapping Knot.)

Some projects, like wall-hangings, lend themselves to fringe. If you'd like to add fringe to a project, trim the cord to the desired length. Working from the bottom up, use a stiff wire brush to separate the cord fibers.

Always purchase enough cord or rope for your project. If you're working from directions on the Internet or from a book, buy the amount specified in the materials list. If you're creating your own project, a good rule of thumb is to multiply the desired length of the finished project by five or six. It's always best to have more cord than you need rather than to run out!

Just like when doing needlework, knitting, or crochet projects, it's important to keep your tension even as you knot in macramé. That's why it's so important to master the skill of knotting before tackling any large projects. Remember, practice makes perfect!

A NOTE FROM THE AUTHOR

Dear Readers,

I hope you enjoyed *Sorry, Knot Sorry*, the thirteenth book in my Anastasia Pollack Crafting Mystery Series, as much as I enjoyed writing it. If so, please consider leaving a review at your favorite review site.

Happy reading!
Lois Winston

ABOUT THE AUTHOR

USA Today and Amazon bestselling author Lois Winston began her award-winning writing career with *Talk Gertie to Me*, a humorous fish-out-of-water novel about a small-town girl going off to the big city and the mother who had other ideas. That was followed by the romantic suspense *Love, Lies and a Double Shot of Deception*.

Then Lois's writing segued unexpectedly into the world of humorous amateur sleuth mysteries, thanks to a conversation her agent had with an editor looking for craft-themed mysteries. In her day job, Lois was an award-winning crafts and needlework designer, and although she'd never written a mystery—or had even thought about writing a mystery—her agent decided she was the perfect person to pen a series for this editor. Thus, was born the Anastasia Pollack Crafting Mysteries, which *Kirkus Reviews* dubbed "North Jersey's more mature answer to Stephanie Plum."

To learn more about Lois and her books, visit her at www.loiswinston.com. Sign up for her newsletter to receive an Anastasia Pollack Mini-Mystery.